Other books by Lauren James

The Next Together
The Last Beginning
The Loneliest Girl in the Universe

THE
QUIET
AT THE
END
OF THE
WORLD

LAUREN JAMES

WALKER
BOOKS

First published in Great Britain 2019 by Walker Books Ltd
87 Vauxhall Walk, London SE11 5HJ

2 4 6 8 10 9 7 5 3 1

Text © 2019 Lauren James
Cover illustration © 2019 Lisa Horton Design

This book has been typeset in Fairfield, Arial, Ubuntu, Verdena

Printed and bound by CPI Group (UK) Ltd, Croydon CR0 4YY

British Library Cataloguing in Publication Data:
a catalogue record for this book is available from the British Library

ISBN 978-1-4063-7551-0

www.walker.co.uk

MIX
Paper from
responsible sources
FSC
www.fsc.org   FSC® C020471

For Chris – for a childhood spent digging
holes in the sand in search of treasure

*Whence, I often asked myself, did the
principle of life proceed?*

Mary Shelley, *Frankenstein*

*We will now discuss in a little more
detail the struggle for existence.*

Charles Darwin, *The Origin of Species*

OPERATOR 1	Hello, emergency service operator. Which service do you require? Fire, police or ambulance?
CALLER	Ambulance, please.
OPERATOR 1	I'll just connect you now.
OPERATOR 2	Hello, this is the ambulance service. What is the nature of your emergency?
CALLER	Hi. Er, my mum – she's got a nosebleed. It won't stop, it's been going for ages. What do – what do I do?
OPERATOR 2	A nose bleed?
CALLER	Yeah, it's – really fast and … sticky.
OPERATOR 2	All right, duck. Try to stay calm. Can you give me your location?
CALLER	Home. We're at home. She's – should I drive her to the hospital?
OPERATOR 2	If you give me your address, I can send an ambulance.
CALLER	Right. It's, er, Maya Waverley. 18 Horn Street, Oxford. How – how long —?
OPERATOR 2	They're leaving now. Stay calm, duck.
CALLER	Oh! Oh God!
OPERATOR 2	What is it? Maya? Are you still with me?
CALLER	I've got it too! I'm bleeding! It's everywhere!
OPERATOR 2	Stay calm. The ambulance is on its way.
CALLER	I'm fine! It doesn't hurt. I've got a towel. It's just – a shock.

CALLER	Hello?
CALLER	Hello? Operator, are you there?
OPERATOR 2	I'm sorry. I just… My nose is bleeding too. I'll – I'll be right back. I'm sorry. I'm sorry. Oh, damn – sorry, sorry, damn.
CALLER	What's happening? What's happening to us?
OPERATOR 2	I don't know. I don't know. My colleague – her nose is bleeding too. Oh, damn.
CALLER	What do I do?
OPERATOR 2	I don't – I'm not sure, ma'am. I think I need to—
CALLER	Hello? Hello? Hello?

EIGHTY-FIVE YEARS LATER

TIME	DATE	LOCATION	OBJECT	NOTES
12.17	04/04/2109	51.508474, -0.121292	Embossed emerald-green plastic wallet, circa mid-twenty-first century.	Found by LMBW.

"We haven't got long," I shout, already jumpy with adrenalin. "I'm going in!"

Before Shen can reply, I fall backwards into the manhole. I'm swallowed immediately by pitch-black air. It smells of warm death down here, rotting and ancient.

I drop far enough that my stomach flips before the rope kicks in and catches me. Holding on to the carabiner clip of my harness, I walk my feet down the curved tiles of the ceiling, guiding the rope through my gloved hands.

Shen shouts to me from where he's crouched on the pavement above with Dad, "Watch out for the sewer alligators, Lowrie!"

"This isn't even the sewers! And that's a myth!" I yell back.

"You can never be too careful." He ducks back out of sight to buckle on his own harness.

My foot hits an old fluorescent lighting tube and smashes it, sending glass into the water below. Wincing, I step off the wall, so

I'm hanging freely from the rappelling line. Then I lower myself down again, twisting around so that I can see the tunnel on all sides. I'm trying to read a sign hanging loose from the wall when I hit the surface of the water with a gasp. It's ice-cold, despite the moist warmth of the air.

Treading water and trying not to shiver, I unclip the rope from the harness and call up, "All OK!" My teeth are already chattering.

The rope is lifted back up, clip jangling merrily.

"Very good, Shen," I hear Dad say. "Slowly does it."

Not wanting to stay in the freezing, foul-smelling water for any longer than necessary, I swim over to the platform and pull myself out. There's a tile on the floor warning me to MIND THE GAP, and the old London Underground symbol – a red circle with a blue line through its centre – covers the wall. Posters dangle from their holders all along the platform wall. Dripping, shredded plastic advertises insurance and movies.

This was part of the Circle line, back when there were enough people to justify running the Tube lines. Now the flooded underground tunnels are just another relic of the past. The small number of us left in London have all but forgotten about them. Shen, Dad and I are probably the only ones who've been down here in the last twenty years.

I reach out to grab Shen's hand as he descends on the rope, guiding him on to the platform, so he doesn't land in the water too.

"Perfect timing," he says, unclipping his harness. "It's raining up there."

I look pointedly at his wetsuit.

He shrugs, grinning. "I don't mind getting wet in the name of treasure-hunting. Drizzle is a different matter altogether, Shadow." He calls me Shadow because when we were little I used to follow him around like one, apparently. It is a controversial and much-debated nickname, but he doesn't seem likely to give it up any time soon.

Dad lowers himself into the tunnel after us. He comes down here a lot to collect plant and algae samples from the water, and we've been coming with him for years, ever since we were big enough to fit in the harnesses. It started because he wanted to get us interested in horticulture, but it kind of backfired because we were both more interested in exploring the tunnels.

I keep hoping we'll be allowed to come here on our own soon, but realistically that isn't going to happen. My parents and Shen's still think that we're not old enough, even though I'm sixteen and Shen is seventeen. For now, we have to make do with tagging along on my dad's botanical outings – although he gets so caught up in his findings that he often forgets about us anyway, so it's almost like being on our own.

"Lowrie, you need to let your rope out a little more slowly next time," Dad says, as he lands perfectly on the platform without getting even a little wet.

"You always say that," I reply.

He huffs at me, unclipping his harness. "Well, you always do it too fast."

"I'm always excited to get started."

"Safety first, exploring second." As he says it, Dad is already leaning into the wall to examine lichen growing on the tiles.

Shen says, "Are you sure it's not 'plants first, safety second, exploring third'?"

"Well. You said it, not me." Dad grins.

I think Dad would choose plants above anything else in the world. Except me, I suppose. And even that would be a close call.

"Go on, then," Dad says. "Be off with you. I don't need your attitude while I'm working."

"See you in forty minutes!" I say, biting back a smirk.

"Twenty," Dad replies immediately as I knew he would.

"Thirty."

"Twenty-five."

"Deal." I salute him, bouncing on my heels.

"And keep your helmets on," he calls after us.

I wave a hand in his direction in lazy agreement.

Shen and I come down here to search for treasure. The Tube lines are full of old decaying junk, washed in from the River Thames, which is what makes them so fun to explore.

Shen is all about the unexplainable oddities: the curiosity cabinet treasures. Things that won't necessarily be registered by a metal detector: ancient fossils, bleached white and smooth by time and pressure; fountain pens from the fifteenth century; ivory and textured silver; anchors from ancient ships, dropped into the Thames when shipments came into harbour.

I'm here for the jewellery. You'd be amazed at what you can find – gold and silver and platinum, embedded with rubies and diamonds and amber and sapphires. Cameo brooches of enamelled silhouettes surrounded by gilding. The kind of thing which takes hours to clean, rubbing cotton buds through the delicate filaments until the texture and design appear.

"I don't know why you bother arguing with your dad for more time," Shen says as he pulls his handheld metal detector out of his rucksack. "You know he's going to take at least an hour anyway, once he finds something good."

I glance back along the platform to where Dad has already crouched down to gather a lichen sample. The plants he studies all look the same to me, but each to their own. "I've gotta practise my bartering skills before the next jumble sale, you know that." Since there aren't any shops any more, the local secondhand sales are the only way to get things, so competition over certain rare items is legendary.

Shen hums. "You can't let Mrs Maxwell get the screwdrivers first again?"

"Don't even joke. I still wish I'd got that chisel. The blade was Japanese steel. I'm never going to find another one like it."

"Just wait. I bet she only wanted it so she could give it to you for your birthday."

"I hadn't thought of that!"

At the end of the platform, we walk down the steps and wade into the grimy water covering the disused train tracks. It comes up to my knees and is so cold that it makes me shiver. I have to breathe through my mouth to ignore the smell.

As we follow the curving metal rails along the line, Shen and

I fall into a companionable silence. The only sound, aside from the swish of the water, is Shen's metal detector, which emits an oscillating beep as it passes over a piece of iron sticking out of the water. We're stirring up thick and putrid sediment as we walk. A rat swims past me, ears flat back against its head. I twist quickly, grimacing, to make sure it doesn't touch me.

As the tunnel drops down at a gentle incline, the water steadily deepens until it's almost at waist height. I grit my teeth and kick off the floor to start swimming. Shen follows me, more slowly. He's always cautious about hurting himself in places like this, whereas I'm more than willing to risk a grazed knee in the name of treasure-hunting.

When the tunnel ahead twists into view, I catch sight of something looming in the darkness. "Look!"

"What was that?" Shen says. He's deaf in one ear. He fell off a horse while practising jumps when we were ten. Sometimes when he's distracted or not paying attention, he misses things people say. I used to get really annoyed that I had to constantly repeat things to him, until I realised he wasn't doing it on purpose.

"There's something there," I say, pointing the torch on my headlamp to show him. The light picks out something large and metal. We both grin at the same time. It's a train. We've never found one before. This alone makes the trip down here worth it.

We swim towards it. For once I'm glad that the water is so deep. It means that we're level with the driver's door. When Shen tugs on it experimentally, it opens, releasing a musty, cotton smell. He pulls himself up out of the water and into the train, hesitating a moment to see if I need help – I don't – before passing through the driver's compartment into the front carriage. After dragging myself out of the water, I take a moment to poke through the booth for anything interesting before following him.

In the main carriage, the floor is covered in padding from the seats. It must have been gnawed on by rodents. The whole place looks as derelict as you'd expect from a vehicle that has been standing in water for decades. I grab the chrome railing running along the ceiling to steady myself, wary that rot might have made the floor dangerous. Then I pick my way down the carriage after Shen.

It's hard to imagine this small vehicle packed full of commuters. I can't even wrap my head around the idea of *seeing* this many people, let alone being squashed up together in a confined space like this. There are only three hundred people in London now.

Eighty-five years ago, a virus stopped humans from being able to reproduce. It infected everyone in the world. No one knows exactly where it came from – whether it mutated from an animal disease or was somehow caused by pollution – but within weeks it had spread across the planet. The symptoms weren't even that bad, nothing worse than a mild flu. It was only in the months afterwards that everyone began to realise that the entire population had become infertile.

The births didn't stop immediately. Eggs and sperm that had been frozen for IVF treatment before the virus spread remained viable. A lot of them were used up in the first year after the virus, before everyone realised how widespread the infertility really was.

By the time people understood how long it might take to find a solution to the sterility, the samples had nearly all been used up. The remaining eggs were kept safe after that, and babies were only born occasionally. Finally, seventy years after the virus first spread, there were only two eggs left: Shen and me.

We are the youngest people in the world. Our parents thought it was only right that we grow up together, seeing as we might one day be the only two people on the whole planet, so his parents moved from Beijing to London.

We've grown up surrounded by a community of people much older than us. The youngest of them are in their eighties and were born from the other frozen eggs. They're the last surviving members of the youngest generation, born in the decades after the sterility. More and more people die every year.

There's no one else at all my age, except Shen. We're just leftovers, really. Being the youngest doesn't mean I'll necessarily be the last person to die. There's no assurance I'll live to my full life expectancy. But I'll definitely be around to watch the population drop below a few dozen. The thought terrifies me. Who is really brave enough to knowingly watch their species go extinct?

So far no one is anywhere close to working out how to fix the effects of the virus. It didn't affect any animal species, just humans, and it appeared completely out of nowhere. Shen's personal favourite theory is that aliens brought a weird space disease to Earth.

Whatever caused it, there's not much we can do except wait and hope that the scientists will create a cure before it's too late.

"Find anything?" I call to Shen, who's opening the door into the next carriage.

"Nothing but mouse droppings," he says warily.

I smile. Shen would never admit it, but he's a little scared of mice. He has no problem with rats, but he thinks that mice are too small and quick. Apparently that makes them "suspicious".

I kneel down to peer under the seats. There's an old newspaper, shredded into dust, a shopping bag and something at the back in the shadows. My fingers hook over it, and I tug it out into the light.

It's a purse. A cheap one, because the plasticky material hasn't rotted as much as the seating. In fact, I can still make out the faded design – the logo for something called *Loch & Ness*. I try the zip, but it's sealed shut with grime, so I run the blade of my penknife along the edge of it and the purse flops open, revealing rows of plastic cards. When I tilt one to the light, I can make out an embossed name: MS MAYA WAVERLEY. I call Shen back and he takes the card from me, pulling out his magnifying glass same time.

"You can look at it later," I tell him, checking the time. "We should probably find our way back to daylight if we don't want to be late for the community meeting."

Everyone comes to the weekly meetings. As far as we know, London is the only occupied city now. As the population got smaller and smaller, people migrated towards the capital cities. Then, when we were about five, it was decided that everyone left should move to one place, to make it easier to keep energy and water supplies running. London was chosen because it's where Shen and I were already living.

I make a note of the purse's location in our Discoveries log-book on my tablet: "Embossed emerald-green plastic wallet, circa mid-twenty-first century." I also note down the coordinates of where I found it. The purse is mysterious, which sometimes makes a discovery more interesting than it being simply valuable. Often, I'll find something weird and take it home just to work out why I like it.

Shen often jokes that only people like us would think sifting through mud and sewers for junk is a hobby instead of an act of desperation. He says we're so used to having everything we need that the only thing really valuable to us any more is the element of surprise. I don't think that's true, though.

We are lucky that we don't have to worry about food supplies or anything like that. Our parents, and their parents before them, planned meticulously for the time when there would be only a few humans left. We definitely don't need to scavenge for items for anything but fun. But I don't think we're ungrateful or spoiled. The reason I enjoy treasure-hunting is because I'm fascinated by history. When you know that there's no future, the only thing that's interesting any more is the past.

I want to know who Maya Waverley was. I wonder if I'll be able to track her down on the old social media sites people used to post on. It would be nice to find out what happened to her.

Once, I traced the owner of a lost engagement ring to the grave she shares with her husband, based on the names and date engraved on the inside of the ring. The gravestone was in a local cemetery, and had been completely hidden under brambles and moss by the time Shen and I tracked it down using the county records. We cleaned it up and left the ring on a chain hanging over the stone. People may die and civilizations may fall, but little pieces of the past linger.

After tucking the purse in my utility belt, we swim down the tunnel until we reach the next platform. We walk up a spiral staircase to the old Westminster station entrance and climb out through a gap in the boarded-up doors. The fresh breeze is a relief after the stale air in the tunnels, but the wind makes me feel even colder in my wetsuit.

We walk towards home along the bank of the Thames. Shen and I are allowed out on our own, as long as we stay in central London, where the buildings are safe. Beyond that, it can be too dangerous. Everything is falling into ruin. Our parents don't let us go out there without an adult.

I call Dad and say, "We found a way out at Westminster. Where are you at?"

He sounds distracted. "I'm still here. I found a – well, I'm not sure what it is, but I think it's in the *batrachospermaceae* family. I'm going to be a while."

I roll my eyes at Shen, who smirks. "OK," I say to Dad, "see you at home."

Dad makes a distracted noise of confirmation, and I hang up.

We head down the foreshore. The tips of my boots dip in and out of the brown waves, leaving half-moon footprints in the sand which quickly fill with water. Even though we didn't find much in the Underground today, we might have more luck in the Thames.

Everything ends up here. People have been dumping sewage and rubbish in this river ever since London became a city. Most of it sank down to the bottom, where it has remained for centuries.

Now, when the population is so low as to be negligible, the river bed has started eroding instead of building up. The Thames is cleaning itself of humanity's presence. The infertility of the human race was actually quite a good move, from an environmental perspective.

Year by year, the layers of history are peeling back to reveal older and older treasures. Shen and I have made it our mission to find as much of it as possible, mudlarking nearly every day. That's what it's called, when you search the mud of the Thames for interesting stuff.

An old robot is plodding along the sand ahead of us. He is so old that grey-green moss and bird droppings fill the crevices of the joints, curving over his round body. He lifts his head as we walk past, but looks back to the ground with disinterest. I try not to take it personally. He is such an old model he's barely functional any more. Mum says he was installed on the riverbank in the twenty-twenties as a lifeguard after a tourist drowned.

He's solar-powered, so for decades he has been walking up and down the river, scanning continuously for anyone in danger. Mum calls him "Mitch", after some lifeguard character in an old TV show. It's a joke that only the adults find funny, but the name kind of stuck.

We carry on, past Mitch, and past the remains of a collapsed Victorian redbrick which the maintenance bots haven't demolished yet. Our ancestors designed bots to keep things safe, even when there weren't many humans left. Eventually, though, when the last of us dies and there isn't anyone around to service the bots, they'll all start breaking down too. Then all the buildings will finish their slow descent into ruin, like this one.

"You can see the rock, look." I point at the building. Slabs of softening concrete have torn away the tarmac of the road above, exposing layers of the earth in lines of soil, clay and sand.

"Isn't it strange to think that in a few million years, all that might be left of the human race will be a millimetre of rock like that?" Shen asks. "I wonder what an alien would make of it, if they visited Earth then?"

I reach down to twist a glass bottle out of the mud. It comes out with a squelch. I've never given up hope that there'll be a message inside one, one day. I rub away the mud to read the name embossed in the glass. Coca-Cola, as usual. "Well, they'd probably think Coca-Cola was a religion, for a start."

Shen gives a small smile and then tilts his head, eyes on the ground. "I read this thing that said that the carbon dioxide we released from burning fossil fuels will last longer than anything else humans have ever made. So I reckon alien archaeologists would be able to work out from the carbon dioxide caught in the rock that *something* happened on this planet a long time ago."

"I wonder if they'd work out that the carbon dioxide came from an intelligent species burning fossil fuels, though," I say, intrigued by this idea. "They might think it was a freak natural event."

I look at the stones at my feet: the shards of slate and glass left in the soil. What would I think had caused them, if I was an alien and knew nothing about humanity? Would I see any difference between sandstone and concrete, or glass and amber, or plastic?

Once, I was 3D-printing a tool box when a fly got stuck in the molten plastic. It's still there, perfectly preserved like a butterfly in amber. Would an alien recognize it as a fake fossil? Maybe the man-made materials would mean nothing to them. Maybe they wouldn't even be looking for an intelligent race.

"The aliens definitely wouldn't know about us, then," I say. "A boy and a girl, living on the outskirts of a collapsed civilization, watching their species go extinct."

Shen swallows, Adam's apple rising and falling. "Nope."

The metal detector lets out a short beep, and he pushes his toe into the silt, flipping over the dirt to reveal a bottle cap.

"You never know, though," he adds. "Maybe us humans will leave something behind. There are caves full of drawings made over forty thousand years ago. The conditions have preserved them perfectly. They're going to survive centuries after the last buildings have collapsed."

"So if humanity does leave a message for the future, it's not going to be from us. It'll be from the first hunter-gatherers." I picture ochre handprints stretching upwards to the sky, welcoming extraterrestrial visitors a million years from now.

Shen grins. His cheeks have turned pink with cold. "I mean, they've probably got more of a right to it than us. Those caves had people living in them continuously for thousands and thousands of years. A lot longer than humans have ever lived in buildings.

We're the dead end in a long line of generations. The ones who broke everything."

I gulp. The thought hits home, probably more harshly than he meant it to. I think about the legacy we're leaving behind all the time: pollution and plastic and buildings and everything else. As one of the last humans, my choices and decisions are imbued with the full weight of the billions of lives that came before me. It feels like my ancestors are watching me, waiting to see how I ensure their legacy, how I remember them.

That's why I like mudlarking, because it feels like I'm actually doing something to record the history that's being lost. I'm so helpless, in the face of the infertility. But I can make sure that someone remembers the lives that came before us, if only for a few more decades.

Overhead, a helicopter thrums as it heads downriver. It must be Alexei Wyatt, on his way back from one of the abandoned cities around England, where he goes to pick up scavenged items in an old army helicopter. He'll be heading straight to the community meeting, which means we've got just enough time to go home and change into dry clothes before we have to join everyone at City Hall.

"What song are we doing today, do you know?" I ask, as we walk. Our choir always rehearses after the meeting. I sing – and weasel a rap solo out of Shen's mama, the choirmaster, when I can. Shen's voice is terrible, so he plays bass guitar instead.

Shen hums a few bars of melody. "That one. Mama was singing it in the shower this morning."

I hum it back to him, trying to remember the name. It's catchy, annoyingly so, and I'm still singing it in my head when I realise there's something wrong with the helicopter. It's tilted at an angle, skittering in the air like a glass about to fall off a table. It looks like it's been caught in a gust of wind – but the air is still and calm.

"That doesn't look—" Shen begins, but before he can finish, the helicopter drops out of the sky. The tail rotor catches on a lamppost on Westminster Bridge, and there's a shrieking explosion of metal.

I take an involuntary step backwards as the helicopter whirls in a tight circle, swung around by the force of its spinning rotors. It's thrown across the bridge and into a support beam. Sheets of metal pull away from the cockpit, and I think that surely it can't keep going, that it must come to a stop soon, but it doesn't. It swings around in another violent arc and collides with the clock tower of Big Ben.

TIME	DATE	LOCATION	OBJECT	NOTES
11.59	12/09/2107	51.494998, 0.068884	Engraved nine-carat gold engagement ring from 1899.	Found by LMBW inside a steel beam on the underside of Woolwich Pier.

I can't believe what I'm seeing.

The clock tower explodes, the whole front panel sheering off. The ancient clock face crumples as a rotor blade stabs into it. Bricks fly towards us, and we both scramble backwards through the mud, away from the explosion.

Shen's hand wraps around my elbow. "Run," he says, and I don't argue. He's always so calm in a crisis, but my heart feels like it's going to hammer out of my chest.

I'm desperate to look back over my shoulder at the rolling fire-ball, but I know I'll trip and fall immediately if I do. Something lunges towards me and I stumble back in shock, tripping and scraping my knee on the ground. It's Mitch. Spindly metal legs have sprouted out of the robot's rusted spherical body, and he scoops Shen and me into his arms, and then starts hopping in long, jolting strides down the riverbank.

I give a little cry of surprise, confused until I realise that his lifeguarding protocol must have been activated by the crash. I'm strangely glad about it, and I hold on tightly. He's running faster than I could have done.

When I risk a glance over the robot's shoulder, I see that the fire is spreading from the tower to engulf the Palace of Westminster, filling the air with the crack and roar of brickwork collapsing.

I can't think. My mind is abuzz with the white noise of shock – that a helicopter crashed in central London; that it crashed into the tower of Big Ben; that we were right there to see it happen.

Mitch climbs a staircase embedded into the concrete embankment and comes to a stop at the top. Still clutching us tightly, his head spins as he scans for more trouble. I wriggle, keen to be free now that we're a safe distance from the crash, and Mitch releases us, lowering us carefully to the tarmac.

"I can't *believe*—" Shen says, staring at Mitch and then at the fire. "*Tamade!*" He always reverts to Chinese when he gets upset.

"I know." My lungs can't seem to remember how to pull in air. I focus on breathing until my chest loosens and the dizziness stops.

"It's Alexei, isn't it?" Shen asks quietly.

I nod.

He closes his eyes briefly, grimacing.

Alexei, our friend. Alexei, who gave Shen and I the best tips for mudlarking, from his scavenging experience. Alexei, whose wife died a few years ago. Alexei Wyatt, who we've known our whole lives.

"Do you think he's...?" I can't even stand to think about what must have happened to him, in that kind of explosion.

Shen blanches, answering my question.

A squadron of emergency response drones is already flying to the building, but they look miniscule next to the growing fire. I can't see how they'll manage to put it out.

Shen takes a deep breath, and there's only the slightest wobble in his voice when he speaks. "Are you hurt?" He braces his palms on either side of my neck, checking my eyes for pupil dilation.

"I'm fine," I say, but I let him massage the joint at the top of my spine. His touch is comforting. "Are you?"

All the colour has disappeared from his face except for an irritated patch of pink at the corner of his jaw, where he must have hit the ground. I rub away the small curls of white that it scraped from the skin. His stubble catches on my thumb.

Behind us, the fire is blazing higher and hotter, but to my surprise, half of the emergency drones are flying straight past the crash and heading towards *us*.

"Are they—?" I ask.

"Yes."

I let out a heavy sigh. We're fine. We're not even hurt. This isn't necessary. They should all be trying to help Alexei.

The emergency response drones swoop in to land, surrounding us in a neat circle. Their laser scanners flicker down our bodies, searching for injuries.

"We're OK," Shen says, but the drones don't listen. They chitter to each other in binary as they cluster around my leg, where there's a tear in the wetsuit. It must have happened when I fell. I can't feel the cut, but red blood shines bright against the fabric. A mechanical arm appears from one drone, reaching out to clean the shallow wound.

"Shouldn't you be putting out the fire?" I ask. It's hardly a life-threatening injury. I'm worried the same can't be said of Alexei's. The bot ignores me and is carefully spraying the wound with antiseptic when a car pulls up next to us. Mrs Bolton jumps out, barely stopping to turn off the engine in her panic. "Are you OK? What happened?" she gasps. "I was on the way to the meeting and I saw the fire." She stares at it in horror.

"There was a helicopter crash…" I begin and trail off, unable to finish.

"Alexei?" Mrs Bolton's eyes widen.

"We think so," Shen says. "We don't know if he was on his own."

My throat tightens. It hadn't even occurred to me that there might have been someone else. *Please, no. Please.*

Mrs Bolton raises a hand to her mouth. "Oh no." Her eyes fill with tears, then she glances at us again, before reaching out to squeeze my shoulder. "The drones will do whatever they can to get him to safety. At least you weren't hurt too. That's what matters." She chokes off another small sob.

Meanwhile, Mitch is still pacing around us in emergency mode, a red light flashing on the top of his head.

"It's OK," I call to him, trying to get him to calm down. "We're safe now."

Mitch doesn't listen, and continues to scan for danger. More drones are flying around the wreckage of Big Ben, trying to reach the helicopter. I try to imagine what Alexei must be feeling right now, stuck inside. My mind skitters away from the thought. I can't bear it.

I hear a squeal of tyres and I'm relieved to see Mum's Rolls-Royce heading towards us. She slams on the brakes when she spots us. "Oh, thank goodness," she says, jumping out of the car. She checks me over to make sure I'm not hurt. I lean against her side, feeling ten times safer.

"Come on, let's get you both home," she says.

"Is Dad OK?" I ask. "He was in the Underground. He didn't get caught in it, did he?"

"He's fine. I called him," Mum says. "He's meeting us at home."

She turns to Mrs Bolton, and they have a quick whispered conversation about what happened. Deep lines of worry form around Mum's mouth when she finds out about Alexei.

"We should get home," she says, looking over at Shen and me.

Suddenly I just want to get out of here. I follow Shen to the car. My steps are off-kilter. I feel dizzy again.

Before we can get inside the car, Mitch pushes past me and slides on to the white leather of the front passenger seat. "What are you *doing*?" I ask him.

He is so old that he doesn't have any communication software installed. He can't speak, so he can only flash an answer at me: blue, whatever that means.

"He probably wants to make sure we're all right," Shen says.

"He did save us," I admit, confused but a little pleased. "We should let him come with us."

"What on Earth—!" Mum says, gaping at the mud-covered robot as she gets into the driver's seat.

Mitch flashes green at her, in a resolute, determined way, making it clear that he is going nowhere.

Mum sighs and lets Mitch stay without complaining, even when flakes of orange rust splinter on to the burled walnut panelling of the car. Her shoulders are stiff with worry, and I don't think that has anything to do with Mitch.

Now I'm in clean, air-conditioned air, I notice that the smoke has settled into my lungs. It's thick in the back of my throat. When I cough, trying to clear it out, Mum's eyebrow jerks upwards, looking at me with concern in the rear-view mirror. I wince. "This isn't going to be good," I lean in to whisper to Shen. Our parents already worry about us far too much.

He taps his ear. "Wrong side," he says.

It annoys me that I can never, ever remember which is his deaf ear. Which is ridiculous, because I know everything about him – every food he likes and dislikes, the meaning of every single expression that crosses his face, all of his favourite phrases. Why can't I remember to sit on his hearing side?

"We're screwed," I whisper into his other ear when he twists, dipping his head to mine.

He hums his agreement.

They're probably not even going to let us leave the *grounds* after this. They're all going to start another discussion about how we need to be more careful, because we're too important to get hurt. Like I've been hearing since the day I was born. But all of that feels inconsequential when I think about Alexei, and that fireball. Maybe our parents are right to want to keep us safe.

CHAPTER 3

TIME	DATE	LOCATION	OBJECT	NOTES
16.43	30/03/2106	51.501621, -0.148714	*Neolithic dark-grey flint, barbed arrowhead with chips on edges, 3000 BCE.*	*Found by SZ. Dug out of the soil while helping Dad plant a new rose bush.*

After the car pulls up outside the gates of the manor, we all traipse inside in silence. There's a Conversation about Safety simmering, but it's bad manners to start before Dad and Shen's parents have a chance to join in.

Mum groans as she gets out of the car. She was born five years after the sterility, so she's almost eighty, and she groans a lot these days – more than Dad, even though he's older. I feel bad for making her worry about us. She shouldn't have to deal with that, not at her age.

We toe off our wellies and peel off our damp wetsuits in the mudroom. Then Shen drops his metal detector into the umbrella stand by the door. It's an ancient porcelain vase which is probably too precious for such treatment.

The dogs race up to greet us, yipping madly. Victoria licks at the blood on my wetsuit. Trying to distract her from it, I reach into my utility belt for a dog biscuit and my fingers scrape over the old purse from the Tube. In all the drama I'd almost forgotten about it. Victoria crunches the biscuit down in seconds, and then sniffs at my pockets for more as Shen crouches to rub Albert's ears.

"Feng and Jia are in the library," Mum tells me distractedly as she unties the silk scarf from her hair and throws it over a statue – a stern rendering of my great-great-great-grandfather. Wisps of blonde hair float across her face, and she blows them away from the corner of her mouth. She still looks pale.

Over the top of my swimming costume, I pull on a mustard-yellow knitted jumper that is hanging on a nearby coat hook. I think it's Shen's – but jumpers are in such high demand here that if you see one, it's fair game. The manor is so big and the heating system is so ancient that it's always freezing cold. Everything has been converted to run off solar power, but the pipes and radiators are the same old ones which have been used since the nineteenth century.

I follow Shen and Mum to the library, slipping along the parquet floor in a pair of warm socks, fresh off the radiator. Mitch comes after us, looking around with interest. I wonder if he has ever been inside a house before, or if he's spent the entirety of the last eighty years patrolling the river. Whatever his reason for deciding to hang on to us, I'm glad. It's reassuring having him here, even if he is leaving a trail of moulted mulch in his wake.

"Shen! Lowrie!" Shen's mama, Jia, says as we come into the library. She stands to hug us, before pulling us over to a chaise longue, next to the heat of the fire.

"You're both OK?" Feng asks, in a rough, worried voice. Feng always dresses smartly, in a bow tie and waistcoat, even in summer, but today his waistcoat is unbuttoned and his bow tie looks askew, like he was in a rush to get here. Jia looks dishevelled too. Her face is drawn and worried, like Mum's.

Jia sits between us, pulling us close, and I can't help but lean into her side. She's always so easy to touch – tugging Shen and me into her arms without hesitating. Mum doesn't hug me nearly as often.

"We've been watching what happened on the news," she says. "If you'd only been a few metres closer… I can't bear to imagine what might have happened."

"We're fine, really," I tell her. There's an annoying quaver to my voice. "Mitch saved us." I nod at the robot who is wobbling along the edge of the room, tilting up on his heels to stare at the golden ceiling.

"You did a good job of keeping them safe," Feng tells him approvingly.

Mitch's head lifts a little, like he is preening.

Neither Feng nor Jia asks us why the robot has come back with us. They're used to us bringing home all manner of strange things.

"Has there been any news about Alexei yet?" Shen asks, nodding towards the newsfeed playing on the wall.

I don't usually watch the news – everyone takes it in turns to host, and I've heard all their anecdotes and stories and jokes a million times before. The last time I watched it must have been when Shen gave a guest lecture on alien conspiracy theories, which is his favourite topic of conversation, bar none. He was very good, but he didn't get the viewership he really deserved.

Hilary Barnett is hosting today. She looks a little overwhelmed by the action – usually she just discusses gardening techniques. "The ... er ... fire has already been put out," she says.

I tap the floor with my foot, urging her to hurry up and tell us what's going on.

An image pops up on the screen of the once delicate carved brickwork of Westminster Palace. The whole building is a charred, destroyed mess. Water is gushing into it from the Thames, and the helicopter is already nearly submerged.

I must have let out some sort of noise, because Mitch comes over and presses against my legs. I pat his shoulder, distracted.

"Doctor Ahmed is treating Alexei at, at – the, sorry." Hilary stops talking and dabs her eyes with a flowered handkerchief. "This is such a difficult time. At the h–hospital as we speak. We're not sure of his condition just yet." She draws in a breath. *"Poor Alexei."*

I shudder. I really hope he doesn't die. We've lost enough people. Just last month one of the ladies in our choir died. I never get used to seeing everyone gathered at the funerals. It makes me realise how old and small the community is now. Every single person who dies brings Shen and me even closer to being totally alone. "Hilary is doing a stand-up job of dealing with the emergency broadcast," I say, trying to smile.

Jia nods in agreement as she gives Shen's hand a squeeze

when he starts anxiously tapping out Vivaldi's *Four Seasons* on the arm of the sofa.

"Good for her," Feng says, as a bot brings in a plate of tea and scones, fresh and hot from the oven. After everything that's happened, the warm, comforting smell makes me feel a bit sick.

In the old days, our manor needed a household of fifty servants to keep it going, but these days it's run by only around a hundred bots. We might live in a world that's breaking down, but, thanks to the planning that went into our future after the virus, we live just like everyone did when London was filled with millions of people. It wasn't as hard to plan as you might think. Even before the sterility crisis, most repetitive jobs had been taken over by automated bots. Banking, deliveries, factories, farms, water-treatment plants and retail have all been computerized for decades, while humans were hired for jobs that required personal interaction, like nursing and teaching. Now, there are even maintenance bots to fix any broken bots, so it's a self-contained system.

Society could probably keep running indefinitely without any human interference at all. All our energy comes from solar panels, and our cars run on electricity, so there's no waste or environmental damage. Our world is perfectly organised. It's just … empty. There's barely anyone left to use the tech and resources.

"Henry was in the Underground at the time?" Jia asks Mum, who rolls her eyes.

"He's fine. Was oblivious to the crash. You know how he gets with lichen," Mum says.

I can tell she's slightly mad at him for leaving us alone. "It's not his fault," I say hurriedly. "Dad didn't know anything was going to happen."

Shen adds, "We'd have been perfectly safe, if – if Alexei hadn't—" He dips his head and bites his lip.

"The thing I don't understand is how Alexei…" Feng starts. He breaks off when Jia throws him a look that I can't interpret.

"Alexei is in safe hands. Doctor Ahmed is one of the best," Jia says to us, and she would know. She is a doctor at the hospital. She and Dr Ahmed are two of only a few human members of staff left. The rest are bots. There are hardly any patients these days, though, so there's never any trouble about it – and Jia conducts the bots around like a symphony orchestra.

I pull a tangle of seaweed off Mitch's head, twisting it between my fingers until it's tight enough to make the skin go white. I know Jia's trying to make us feel better, but I can't stop thinking about the crash: the heat of the flames, the searing metal, what would have happened to us if we'd been any closer. Poor Alexei.

Mum butters a scone and applies a neat layer of Dad's home-made blueberry jam and clotted cream, before passing it to me with a china teacup full of hot, sweet tea, and a slice of lemon on the saucer. "Eat that, love. You need the sugar – you've had a shock."

I'm not hungry, but I pick it up anyway and attempt to take a bite, while Mum butters another one for Shen. The heat of the insides catches my fingertips.

While we're eating, Jia kneels in front of us, shining a light in each of our eyes in turn. "Dilation is normal," she says. "No sign of concussion. Are you cold? Nauseous?"

We shake our heads. I can't believe she's this worried about us when Alexei is injured. What does it matter if we feel a bit nauseous when he might *die*?

"Now sing an octave," Jia says.

We give it our best attempt, but we're out of tune – both with each other and what we're supposed to be singing.

"What does that even tell you?" I ask.

"Nothing. I wanted to see if you had been doing your choir warm-ups." Jia grins.

"I'm not even one of the singers," Shen says, miffed. The chandelier dangling from the ceiling casts pale light over him, making him look tired and thin.

"Lucky for us all," Feng says dryly.

Despite my worry, I choke back a laugh.

Shen gives a long sigh. He really is a terrible singer, though – and he hates it. He's not good at dealing with failure.

A satisfied line appears at the corner of Jia's mouth. Clearly, she's just got her answer to the real test. We can't be too affected if we're laughing and grumbling.

"It looks like Lowrie's leg is the only injury," Jia says to Mum and Feng. "They may also experience some mild post-traumatic stress disorder, but we can treat that as and when it occurs."

"I'll put away the blue lights, then," Mum says, pretending to turn off a police car's emergency siren. "Thanks, Jia."

Mitch is still pressed against my legs, smearing muck on my jumper. He holds still as I wipe the bird droppings off his chrome oval head with a rag from my utility belt. If he's going to be around for a while, then I can at least make sure he doesn't ruin any priceless antiques. "Can I go and shower?" I ask when I've finished. I need a bit of time to process everything somewhere our parents aren't watching every reaction for a sign of shock.

"Eat a crumpet," Mum says, "and you can both go."

When the tea tray is full of nothing but crumbs, we stand up. Mum follows us out of the library, calling, "Lunchtime, darlings!" to the dogs. Mum never cooks, as the bots do all the cleaning and cooking and tidying, but she makes an exception for her dogs.

I chase Shen and Mitch up the left side of the double spiral staircase towards the east wing, pausing to rub the petals of my favourite bronze rose on the bannister. I need the luck today.

When we get to my room, Shen flops on my four-poster bed while I run the shower. He's been quiet since we got back. Mitch is the only one who doesn't seem worried. Instead, he's busy exploring. The lights on his head flash purple when he pushes open the door of my walk-in closet to see what's inside.

Dad and I turned it into a workshop years ago. There's a long workbench with a Belfast sink for washing dirty equipment, and the walls are covered in hooks for my tools to hang from. Their matching pale-oak handles hang on the white walls in an inter-locking geometric pattern which is deeply satisfying. Under each hook, I've painted a light grey outline of the shape of the tool which goes there – so I know where everything belongs.

It's my favourite room in the manor. Dad calls it my "growlery", because I always come in here when I need to sulk. Organising the tools and hanging them back over their outlines – clean and sharp and ready for the next adventure – is my favourite thing to do, bar none. There's even a gold plaque on the door, with the rules of entry. Feng and I made it. (I was eight, so the rules aren't particularly polite.)

> ## THE RULES OF LOWRIE'S GROWLERY
> 1. ALWAYS KNOCK BEFORE ENTRY.
> 2. DO NOT TAKE TOOLS WITHOUT LOWRIE'S PERMISSION EVER.
> 3. SHEN ISN'T ALLOWED TO COME IN UNLESS I'M HERE.

Mitch rises up on his long, retractable legs, peering at the tools with interest. I watch him for a moment, then stand in front of my bathroom mirror, frowning at my mud-caked hair. It's usually a light blonde, but the mud is giving me a good sense of what I'd look like if I were brunette. I'm going to have to wash it at least twice.

I poke at the neat little oval patch above my right temple that's gone prematurely grey. It appeared abruptly last year and has been growing steadily larger ever since.

Shen squints at me through the doorway. "Is that my jumper?"

I shrug, defensively. "I was cold." His jumpers are always so much better than mine and have enough spare material in the sleeves that I can wrap my palms in them. They always smell good too. "Aren't those my slippers, anyway, Zhang?"

He wriggles his toes in my lambskin slippers, looking more pleased than ashamed.

We take turns to shower. There's a lump of something disgusting tangled into a knot in my hair that even a double wash can't remove, so I cut it out with my penknife, dropping the gunk into the bin without inspecting it too closely. If it's from the tunnels, I'm not sure I want to know.

After showering, Shen settles into the oxblood Chesterfield armchair nestled between the bay windows, rubbing a towel at the back of his neck. His damp hair lies flat. "Feel better?" he asks.

I fall back on the bed, sighing. "I can't stop thinking about it. The crash. Alexei."

"I know," Shen agrees. He hesitates and says, "Do you think it was an accident?"

I raise my eyebrows. "What do you mean?"

"I just don't know how you could crash a helicopter that drives itself. It would have sensors to guide it away from buildings. It's all coded. It shouldn't be possible."

"He probably programmed the flight path wrong or something."

"I guess," he says. "I'm sure Baba thinks something is off too, though…" He lets his sentence trail off. Then his posture loosens, and the anxiety slips out of the lines of his shoulders. "I'm probably worrying about nothing."

"I can't believe Big Ben is just … gone now," I say. It all feels so surreal. I close my eyes, suddenly exhausted. The room smells like Dad's homemade mint shower gel. Albert – who has some kind of internal nap sensor – slinks into the room and jumps on to the foot of the bed, woofing gently.

I can't seem to relax enough to sleep. I keep reliving the moment of the helicopter crash in my mind. The bright heat of the explosion on my cheeks, the shock of the belief that I was about to die. I feel twitchy and on edge. I need something else to think about. Sighing again, I fetch the old purse we found from my utility belt and take it back to bed.

I turn one of the plastic cards over in my hands and rub free a particle of grit embedded it in. We've learnt about these cards. They were how people used to pay for things. The faded curl and spiral of Maya Waverley's signature fills a white strip on the back of the card. I wonder who she was; where she lived; when she died.

Intrigued, I type her name into the archive of an old social media site, just to see if I can track her down. A lot of the internet disappeared before I was born. Huge numbers of news websites, social media archives, reference sites, emails and more were lost as the companies that hosted the data closed down, one by one. They vanished like they'd never existed. Luckily, a few long-term internet archives are still online, and they make up a series of tiny islands sticking out of the ocean of online data that's been lost to time.

Feng showed us how to access them years ago. Whenever Shen and I want to research something, we can hop from island to island, searching for quotes from articles, or looking at screenshots of videos that no longer exist, and reading transcripts of code from websites that haven't been available for decades. It's enough to get the context of what actually happened, even if we can only view the eroded copy of a copy of a copy of the original facts. It's hard to work out exactly what is being talked about most of the time, though.

Out of all of the strange things I've learned about the past, social media is the weirdest. I can't believe how much private information people used to post online, for anyone to read! I can't ever imagine doing it myself.

I scroll through the results for *Maya Waverley*, searching for anyone with that name who lived in Britain. It's a rare name, but there are still too many results to narrow it down in any obvious way. While I'm searching, Shen picks a book from the stack on my bedside table. His reading pile always ends up in my room, supposedly because my armchair is the best reading nook in the manor. I think it's more likely to be because I have the best snacks. He checks the spine and then flips to the back. Shen always reads the acknowledgements first.

He's got his research face on, and I wonder if he's looking up the helicopter crash, or the train in the Underground, or something else – something about aliens, knowing him. I'm pretty sure that he's the world's leading expert in faux alien sightings throughout history. He knows every single case study by heart.

I flick through the cards in Maya Waverley's purse again, looking for anything which might help me pick her out of the results. At my feet, Albert whines, chasing dream rabbits. There's nothing on the cards, but the purse is embossed with the words "*Loch & Ness*". I don't know what that is, but I go through the search results again, this time checking the profiles to see if any of the Mayas made reference to it. There is one:

Maya Waverley
18 February 2024
New *Loch & Ness*, new *Loch & Ness*!! Would it be bad if I stayed up until 9 a.m. to watch it when it goes live online?

Loch & Ness must be a TV show, then. I'll have to see if we have a copy of it in the archive. Dad stored a lot of old shows when the biggest internet memory banks were about to shut down, for Shen and me to watch one day.

I look at the search results again. This Maya lived in Oxford, which is near enough to London that she might have been visiting and caught the Tube, leaving her purse behind by accident. According to her info, she was born in 2005. She would have been nineteen when the virus spread. She would be one hundred and four by now. I've never heard of her, though, so she's definitely not still alive.

I skim through her timeline, reading some of her public posts. I'm not really sure what I'm looking for, except a distraction from thinking about Alexei.

Maya Waverley
19 February 2024
Me, grandly, crawling into a tangle of bedsheets at 9.45 a.m. after silencing my alarm: a productive day well spent. So glad I get to go back to sleep now.

> **Riz Stevens** I silenced my alarm seven times this morning, and I'm not even sorry.

> **Maya Waverley** That's pure determination right there.

I like her. She's funny.

It's both overwhelming and incredible she lived so long ago but I can still read the posts she wrote: things that she probably didn't intend for anyone to see except on the day she wrote them. It makes me wonder what will be left of me in eighty-five or even two thousand years. There'll be no one around to discover any messages by then, of course – but the idea of leaving a record is still appealing.

Did people imagine their grandchildren and great-grand-children one day reading the things they posted online? Back then they probably took it for granted that they would have grandchildren.

All that's changed now. I've always assumed I *won't* have kids. I mean, aside from the virus, who would I have them with? Everyone always jokes about how Shen and I will end up together, like some kind of Adam and Eve of the apocalypse. It's partly because our parents want us to be happy, and for them, that means getting married and being together for ever, like they've done.

But that can't happen. I absolutely won't let it. If Shen and I date, then there's a chance we'll break up. I can't risk that. He's all I've got. It's safer for us to stay as we are, as friends. There's no chance I'll lose him that way.

I don't know what he thinks about it. I've never wanted to risk asking. But I'm sure he feels the same. He must do. He would have said something ages ago, if he didn't.

CHAPTER 4

TIME	DATE	LOCATION	OBJECT	NOTES
14.22	04/04/2109	53.410551, -6.362114	Social media profile for Maya Waverley.	Found by LMBW saved on an internet archive of data over eighty years old, then stored in the London memory banks.

That night, after Shen and his parents have gone home, I can't sleep. I lie in bed and try not to think about Alexei, while watching Mitch's lights flash across the ceiling.

Mitch seems to have taken it upon himself to be our personal bodyguard. He followed me around all day, and he's now standing guard in my room, leaning against the wall next to the growlery.

"At least do something useful if you're going to stay," I say, half joking, but Mitch must take me seriously because after a moment or two, I hear a noise. He's started sorting through a bucket of rusting iron scraps.

Even though the clinking sound is kind of soothing, I still can't sleep. In the end I decide to read some more of Maya's posts instead, skimming through them in search of anything interesting. I come to one that pulls me up short.

Maya Waverley
21 February 2024

My mum has had a nosebleed for about two hours now. It's awful, we can't stop it. We've tried every tip online – ice, towel, standing up, etc. But it hasn't stopped. Do we call an ambulance, or am I massively overreacting?

> **Ashley Samson** Yes, call! That sounds really bad, Maya. Hope she's OK xx

---

Maya Waverley
22 February 2024

It feels slightly futile to throw another post into the writhing sea of social media posts discussing this, but I'm going to do it anyway just because it's three in the morning and I can't sleep without processing this in some way.

Yesterday, my mum got a nosebleed. I called an ambulance, and it turned out that not only was the operator's nose also bleeding, mine was too. I hung up and checked online, but there was nothing on the news.

It was only when I checked social media and saw everyone posting about it that I realised this was happening everywhere. It wasn't just a local or national thing. All over the world, friends and family and strangers were posting about their noses bleeding.

I know everyone is saying this, but at that point I honestly thought I was going to die. I started planning what I wanted to do with the time we had left. I hugged my mum and told her I loved her. I did the same to the cat, who hissed at me and ran outside (thanks, Jeff). I tried to call my dad, but the call didn't connect (probably because everyone in the country was doing the same thing).

At that point, my panic kind of transitioned into this horrible acceptance. Mum suggested we make cups of tea, and I agreed instantly. We sat in front of the TV and refreshed social media, waiting for the nosebleeds to make it on to the news. It took about twenty-five minutes.

By then, my feed was full of everyone online saying goodbye to each other. I've replied to everyone's messages in private, but you should all know that quite a few of you made me cry. I was a mess: tears and blood and spilt tea all over the place. I thought I was going to die and it wasn't even going to be dignified.

Dad came home, his shirt soaked through with the horrible blood. It was all sticky and matted in his beard too. I think that was worse than anything else.

Around this time, all our phones beeped. An emergency alert had been sent out warning people to stay in their homes in quarantine. I'd heard of phone alerts in hurricane zones, but I had no idea that the government could do that in the UK too. That ranks up there amongst the most horrifying moments of my life.

The bleeding had slowed down by then, so we all showered and watched the news for a bit. That made it about a hundred times worse: you could tell that no one had any idea what was going on. Everyone was just speculating in increasingly horrifying and imaginative ways. We collectively agreed to turn off the TV. I'm going to be honest here and say that when it became clear, after several painful hours, that there was nothing we could do except wait for news, we all decided to go and have a nap.

I lay in bed trying not to refresh my feed. Eventually Jeff joined me and I might have (definitely did) cry into his fur for a while. I tried to read, but I remembered I was reading a book about an apocalypse and actually threw my eReader at the wall in horror. I must have fallen asleep, because when Dad woke me up, it was dark. There'd been another alert: the virus wasn't life threatening but the quarantine was still in place.

I don't remember feeling relieved at that. I was still kind of keyed up. My parents must have been too, because we all directed our panic in another direction. We checked the cupboards and tried to work out how much food we had, and how long it might last if the quarantine continued.

Dad was furious for a bit, because he had nearly gone to Costco a few days before, and we could have been overflowing with bulk goods. The process was delayed by a hysterical screaming match about this from all parties (none of us had shouted when we thought we were going to die, so we must have all been feeling a bit better, even if it didn't feel like it at the time).

There was a siren outside, and we all ran out to see what was going on. An ambulance was going past. It didn't stop.

Dad suggested at that point that we go to Costco, but I refused to start scavenging for supplies five hours into the end of the world – so we made jacket potatoes and watched a film instead. And then we went to bed, like it was a normal day, because what can you do at that point except give up?

That was my first day of our new normal. Nothing will ever make this easy, but I think writing this out did help a bit. I'm so sorry this was so long and I apologize if you felt you had to read it all. I just needed to say something, even if it's the same as what everyone else is saying. This is something we're all going through, and I think it does help that we can go through it together. I can't imagine how hard this would have been without social media.

Maya Waverley
24 February 2024

So much for feeling calmer! Today I can't stop showering and showering, trying to get the virus off me. I know that's not how it works, but it helps somehow to turn the water up as hot as I can, until my skin turns pink. I ignore the pain and scrub at my face until it feels tender, gargle mouthfuls of soap and spit it out in the drain. I still feel infected, like the virus is all over me. I don't know what to do.

I read the entries in a state of shock. There are so many things Maya mentions that I didn't know about. I had no idea that people had nosebleeds when they caught the virus, or how panicked everyone was when they caught it and didn't know what was happening. I can just imagine the endless, sticky blood. It makes me feel sick.

I'm going to have to tell Shen about it tomorrow. I can't believe our parents never mentioned it, when they told us about the virus. They probably thought that it was a bit too nasty for kids to hear about.

I skim through more of the posts, looking for anything else interesting. There's one from two days before Maya caught the virus that makes me smile.

Maya Waverley
19 February 2024

Whenever I watch *Loch & Ness*, I'm hit
by the continuous realisation that I want
to date BOTH Lyra Loch and Jayden Ness,
and I can't, in fact, date either of them.
Frankly, it's ruining my life.

Does that mean Maya was bisexual, like me? I guess it does.

Something lights up inside my chest. There's no one my own age I can talk to about this stuff, and just seeing Maya living her life and posting about boys and girls makes me feel less alone. There are other gay people around, of course, but they're all older couples, who've been together for decades. Shen understands, or at least tries his best to be supportive, but it's not really the same as having someone who can actually relate.

I'm so glad I found her account. It's made me feel calm enough to finally be able to sleep.

"Good night," I call to Mitch.

He flashes a serene sky blue at me.

I drift off to sleep to the sound of metal scraps quietly clinking together.

CHAPTER 5

TIME	DATE	LOCATION	OBJECT	NOTES
10.10	11/07/2106	51.504393, -0.161654	First-generation black iPhone with a cracked screen. Contained a Vodafone SIM card, 2007.	Found by SZ. Dredged from the Serpentine accidentally during an unfortunate kayaking collision incident (Lowrie's fault).

Mitch is still hanging around my bedroom the next morning. I'd been wondering if he would get bored and leave during the night, but I wake up to find him stretched out on the floor next to a pile of perfectly organised metal. He even follows me down to breakfast.

The butler bot, Fitz, beeps at him disapprovingly. Mitch flashes some lights at him, trying to communicate the only way he can. Fitz clearly doesn't understand, because he beeps at Mitch again. There's a brief standoff, then Mitch gives in and backs out into the hallway, out of Fitz's territory.

I help myself to muesli with honey and raspberries from the buffet table. All the food is made by the bots and kept carefully warm under silver domes. Then I sit across the table from Mum. The mahogany breakfast table is laid out with gold cutlery, antique porcelain, and crystal glasses, which I was finally given permission to use last year after a decade of begging. They make orange juice taste extra sophisticated.

Dad is dozing in his chair by the window, a plate of eggs slowly sliding down his chest with each snore. Albert is waiting at his feet, practically open-mouthed in anticipation of falling food.

"Where are you going?" I ask Mum, eyeing her khaki trousers and gilet. She's not wearing her usual silk blouse and tweed skirt.

"I'm going out to the crash site to see if we can work out how it happened," Mum says, pouring coffee.

"With Mrs Maxwell?"

Mum nods.

Mum and Mrs Maxwell are sort of our unofficial investigators. Not that there's ever much to investigate. Usually, they just organise pot-lucks for the community meetings and act as the designated drivers for parties. I think Mrs Maxwell used to be a police officer, back when there was still a need for the police, so people tend to go to her if they need any help.

"Has there been any news about Alexei?" I ask, selecting an apple from the fruit bowl. It came from orchards in the grounds which have been there for at least a hundred years, but still grow the sweetest apples.

"Not yet. He's still unconscious."

I grimace. Poor Alexei. "What are you hoping to find at the site?"

Mum shrugs. "I don't know, to be honest. The fire probably destroyed most of it, but Mrs Maxwell likes to be thorough." There's a slight edge to her voice and I can't work out why. Then

I remember what Shen said yesterday about the crash maybe not being an accident. Is she worried about that too?

I take a bite of my apple, then say, "Can Shen and I come? *Please?* It'll be educational."

"I can't wait for you to get Shen out of bed." She frowns at her plate, and I realise with a shock that she's really worked up about this. She almost looks nervous. I'm all the more curious to go to the crash site, to see what could have got her in such a state. Has the collapse destroyed the whole of the Palace of Westminster, or something?

After a long pause, she sighs and says, "I suppose you can meet us there, if you want. We'll be there all morning. Bring some of your tools, in case Mrs Maxwell doesn't have everything we need."

"We'll ride the horses over. Thanks, Mum! You're the best!"

She smiles, carefully buttering a crust of bread and feeding it to Victoria, who props the toast between her paws and licks off the butter.

I call Shen, knowing that he won't answer. He'll still be deeply asleep, but he usually wakes up if I call enough times. He's a night owl, which I find completely confounding.

The call rings and rings. After a minute or two, I hang up and try again. I reach for a croissant, eating it while I wait.

"Shen!" I shout around a mouthful of pastry, when he finally answers. "Get out of bed right now! We're going to the crash site!"

"Make sure you tell him to wear lots of layers," Mum says as she leaves the room. "It's chilly today."

I roll my eyes but pass on the message.

Shen yawns loudly in my ear, mumbles something and hangs up.

"Don't go back to *sleep*!" I shout, but it's too late – he's already gone.

Dad wakes with a snort and catches the plate of scrambled eggs just before it tips into Albert's expectant mouth. "You look nice, Lowrie," he says, yawning.

Albert gives up all hope of eggs, and goes to eat the well-licked toast that Victoria has abandoned instead.

"I curled my hair," I say, pleased that the effort was noticed.

"You used to be such an ugly baby," he says, sighing nostalgically. "I don't know how you ended up so beautiful."

"Thanks. I think," I say, squinting at him with suspicion. I'm pretty sure he just insulted me.

Dad notices Mitch, standing in the doorway, and perks up. "Hello, little fella," he says surprised. He turns to me, questioningly.

"He followed me home from the foreshore yesterday," I explain. "He saved Shen and me from the explosion."

Dad nods, impressed. "Is that some *xanthoparmelia thalli* on your head?" he asks Mitch. "Come over here and let's have a look."

Mitch reluctantly slinks over and lets Dad pick through the different lichens covering his metal head.

I watch, captivated, and realise I've absent-mindedly eaten another croissant.

"Mum's showing Shen and me the crash site this morning,"

I tell Dad, as he scrapes off a sample of lichen with an antique, ivory butter knife.

"You are an old one, aren't you?" he says to Mitch, then takes in what I said. He looks surprised. "She is? Oh. Well, I suppose your mother knows what she's doing. Make sure you're back for class. Whose turn is it this afternoon?"

"Yours," I say, sliding my socked soles over the smooth carved wooden feet of the chair.

He groans, staring longingly into the empty cafétière. He always forgets which day he's teaching, and usually prepares a hasty lesson plan at the last minute.

Shen and I are tutored by our parents. Dad teaches us life skills – sometimes that's everyday things, like cooking, sewing and DIY, but other times it's more serious subjects, like farming methods and basic mechanics. Mum teaches politics and English; Jia teaches history and medicine; and Feng teaches science and maths. Whatever we're learning, Shen loves it. He soaks up information like a sponge, and goes off and researches everything in his spare time. He asks a lot of questions too, whereas I'd rather be out digging up fossils. I can't see the point of learning any of it, except for what Dad teaches us.

He tells us things we might need to know one day, decades from now, when there might not even be bots to help us. He gives us survival skills to prepare us for a time when we may be the only people alive in an empty world.

I understand the point of those lessons. Worryingly.

Though I'd much rather not have to study at all.

"We can skip school today," I say, hopefully, as he tips out the dregs of cold coffee into his cup and drinks from it, wincing. I think that secretly he hates being a teacher even more than I hate being a student. Not that he'll admit it.

"On your bike," he says, affable as always, and gives his eggs to an ecstatic Albert.

I give him up as a lost cause and go upstairs to get ready.

Lowrie MBW [9.46]:	Are you on your way? I've eaten every single croissant on the buffet table. I need you to save me from myself.
Lowrie MBW [10.14]:	We're going to run out of time before class if you don't hurry.
张申 [10.33]:	10 min.
Lowrie MBW [10.34]:	You went back to sleep, didn't you?
Lowrie MBW [10.46]:	Why do you do this to me every single day? Why am I always surprised?
Lowrie MBW [10.48]:	Good morning, by the way
张申 [10.49]:	no morning is ever good.
Lowrie MBW [10.51]:	This is exactly how I feel when you send me sixteen messages at 4 a.m.
张申 [11.03]:	xixixi. nearly up.

I go to the growlery to pack some tools while I wait for Shen. I've learnt to always be over-prepared after we found a sealed wooden chest by the river but didn't have any tools to open it. By the time we had fetched some and gone back, the tide had washed it away.

I fill my utility belt with the essentials – a penknife, screwdriver, chisel and spanner. Then, as I'm still waiting for Shen, I rub beeswax into the pale-oak handles of my tools, and use a whetstone to make the edges of the blades as thin and sharp as possible, buffing the metal with a chammy cloth until they gleam. When I'm done, I catch sight of Mitch's dirty back as he pokes through my drawers. He definitely needs a polish too, even if Dad likes the lichen.

"Come here," I say, holding out the cloth. When he realises what I want to do, he tries to run away, but I manage to back him into a corner, and give his head a bit of a polish. I notice for the first time that there's a small, brown nest in his shoulder socket. The cracked shells of several pale blue eggs, each no bigger than a fingernail, are nestled in a bed of moss. It's kind of sweet. Mitch must have been so careful not to disturb the birds until they had hatched. I leave the nest there, polishing around it.

"You shine up quite nicely," I say, approvingly.

He flashes a sullen orange at me.

Shen still hasn't arrived, so I carry on tidying up. I wipe down my workbench, cleaning up the ever-present layer of sawdust and polishing the glass of a photo of Shen and me on the wall. It was taken on the dancefloor at last year's New Year's Eve Gala. We have big parties fairly regularly. Mum says it's to keep morale up, but I think she just likes organising them. I'm wearing a black tuxedo jacket over a deep-crimson silk voile ball-gown, and Shen is in a white suit with a skinny black tie loose around his neck. We're both smiling, eyes creased into laughs while Shen dips me backwards over one arm. I remember that seconds after the picture was taken I had spun him around and dipped him in return.

It's one of the last times I wore a ball-gown. A couple of months ago I started wearing suits to events instead – mainly because I hate having to shave my legs all the time. Feng was particularly excited by my decision to wear suits and got his specially created tailoring bot to fit me for dress shirts.

Shen messages me to say that he's just leaving, and that I should make him a bagel and meet him at the stables.

Dad has gone outside with the dogs, so I stand alone in the empty morning room while the bagel toasts. Bored, I open up Maya's posts and carry on reading. This time, I scan through some of the more light-hearted ones from the month before the virus, where she's joking around with someone called Riz.

Maya Waverley
7 January 2024

This ad is so dumb and funny, I love it:

Borough of Westminster

**Introducing ... the all new,
all powerful lifeguard bot!**

Sentient and fully automated, these robots will
patrol the Thames in search of anyone in distress.
They can swim, they can run, they can even fly!*

If you see someone in danger of drowning or
otherwise in need of riverside assistance, don't
hesitate to call the bot helpline on 999–BOT, to
bring the lifeguard directly to your location.

*limited distances in clement conditions.

**Initiative supported by the Mayor of London
& the Borough of Westminster as part
of the 2024 electoral campaign.**

> **Riz Stevens** Do you think one will burst through
> my window the next time I fall asleep in the bath?
> Because I would not be opposed to that.
>
> **Maya Waverley** Only if you vote for the mayor.

I grin. I'm pretty sure they're talking about Mitch. You wouldn't know that the robot was once considered the height of new technology, based on the way he accidentally burst a tube of my wood glue when we were upstairs.

"999-Bot?" I ask Mitch experimentally. He gives no visible reaction, which I decide is inconclusive.

I scroll forward through the posts, trying to find out more about the sterility crisis. I want to get as much information as I can about the nosebleeds, so that I can tell Shen about them.

> **Maya Waverley**
> 17 March 2024
>
> I had the most horrible dream last night. I dreamt I had
> a nosebleed. I was crying and tears were rolling down
> my cheeks, merging with the blood that was flowing
> from my nose. It dripped into my mouth, warm and salty,
> coating my tongue and sliding down my throat. I couldn't
> swallow it, and it cooled into a thick mass, choking me.
> Then my alarm went off, and I woke up. When I tried
> to wipe away the blood, there was nothing there.
>
> Every morning, I can't stop myself from checking my reflection
> for blood as I clean my teeth. I spit into my hand a few times
> a day, checking to see if the saliva is clear. I don't know
> how to make myself stop expecting it to happen again.
>
> **Maya Waverley**
> 7 April 2024
>
> Wow. This is so weird. It makes sense though. I'm still
> having nightmares about the virus. I definitely wouldn't

want to have a baby right now. I can see how other people might feel the same way and put off trying for a bit.

NEWSBREAKING.COM

DOCTORS REPORT DROP IN WOMEN CONCEIVING BABIES

NHS doctors are reporting a 60% drop in the number of women making appointments with their doctors to start antenatal care.

The NHS believes that women have stopped trying to conceive in the wake of the virus which spread throughout the world in February. This has sparked concerns that people previously hoping to conceive have started using contraception, possibly out of fears that the virus, which caused nosebleeds, might affect the baby. The virus is of unknown origin and has yet to be fully understood by virologists.

The NHS has made a statement encouraging women to book appointments with their GPs if they think they might be pregnant, or have concerns about beginning a pregnancy while the virus is still in their system.

Maya Waverley
22 May 2024

Please, please, can we all stop with the nosebleed memes? It's really not funny. I know you're trying to process your grief in a cacophony of blasé and humorous ways, but if I mute one more of you, there'll be no one left on my timeline.

Maya Waverley
25 May 2024

I just saw the news. Is this real?! What the HELL. How can a VIRUS do something like this? How can that even affect fertility? I thought women had just stopped trying to get pregnant! Not that the virus had made us all INFERTILE. This is a whole other level of awful. I cannot even begin to imagine anything worse. What do we do? How can this have happened?

Maya Waverley
26 May 2024

I really wanted to be a mum one day. It hurts so much that I might never get that chance. And I'm one of the lucky ones – I'm young enough that, even if this crisis takes a decade to fix, I might still get a chance to have kids. But my friend Ashley has been trying to have a baby for years, and now it looks like she's lost her last chance. My heart hurts for all of the women like her. I really hope that the doctors solve this quickly. **#TogetherandUndefeated**

Riz Stevens
26 September 2024

Debating whether it's more feasible to spend the rest of my life in cheerful ignorance or continuous weeping. Both seem equally reasonable responses to the news today.

> **Maya Waverley** Every time I watch the news my brain starts shuddering like a wet dog in a clean Porsche. Everything is going to rot and there's nothing any of us can do to stop it.

>> **Riz Stevens** This. This is exactly it.

Maya Waverley
2 October 2024

I just signed this petition:

PETITIONFORCHANGE.ORG

GIVE IVF SCIENTISTS UNLIMITED FUNDING

Nothing else is more important than solving the sterility crisis. I want the EU to give unlimited resources to all research groups working on fertility and IVF treatment. As many scientists as possible need to pause their current work and start researching the problem too. Please sign this petition to bring this to the attention of the EU!

CHAPTER 6

TIME	DATE	LOCATION	OBJECT	NOTES
17.39	04/04/2107	51.464031, -0.207841	CREAM CERAMIC POT displaying the ROYAL SEAL AND the LABEL: "MRS STAPLETON'S SOOTHING SYRUP! TREATS CATARRH AND THROAT TROUBLES. PRICED AT 2 SHILLINGS. CONTAINS MENTHOL, COCAINE, OPIUM, FORMALDEHYDE, CHLOROFORM AND AMMONIA. TAKE A DOSE THRICE DAILY, ONCE FOR CHILDREN". 1849.	FOUND BY LMBW, LODGED UNDER THE FLOORBOARDS IN THE OLD MAID'S QUARTERS. SHEN HAS TAKEN IT HOME AND PLANTED A SUCCULENT IN IT FOR HIS BEDROOM.

I meet Shen in the stables and hand him a bagel and mug of green tea. Albert parades around with a fluffy toy in his mouth, showing off, as the horses nicker at us, lifting their noses in search of oats.

"Thanks, Shadow," Shen mumbles, sipping at the tea. He's wearing his riding clothes – cream jodhpurs and a pressed white shirt that makes his shoulders look especially broad. He's drowsy-eyed and soft-faced, with pillow creases on his cheek.

"I thought you'd be excited to see the crash site," I say.

"I am. I'm not awake enough yet."

Mitch flashes purple at Shen in welcome, who taps his

67

knuckles on the robot's forehead. "Shiny," he comments.

Mitch's purple turns pink in delight. I'm starting to guess what his different colours mean, but I have no hope of understanding what the length and order of the flashes represents. Sometimes I think it's like Morse code – long and short flashes, making letters – but other times it goes crazy, flashing in no order whatsoever. I've started treating the lights like Victoria's wagging tail – it means he's happy, even if I don't know exactly what he's trying to say.

"Do your mum and Mrs Maxwell think there's something odd about the helicopter crash as well?" Shen asks. "Is that why they've gone there?"

I shrug. "I think they're doing their job properly, that's all."

He squints. "I guess we'll see." Then he bites into the bagel and sighs, leaning back against the door. The smell of the stables, all musty hay and manure and saddle soap, makes me long for it to be summer. Every year we spend days doing nothing but messing around with the horses in the meadow in Hyde Park, in amongst the fields growing oats, potatoes, rapeseed and vegetables.

After hours of riding practice, we always drop, exhausted, into the long grass, where we strip the husks off the stems of the crops with sharp pulls and then scatter the seeds. The horses graze as I try to catch tiny grasshoppers, feeling the vibration of their legs against my palms. Around us, white butterflies swoop and dive around golden buttercups and sprays of cow parsley. Baby rabbits creep closer and closer as they nibble on clover and dandelions. If I had to describe heaven, I imagine it's probably something like that.

"I read more of Maya's social media account," I tell Shen, while we tack up. "She said that the sterility virus caused a nose-bleed. Did you know that?"

He grimaces. "No. Really? That sounds grim."

"Yeah, it sounds like Maya thought she was going to die." I pull on my tweed hacking jacket and riding hat. I've known about the virus my whole life, but I've never really given much thought to what it was actually like for people to go through it. It must have been scary and overwhelming to realise that practically everything had changed overnight.

"I think I can see why our parents never went into specifics," Shen says, as he gives me a leg up on to Elizabeth's back. "I guess they thought the details would be too much for us. That maybe they would freak us out."

That's possible. The idea that they kept this stuff from us has worried me more than I would have expected. I wrap the leather reins around my hands, pressing my thumbs against the lines of even stitching. The horse whinnies softly, already hopping on her front hooves in anticipation, and the sound of it calms my thoughts a bit.

As Shen passes up my rucksack, he says, "How many tools have you got in there? It weighs a ton."

"A few. Just in case," I say, defensively. I could probably have left the propane fire-starter behind, but I definitely need the hammer and chisel, and the trowel for digging on the fore-shore, and the pickaxe. Those are all basic items. It's a completely normal amount for anyone. Probably.

"We should ask them about the nosebleeds tonight," he says.

I nod. "Maya also posted about a campaign to give scientists more funding to try and solve the fertility crisis. I want to know more about that too."

I've always taken it for granted that the fertility research occupies most of everyone's time. Our lives all revolve around it now, with most people working on it in some way, whether that's in the lab, like Jia, or by analysing spreadsheets of data and DNA code, like Mr Kowalski and Ms Bard.

I wish I was clever enough to help with it. But the world's top scientists, including Jia, are doing everything they can to fix the sterility without my interference. They're working on things so complicated that I can barely understand them.

Jia used to give lectures before her university closed down, and every year she tries again to explain her speciality to us in the hope that we'll be ready to understand her favourite module, applied clinical embryology. You'd think that after hearing about it sixteen times, I'd at least vaguely know what it's about, but all I know is that it involves IVF – the rest is an ill-defined mystery.

At most, I could help the scientists with their washing-up, and I'm pretty sure there are already bots for that. As I'm not going to suddenly discover a previously unnoticed talent for biology any time soon, all I can do is wait until they fix the problem. Sometimes I feel like being the youngest person on the planet is more propaganda than anything else. I'm hardly going to save humanity at the last minute or anything.

"Do you think I should let Mitch ride on Elizabeth with me?"

I ask, staring at the robot. It's probably not fair to leave him behind when it's so clear he wants to stay with us.

Before Shen can answer, the robot extends long thin metal legs out of his body, rising so tall that his head is the same height as mine, even on horseback.

"I think he wants to run," Shen says, grinning. When he mounts William, his jodhpurs stretch tight over his thighs as he flicks his black coattails out and settles into the seat.

"Do you think you're able to keep up, pal?" I ask Mitch.

He flashes orange and looks offended by the implication.

I send Mum a message to let her know we're on our way.

She replies immediately: *You got Shen to wake up before noon? Miracle of miracles!*

I slip easily into a rising trot, lifting and falling from the saddle in time with Elizabeth's movements. I've lost my riding muscles over the winter, and I can already feel the burn in my thighs. Elizabeth eyes Mitch suspiciously at first, but she soon relaxes and lets him run alongside her.

We pass an abandoned old building that maintenance bots are in the process of demolishing. Slabs of softening concrete have fallen into the road, revealing the rooms inside. The old owner's things are dusty but have remained in almost perfect condition: wardrobes filled with suits and dresses still on their hangers, and bookcases lined with books, crisp and yellowing and long forgotten.

Most people had no living relations to leave their things to when they died, and no one else needed their possessions or houses. It got to the point where the authorities just unplugged their fridges, turned off their computers, washed their dishes and closed the houses up for good.

Those houses are like time capsules now, full of perfectly preserved museums of lives, caught in a moment in history. We sort through them sometimes, trying to find things that are still in good condition for the second-hand jumble sales, but there are more things in the world than people to use them now. Even in a community of scavengers and salvagers and make-do-and-menders, we can't possibly find uses for everything.

We take as many of the photo albums, birth certificates and DVDs as we can to the British Museum, filling the basements with boxes of stuff. They wait alongside Egyptian relics and Greek statues for some future explorer to sift through in awed confusion, using them as a guide to our civilization. It's social archaeology, of a sort.

The world is already so different to how it used to be before the sterility. Even if the scientists do find a solution soon, it's only going to change more. If we're not careful, we'll wake up one day in a place with no resemblance to the old London at all. I know that culture had its faults, but it hurts that the world I see in movies can never be replicated.

I can never walk along Piccadilly at Christmas and see it decked out in fairy lights and bustling with shoppers. The only traffic at Fortnum and Mason these days is the flock of geese that have settled in the ruins of the building.

I can barely even imagine what my life might have been like

if I'd been born in Maya's time. We live in the quiet at the end of the world. The slow winding-down clockwork motions before life stops completely. Time is slipping through our fingers.

When the horses step out on to the foreshore of the Thames, their hooves sink deeply into the sand. It occurs to me that now we're back by the river Mitch might leave again. He's probably bored of hanging out with us now that we're not in danger. To my surprise, I'm disappointed by the thought. For some reason, I want him to stay with us, for just a little longer.

Mitch sticks close to Elizabeth's side, though, running in a bow-legged hop. Ahead of us, a brook cuts across the shore. It used to be one of the dozens of underground streams below the city, running into the Thames. The pavements collapsed years ago, making it more difficult to get around the city and revealing the water to the air again. The water's deep and crystal clear, cutting through the sand in the way it would have done before the city of London ever even existed.

When I lead Elizabeth into the chest-deep water of the stream, she hops around in excitement. I hold on tight with my knees, half-riding, half-floating on her back as she swims to the opposite bank. She lets out little snorts of delight as she ducks her nose into the water, shaking her head and wriggling in pleasure.

Behind us, William throws himself in headfirst with an enormous splash, sinking a few metres before he starts to swim with much less dignity than my horse. Shen nearly falls off, only just catching himself on William's mane.

The horses are climbing up the far bank of the brook when

Mitch backs up and takes a running jump at it, leaping over without getting wet at all.

"What the … hell?" Shen says.

"What kind of programming do you *have*?" I ask Mitch, trying to think of any situation where a long-jumping robot would be necessary, apart from right here and now.

Mitch flashes green, seeming pleased with himself. I can't believe that just yesterday I thought he could barely manage to totter along the shore. Now it seems he is a world-class gymnast.

"Did Maya's account tell you anything else?" Shen asks, as we carry on.

"I haven't had chance to read any more of it just yet. I'm so glad I found it, though. I think I'm going to save all of the data from her accounts to a hard drive, so we won't lose it if any more of the internet servers go offline. It won't be lost if it's stored on a physical device."

He tilts his head. "I don't know about that. I think the only way to really guarantee it's saved is to print it out. Digital data is actually more fragile than books and newspapers. Loads of footage has been lost from the nineteen-eighties because video tapes decayed before anyone noticed. Any data on hard drives might be erased completely only a couple of decades after we go."

"Really?" I say, surprised.

He nods. "It's strange, isn't it? Thinking about what might survive after we're gone. It's never the things you'd expect."

"Yeah! It's odd that an old paperback might be readable long after a tablet breaks down."

Mitch jogs over to me and holds something out. I take it, bemused. It's half of an old CD, cracked down the centre and bearing the words GEANT PEPPER in bubble letters. It's covered in sand.

Thanks!" I say, confused but delighted. It's a useless gift, but I'm kind of pleased he likes me enough to give me something at all.

CHAPTER 7

TIME	DATE	LOCATION	OBJECT	NOTES
10.24	12/06/2106	51.475390, -0.226148	Rusted iron shaft from an agricultural plough.	Found by LMBW. Tripped over it in the sewers at Putney, leaving a scar on Lowrie's left kneecap.

I smell the crash site before I see it. There's a line of smoke meandering through the air from the smouldering wreck of Big Ben, and small patrol drones are circling above it. It's even worse than I'd been imagining. The ancient parliament building has collapsed, and Big Ben's tower has crumbled into the water, exposing the charred innards.

I try to work out how deep the crater might be judging by the radius, but my maths isn't good enough. Deep, anyway. The only part of the helicopter that's visible is one long rotor emerging from the water.

Mum and Mrs Maxwell are standing on the edge of the explosion perimeter. After leaving William and Elizabeth loose to graze the grass and weeds growing from crevices in the cracked tarmac, we pull off our riding hats and walk over. "Hi, Mrs Maxwell!" I call.

"Hi, Lowrie, Shen!" she says. Mrs Maxwell has completely

white hair, from root to tip. I've always wondered what it would look like if it was dyed teal or pink or indigo. When she's not policing, she writes nostalgic novels with titles like *The Only Way Is Love* and *A Child for Us All*. I stopped reading the last one at the line "The question, unasked on everyone's lips, was obvious: how could a child be born now, so long after the last birth? And who amongst them could possibly abandon such a precious life?" Far too cheesy for me, but Shen loves her books.

"Grab a hard hat from the pile and come over," Mrs Maxwell tells us, before turning back to watch Mum, who is holding some sort of device out over the water.

"Uh-huh," Shen says, smiling and walking straight past the helmets.

I grab two helmets and push one into his hands. "You didn't hear that, did you?" I say in an undertone. "She wants us to wear these."

"No," he admits. "She always talks in a mumble." He wanders over to Mum while Mitch stands at the edge of the crater, staring down at his reflection in the water.

I start to follow Shen and then turn to ask Mrs Maxwell something. I'm surprised to see that she's gone pale and looks a little queasy. "Are you all right?" I ask, alarmed.

"Excuse me. I'm feeling hot all of a sudden." She fans her face.

"Do you need to sit down?"

She shakes her head firmly. "I'm fine. It's just a passing hot flush."

Mum looks over at her, frowning.

Mrs Maxwell smiles and shakes her head very slightly at her.

"I feel better already," she says with another smile. "Let's go and see what your mum's doing, shall we?"

She still looks pale, but I decide not to say anything. I clear my throat. "So, what are you looking for?"

"The black box," Mum answers. "We're hoping it will have recorded the last moments before Alexei's crash. The hard drive is designed to be indestructible, so it should still be readable – if we can find it in the water with the scanner."

"So there is a way to preserve data for the future," I say, and shoot a look at Shen.

He beams at me.

"I hate this thing," Mum mutters, jabbing the screen of her device.

"What is it?" I ask.

"It's a sonar imaging scanner, although that's as much as I can tell you." Mum is not the best with technology. She's more of a books person. She so rarely has to do anything with complicated tech that it doesn't usually matter, though.

Shen peers over Mum's shoulder, hooking his aviator sunglasses over the first button of his shirt. When he pokes at the screen, she nudges him out of the way. "Don't do that, you'll break it."

"I don't think I will." He taps the screen again, and the device makes a noise that sounds encouraging.

Mum pushes the device into his hands, looking relieved. "You do it, then. I can't get the bloody thing to work."

Shen taps it for a moment, then holds it up to show us a model

78

of the helicopter below the surface of the water.

"Excellent!" Mum studies the image for a moment and then says to Mrs Maxwell, "I think if you approach from this side, it should be safe."

I realise what they're planning to do when Mrs Maxwell peels open a large carry case to reveal a scuba-diving kit. I gasp so loudly that Elizabeth comes over to check up on me, nosing at my shoulder in interest. "Mum!" I say, "Oh, Mum, can I go instead? Please? I've dived loads of times, and Mrs Maxwell isn't feeling very well!"

"I don't think that's a good idea, Lowrie. You're here to observe, not to get involved. Besides, you don't even know what we're looking for."

"It's probably a box that's black – right?" I grin. "Come on, otherwise you'll have to go, and you know you don't like getting your hair wet," I tell her slyly. "It dries frizzy afterwards."

Mum doesn't look convinced, but Mrs Maxwell smothers what I think is a laugh.

I tilt my chin at a precise forty-five degree angle and stare down my nose at my mum, disgruntled.

Mum sticks out her tongue at me. "All right," she sighs. "You can go. Shen, do you want to go too? There are two kits."

Shen nods several times in a row, delighted.

"Was that a yes?" Mum asks, grinning.

I pull off my hacking jacket, which is an antique I'd rather not soak in murky crater water, while Shen rolls up his shirt sleeves. He reveals wide forearms covered with a smattering of dark hair.

On the pale underside, blue veins trail the bulge of muscles. For some reason, the sight of them makes me feel a bit warm. I look away and focus on taking off my boots.

"Don't go inside the helicopter, that's too dangerous," Mrs Maxwell says, projecting a diagram of the helicopter on the ground using her tablet. "You should be able to get the black box out from a hatch on the outside." She points out where it should be.

"Got it," I say.

"You know you can't keep the black box, don't you?" Mrs Maxwell adds. "The footage will show us what happened in the last moments before Alexei crashed. It might be … upsetting."

My gut twists. I don't want to see that anyway.

"What if we find something else? That isn't connected to the crash, I mean," Shen asks.

I nod at him, impressed by his negotiation tactics. I bet there were loads of forgotten treasure vaults inside the Palace of Westminster. We might even find some jewels under the rubble.

"That's all yours." Mum fishes a sugar cube out of her pocket and holds it out to William on the palm of her hand.

"How about you two get yourselves ready, and I'll tell you if you go wrong?" Mrs Maxwell passes out tubes and masks to us. "You both did well the last time I took you out diving."

Shen and I both have a million hobbies because our parents have always let us try anything we wanted – and there's always someone around who can teach us things. As well as scuba diving, we've had lessons in pottery, croquet, ballet, dressage, fencing, punting, cricket, golf and a dozen other activities. Most of our experiments didn't stick, but Shen tried bass guitar once and never stopped, and I box with a punching bag in the orangery whenever I can't sleep.

I think that everyone is so eager to teach us about their passions because otherwise their hobbies will die with them. No one in the future will ever experience the joy of playing darts if they can't manage to get Shen and I interested now. Even if Jia finds a solution to fix the sterility, these skills might still be lost for ever, like extinct languages disappearing with the oldest members of a small community.

It took a long time for me not to feel guilty when I disliked something (see: painting, dressmaking, extreme frisbee), but I realise now that it's not my job to shoulder the entire weight of humankind's creativity and passion. I only have room to carry my own, and scuba diving is something I love doing.

Under Mrs Maxwell's careful watch, I attach the oxygen tank to the buoyancy jacket, opening the valve to make sure the pressure is full.

"Don't forget to check the mouthpiece is clear," Mrs Maxwell says, when I put it on. "Shen, I think your tube is a bit twisted."

When I'm certain the equipment is working, I make the "OK" sign at Mrs Maxwell before turning to Shen, who looks bug-eyed in his mask. A tuft of his hair is caught under the strap, making it stick upwards in a plume.

"Good luck!" Mum calls.

We step off the edge of the crater into the water. It's cold and it trickles down my back, making me shiver. I wish we had our wetsuits.

I swim in breaststroke behind Shen. His tuft of hair has disappeared now that it's wet, to my disappointment. I carefully extend my arms and legs in slow motion, in case there's something sharp out of sight. The mud hasn't settled after only one night, and the water is dark and cloudy. Wriggling insects swim past my mask.

There's a fast movement ahead of me, and I almost jump out of my skin, until I realise that Mitch has dived into the water too. He spirals around us, his path lit up by beams of white light, making it easier to see the way ahead. When I wave at him, he waggles skinny metal fingers back at me.

The twisted hull of the helicopter appears in the darkness ahead of us. We shine our torches around it, searching for the compartment of the black box.

The whole craft has been bent out of shape by the crash, but there's something bright orange sticking out. When I swim closer, I see that it's a tab. I run my finger along the edge. There's a compartment, about the size of a tea tray, set into the side.

It doesn't open when I pull at the tab, so I use a chisel from my utility belt to ease it open where the distorted metal has sealed it shut. I tap the sharp edge along the seam of the hatch, hitting the end of the handle with my fist. Slowly I manage to ease the door loose.

Inside, there's an orange metal box with the words FLIGHT RECORDER – DO NOT OPEN written on the side in black letters. Success.

I wave to catch Shen's attention, and he swims over to help me slide out the black box. It's heavy, even with two of us, and I'm wondering how we'll manage to carry it to the surface when Mitch tugs it from us and shoots off.

He is so cool, in a weird way. I'm glad the robot has decided to hang around. There are so few people I can be friends with that it's nice to have him around, even if I can't understand what he's saying.

We swim after Mitch back to the surface, and I pull myself on to the ground, shaking the hair out of my eyes and spitting out a mouthful of pale green water. It tastes thoroughly organic, in an unpleasant way that reminds me of algae.

"Good work, kids," Mrs Maxwell says, handing us towels. "That was all very careful and cautious. Lowrie, keep an eye on your legs when you're swimming, though – you nearly kicked Shen in the face at one point."

Shen shakes his head in mock disappointment at me. His shirt is sodden, clinging and almost see-through. He rubs his forehead with the back of his forearm. Sunlight spills over him, dripping down the lines of his shoulders.

"Right, let's take a look at this box," Mum says.

"It's not even black," Shen says, bemused, crouching to inspect the orange wrought-iron box.

"How do we get inside?" I ask, brushing a wet leaf off Shen's wrist. The hair on his arm is dark and sleek against the skin. I rub it idly, watching it go fluffy and soft as it sticks up. I wrap myself up in a towel, shivering at the cool breeze.

"*You* don't," Mum says.

I frown, but I don't argue.

We're helping to pack up the scuba gear when Mrs Maxwell abruptly sits down on the ground. She looks dizzy again. "I think—" she says, and falls forwards, shuddering. Her head jerks to the side.

"Mrs Maxwell? Are you OK?" I ask, running over to her.

She blinks, and her eyes take a moment to focus. Her hand is trembling. "I need to…" She shakes her head, as if unable to speak. "I feel a bit … funny."

"Lowrie, Shen, go back to the house," Mum says, eyeing Mrs Maxwell with concern. "I'll take Mrs Maxwell to Jia, so she can check her out. I'm sure it's fine." She rubs Mrs Maxwell's arm kindly. "Just tiredness."

Mrs Maxwell nods. Her face is scored with worry, though, as she lets Mum help her to the car.

"I hope you're OK," I call after them, but Mum's already starting the car and pulling away. "That was weird," I say to Shen, when they're gone. "Do you think she's getting sick? Or perhaps she's epileptic?"

"She might have just not had any breakfast. But imagine what could have happened if she'd gone diving."

I hiss through my teeth, very relieved we went in her place.

"Mama will sort her out, though, I'm sure," Shen adds. "Come on, we'd better get back. Your dad's lesson is starting soon."

TIME	DATE	LOCATION	OBJECT	NOTES
13.04	15/09/2108	51.473717, -0.177296	Brass luggage tag from the uniform of a World War II soldier, labelled with their name and address.	Found by SZ buried under ten centimetres of sand and picked up using Shen's metal detector. We tried to track the soldier down, but we couldn't find any record of him online. The archives must have been lost.

"I think I have a new best friend," I say, as Shen and I ride the horses back home. I point at Mitch, who's still following us. He is definitely planning on coming home with us again, and I can't help but feel slightly smug about it. It definitely means he likes us!

Shen huffs a sigh. "You replace me so quickly? How fickle your affections are, Shadow."

"What can I say? He's got more stimulating conversation than you."

"He can't even speak."

I shrug lazily with one shoulder, guiding Elizabeth around an old fossilized tree trunk emerging from the silt. "And?"

Shen shakes a fist at Mitch. "You won't get away with this, you blaggard. I'll win her back yet, just you wait."

Mitch is busy examining something in the sand and doesn't even seem to notice. We startle a heron as we pass. It jumps into the air, crossing to the other side of the river with slow, sweeping flaps of its wings.

I wonder if Mum will try to get into the black box, once Mrs Maxwell has recovered. I wish she'd let us help with that.

"Do you think a black box would work – as a way of preserving data for the future, I mean? Could humans use one to leave some kind of message? For a future species on earth?"

"You think another species will evolve to that level of intelligence, after we die?" Shen asks.

I shrug, watching a dolphin jump in the river, spraying water behind it. "It's happened before, with humans. It's not entirely impossible. My bet is on corvids. Crows are, like, crazy smart."

"Octopi," Shen suggests, warming to the subject. "I read this thing that said they evolved totally separately to mammals, so they're very intelligent, but their brains work completely differently to ours. They're as close as we'll probably ever get to communicating with an alien race."

"I hope an octopus finds a black box one day, then," I say, twisting in the saddle to grin at him. "Think how confused they'd be when they tried to read it."

I can't even imagine how hard it would be for aliens or octopi to understand English. It's almost impossible for archaeologists to reconstruct ancient Egyptian recipes or put long-lost Roman songs to music. And that's humans trying to understand other humans, whose brains worked in the same way.

"What an oversimplistic transcription system," Shen says, in a high-pitched, wavering voice which I think is supposed to be an imitation of an octopus. *"Don't they know how much more information they could record with an eight-dimensional coordinate base?"*

"Why would you create a writing tool that only uses one tentacle?" I add, in the same voice. *"What were these creatures doing with their other seven?"*

"Why did they stare at these tiny glowing screens all the time? What a strange god to worship!" Shen laughs, snorting.

There's a screech above us and I peer up at the sky, wondering if it was a crow. I'm suddenly feeling a little paranoid about what they might be plotting. Octopi might be smart, but so are crows – too smart for their own good – and there are hundreds of them around here, according to our last annual wildlife survey.

It also revealed that central London is home to four families of wild boars, one hundred and seventeen pheasants, approximately fifteen thousand pigeons and a set of highly argumentative badgers (they picked a fight with Victoria, and she was *not* the winner). If the crows are going to take over the planet, they're going to have a lot of competition.

We're nearly home when Mitch flashes a bright crimson and hops from foot to foot. "What is it?" I ask, startled. "Are you OK?"

Mitch signs something in a long series of coloured lights of varying lengths that are clearly instructions.

I nod, pretending I have any idea what he is saying.

Then he swerves across the sand like he is sniffing something out. Finally, he stops at a dip in the ground. His head swivels around a full 360 degrees, like an owl. He flashes green at me in a way that very clearly means, *Well? Come on, then.*

I dismount immediately. Even though I'm desperate to get home and change out of my wet clothes, I can't resist the call of treasure. "He's found something!"

I duck my head, eyes straining for any sign of incongruity in amongst the clay and stones and lumps of concrete.

Shen retrieves his metal detector from his rucksack and waves it over the area. It beeps loudly. He grins at me, and I smile back. The excitement of finding something is irresistible. Every single time, my tummy flips.

I dig at the ground with my trowel, prising out a chunk of slabbing and a curl of plastic. Finally I pull out something hard and round encased in a lump of clay. A chunk of soil slides away, revealing a silver necklace, inlaid with pearls, caught on a tangled chain.

I gasp.

Mitch flashes a purple light of pure happiness.

"Have you been scanning for objects this whole time?" I ask him. "For years and years, whenever you walk along the beach?"

The lights on Mitch's headplate all flash green twice, in a smug fashion.

Shen's eyes go wide. "You mean…" He trails off.

A laugh bubbles out of me. "We thought he was bumbling along, staring at the ground. But he was mudlarking. Just like us!" I stare at Mitch, seeing him with new eyes. How did I never realise how cool he is? "Good bot," I tell him. "That was very impressive."

Mitch wriggles with glee.

"High-five, buddy," I say to him. "We make a good team."

He holds out a claw-hand appendage, and I crouch to tap it lightly with my palm.

"That works, I guess," Shen says, not entirely convinced.

"You're just jealous, Zhang," I declare, standing back up. "We're best friends for life now." My socks choose that moment to disgrace me by squelching obnoxiously in my wellies, which slightly undermines my smugness.

Shen laughs, and we carry on walking, letting the horses follow us down the shore rather than riding them. After a moment or two, I spot something white in the sand at my feet, and bend to tug it from the ground. It's a cream pottery pipe stem: long and thin and boring. I throw it into the river, trying to make it skim across the water. Mitch dives in after it, like a dog.

I carry on walking, noticing a dip in the sand ahead, which is sometimes a sign that there's something underneath. I scrape away at the dirt to reveal the mud below. The silt is grey on top and shockingly black underneath, like the layers of a mushroom.

To my surprise, there's a footprint under the mud, clearly indented with toes and a heel mark. That's weird. Has someone been walking here barefoot? But how come the footprint was buried? Besides, the mud here is so solid that I can't even dent it when I press my fingernail in. It wouldn't leave a mark at all if I walked here now.

"Shen! Come and look at this," I say, scanning the sand for any other marks in the bed. There's a whole path of them all along the foreshore. "What is this?"

Shen pokes at the footprint. "You know, I read this thing that said that prehistoric footprints have been found around here. They get revealed as the tide erodes the sand. Maybe this is a set of footprints from one of those hunter-gatherers."

"Oh, *wow*."

I can just imagine a hunter-gathering lady wading through an ancient version of the Thames, searching for mussels and crabs for dinner, toes sinking deep into the riverbed. She must have returned to her home to cook the harvest over a fire, but her footprints are still here, hundreds of thousands of years later – if only for a few more hours. They'll be erased as soon as the tide comes in. It was only luck that we were here to see them, in the brief period between them being revealed and erased for good.

All that history – all that time – wiped away in one moment. Just like us. Humans will be as easily lost as these footprints, when the last of us dies. Our lives are particles on a riverbed being lost by the waters of time. Here and then gone in a moment. Nothing, in the grand scheme of things.

★ ★ ★

Maya Waverley
17 October 2024

Today I was served by a real person instead of a shop bot, and it actually took me by surprise. It felt so weird.

> **Riz Stevens** We chose my nan's care home because the staff there are fully human, and it really does make such a difference to her happiness.

>> **Maya Waverley** It's one of the main reasons I'm studying nursing, because I really think it's

one of those jobs that people should do instead of bots. You need the human contact.

Maya Waverley
20 October 2024

I just bought a FUND THE SEARCH hoodie from <u>here</u>. The proceeds are donated to a charity supporting fertility research, and the designs are really nice. The dresses have pockets! Definitely check them out.

> **Riz Stevens** When I first I bought some skinny jeans from the men's section it blew me away. Have you SEEN the size of the pockets men get? I could have been using them long before I realised I was a guy. You should get some.

> > **Maya Waverley** Riz, omg. I'm going to the shopping centre immediately.

Maya Waverley
22 October 2024

Oh my God, read this.

NEWSBREAKING.COM

WARNING: CHILDREN ARE BEING STOLEN FROM SCHOOL PLAYGROUNDS

The government has issued a national warning after fourteen children were kidnapped at knife-point from school classrooms up and down the country yesterday.

Six schools were attacked in total, in Liverpool, Birmingham and Chelsea. One teacher at a school in Liverpool said that three men in balaclavas and armed with knives had burst into the classroom during the last lesson of the day. Six children were taken in that attack.

"I have never been so terrified in my life," she said. "I

didn't think things like this happened in this country. I should have done more to stop them, but I just wasn't expecting it. I'm absolutely devastated."

All schools are closed until further notice while emergency measures are put in place.

The prime minister told press that she encouraged everyone to remain calm, saying, "This is the work of a few very upset and confused individuals. We urge them to think about the parents of the children who were taken. Please let them go home safely. There is no reason to make an irreversible decision which you will regret for the rest of your life, when all signs point to the sterility being fixed within a timeframe of three to four months."

The latest reports from scientists working on the sterility indicate that no progress has yet been made on reversing the effects of the virus, despite the prime minister's statement.

If anyone has seen any of the missing children, or noticed suspicious behaviour in their neighbourhood, please call the police immediately.

Maya Waverley My surprise at this might be exceedingly naïve but WHAT THE HELL? How can this be happening?! How are people so desperate for kids that they'll STEAL THEM? Is that actually a thing that is happening in the world right now at this very moment? Are we suddenly living in some kind of Stephen King novel? Am I the only one who thought that the human race could survive for more than five minutes without making an abject embarrassment of ourselves?

I'm going to make an obvious and unnecessary statement here, but I wish everything would get fixed so that life could go back to normal.

CHAPTER 9

TIME	DATE	LOCATION	OBJECT	NOTES
14.10	05/04/2109	51.473717, -0.177296	Filigree silver necklace with locket containing an enamel cameo of a Tudor woman in a blue-and-orange French hood, with a pearl necklace looped around her neck.	Found by Mitch. We have a new mudlarker to add to the discoveries logbook!

When we get home, we rub down the horses and let them out in the meadow, then go upstairs to get changed out of our wet clothes. I pull on a Fair Isle wool vest and then read some more of Maya's posts while I dry my damp hair.

I get so caught up in her horrifying posts about kidnapped children that I realise Dad's lesson is about to start, and I'm going to be late. I rush downstairs, taking a shortcut down the old servants' staircase. Our manor is over four hundred years old, so there are all sorts of long forgotten structures and hidden passageways. It's possibly the best place in the world to play hide-and-seek.

Once I found our manor in a book called *Debrett's The Stately Homes of Britain*. There was, somehow, even more gold gilding in the old photos than there is here now. One of the pictures showed a room with mirrored ceilings that I couldn't identify, and Shen and I spent weeks searching for it, convinced it was a secret room hidden behind a wooden panel somewhere.

Eventually I showed the book to Mum, who peered at it with her reading glasses for approximately four seconds before saying that the caption noted that it was a picture of the house on the next page. I'm still embarrassed about that one.

I run across to the greenhouse, arriving only a few minutes late, with Mitch at my heels. Shen is already there, helping Dad plant up seedlings.

"Sorry I'm late," I gasp. Victoria is asleep on the floor, and she thumps her tail in welcome. "I was … wiping the mud off Mitch?" I look dubiously at the robot, who does look suspiciously dry and free from mud, though no towels were involved. I hope he didn't roll around on my bed to dry himself off, like the dogs do.

In a very clear attempt to avoid my gaze, as if reading my mind, Mitch bends to inspect Victoria. The dog presses her nose to his face, sniffing curiously. She snorts and lies back down, leaving a wet spot behind on Mitch's face. To my surprise, dog and robot settle down on the floor together in an untidy, cosy heap.

"Well, don't you look like you've had a good morning," Dad says, taking in my dusty clothes, as Shen pulls a cobweb from the servants' staircase out of my hair.

"We were shadowing Mum's work as a public official," I say primly, and slide on to the wooden bench in front of the tomato plants.

"I'm sure," Dad says, voice dry. He pushes compost down around a bulb. "Lots of swimming involved in that, is there?"

"More than you'd imagine," Shen says.

"Did you tell Dad what happened to Mrs Maxwell?" I ask him.

It's Dad who answers. "Your mother messaged me. Mrs Maxwell is fine. She's sleeping it off. Apparently, it's happened to her before, and it's nothing serious."

"Is it epilepsy?" I ask.

"Something like that. Now, we've got work to do. Let's pick up where we left off on Monday. Can either of you tell me the optimum crop rotation pattern for legumes?" Dad asks, brushing the soil off his hands on to his jeans.

A cleaning bot buzzes around his wellies, vacuuming up the mud. I can usually track Dad down at home by following the sound of chittering bots as they clean up the trail of compost that's always left in his wake.

I pull on my horn-rimmed glasses and squint at the slides Dad projects over the terracotta-tiled floor, trying to remember what he was telling us four days ago.

Shen, unsurprisingly, immediately answers perfectly.

I zone out. These lessons are always about the same things. I wish we could learn about something new, like cinematography or economics. But none of that's relevant any more.

If I wasn't the youngest person on the planet, I wonder what I'd have done with my life. Would I still be interested in engineering? Or would I want to be an actress, or a teacher or a world traveller? There are so many options that are closed off to me – things that I've never had a chance to consider trying. I would probably be a completely different person if I'd been born a hundred years ago.

"Now, storage conditions are really important here. Lowrie?" Dad says, cutting into my thoughts. "Can you remember how to store seeds long term?"

I start, tuning back into Dad's lesson. "Er ... somewhere cold and dry?"

He nods. "A cellar or basement is a good choice, because it stays cool naturally."

"But cellars flood," Shen points out, making a vague twirly gesture as he speaks. "Just look at the Underground. It's all collapsing. You could store seeds there for a while but not for ever."

There's a curving shadow on the underside of his wrist where it rests on the arm of the bench. I realise I'm staring at him and look away quickly. I always end up staring at Shen's forearms. However much I tell myself to stop, I never can. It's not something I'm prepared to analyse. Shen and I are just friends. Absolutely nothing else.

"That's an excellent point," Dad says. "Have you heard of the Snowdon vaults?"

We both shake our heads.

"In a mountain in Wales," Dad goes on, "there's an archival bunker built from tunnels, designed to preserve supplies – including seeds – in case of an emergency that destroys the environment. It wasn't built that long ago, but because of climate change, the sea levels have risen so much that it's already at risk of being flooded. Even when we try, we can't predict what future conditions might be like."

"Lowrie and I were actually talking about this earlier," Shen says. "We were wondering how we'd leave a message for a future intelligent species to find, because everything decays too quickly, especially electronics. There's nothing that will survive long enough to last more than a few thousand years."

"It is a tough question," Dad says. "Did you come up with a solution? If you were going to make a time capsule designed to last that long, how would you do it?"

"I'd engrave a silicon wafer at the nano-level," Shen says, immediately. He must have been thinking about it since our last conversation.

"What would you engrave on it?" I ask him, interested now that the conversation isn't about agriculture.

"I'd start simple. You'd have to assume that whoever found it couldn't understand our writing or language. So I'd put a dot with the number one under it, and then two dots with the number two under them, et cetera. That would catch their attention. Once I'd established a method of communication, I'd build up from there, with a message about what life is like now."

"You have really thought this through," I say.

"Of course I have! What do you take me for!"

"What would you put in one, Lowrie?" Dad asks.

I think for a moment. It would have to be something that you didn't need language to understand. And not technology – whatever Shen thinks, no octopus is going to be able to operate a silicon chip. It would need to be old school. Maybe not a slate or tablet but something made of paper.

"I'd put in one of those flip books," I say. "You know, where there's a line drawing on each page, and when you flip through it, it looks like it's an animation?"

"Oh, those are cool!" Shen says. "That's clever too. You might not be able to read a video file without the right equipment, but anything can flip through pages and put together the movement."

"Plus," I say, as Dad pulls up a blank screen on his projector and writes our ideas in a spider diagram, "if it was a drawing of a human running or dancing or something, it would give them an idea of what we looked like."

"You're assuming that a future species could easily mentally translate two-dimensional images into a three-dimensional being," Dad points out.

"Well, even if they couldn't, I think it's more likely they'll be able to see that it's a message than Shen's chip. They might throw your silicon wafer away without even realising there was anything on it."

"We should probably include both, then," Shen says, as if we're actually going to make a time capsule. I imagine we probably will.

"So where would you store them?" Dad's getting excited now, I can tell. "Shall we do this as an assignment? Why don't you research the Snowdon vaults as a starting—"

Before he can get any further, Shen's father slides open the glass door of the greenhouse. "Sorry to interrupt," Feng says.

"Henry, can I speak to you for a moment?"

Dad follows Feng outside, and we watch through the glass door as they have a hushed discussion. Dad's expression gets more and more anxious.

When they come back inside, I ask, "Is everything OK?"

Dad and Feng look at each other over the top of our heads, and I can tell there's some kind of silent communication going on. "Your mum needs my help with something," Dad says after a moment. "It's nothing to worry about."

I nudge Shen's ankle with my foot, raising an eyebrow at him meaningfully.

"Why don't you two come with me?" Feng says, before either of us can ask any more questions. "We can spend the rest of your lesson in the workshop. I need the help, anyway," he adds. "My angle grinder has broken." He looks pained.

I don't think Feng likes things failing. The only time I've ever seen him lose his temper was when the car broke down when we were on holiday and he couldn't get it started again.

"Oh, I can fix the angle grinder," I say, immediately distracted by the talk of tools. I open up my utility belt, checking I've got my screwdrivers with me.

"Interesting that you just happened to have that with you," Dad comments lightly, eyeing my tool kit. He smiles, but there's a deep frown line on his forehead.

"You can never have enough tools, that's what I always say," Shen tells him.

"You do *not*," I say, outraged. "That's what *I* always say."

Shen and Dad smirk at each other.

Shen might be the best at intellectual things, but fixing stuff is *my* speciality. Smarts versus skills, we call it. Both methods have been known to fail on occasion, which is why we're the perfect team – we've got the best of both worlds.

"I'll find some reference material for designing this time capsule for our next lesson," Dad says, following us out of the greenhouse. "Do some research on it for your homework. I think we've hit on something really interesting here."

We go to the workshop, where I help replace the blade on Feng's angle grinder. The black box is sitting on the workbench. He must have been trying to get inside it when the blade broke. "Have you not been able to open it yet?" I ask, nodding at it.

"I've been having some trouble," Feng admits.

"Do you need some help?"

"No," he says in a hurry. "No need. Now you've mended the grinder for me, we can carry on fixing the broken bot from our last session. Shen, can you take a look at the error log? I've pulled it up on my tablet."

"We're going to have to cut off the old component," I say, trying not to stare longingly at the black box. I clamp the bot on to the workbench, before selecting a saw.

"Don't forget to pull down the extractor fan, and prepare yourself for the pushback," Feng tells me, guiding my hands into the correct position on the saw handle.

White sparks fly into the air as the metal is sliced open with a sharp squealing sound. While I work, Shen says something to

Feng quietly in Chinese, and Feng lets out a hearty laugh. I smile under my mask. It always gets me when Shen talks in Chinese. Usually it's a sign he's anxious, or upset, but when he does it to tease, to joke around ... it's my favourite. I really, really like it.

The three of us have spent hours and hours together like this. A few years ago, Feng even taught us how to build a bot from scratch during his science lessons. Shen and I decided we wanted to build one that could make candyfloss on demand. I helped Feng construct the internal components – attaching circuit boards and wiring up batteries – and Shen, who isn't very good at the mechanical side of things, programmed the software.

It took a long time to make, and Feng put up with many emotional breakdowns and arguments and storming-offs with amazing patience. Shen and I argue a lot when we're doing projects together, because he always wants fancy things like dovetail joints, whereas I'm more of a hammer-and-nails sort of girl.

We finished it in the end, but the candyfloss turned out to be more similar to sticky treacle than air-like fluff. Even so, we were incredibly proud of it. There are bots everywhere, doing everything, so it's nice to know that we could put one together if there was an emergency.

I focus on the bot I'm working on now. The saw has gone through the metal and the back of the bot comes off. I shine my headlight inside it, looking for the broken part. I think I'm going to have to replace a transistor.

"Shen, can you grab some soldering wire for me?"

He's inspecting the bot's code and doesn't move.

TIME	DATE	LOCATION	OBJECT	NOTES
14.17	05/04/2109	51.455206, 0.292369	White clay tobacco pipe with a boar's head on the bowl. Late sixteenth century.	Found by LMBW. The stem snapped when I pulled it out of the sand, but it's still pretty. Dad is using it as a marker for his daffodil bulbs in the border by the gazebo.

After we've fixed the bot, which trundled off happily to join the others in the garden, Shen and I go to the theatre room. It's where we usually end up when we're studying, because it has the comfiest chairs in the whole building: fully reclining velvet ones with padded heated seats, built-in massage units and wide arms with cup holders. There's even a pool table to play on whenever we need a break. It's also really warm, because it's right on top of the pipes for the heating.

There's a cleaning bot polishing the floor, and Mitch wanders over to it, flashing green in greeting. It turns around, ignoring him. Mitch follows it determinedly, lighting up in a rainbow of different colours.

"Look at Mitch," I say to Shen, who's reading something on his tablet.

Mitch extends two fingers and clicks them together, trying to copy the order of the beeps the bot makes as it moves.

The bot stops and stares at him, and for a moment, I think it is going to reply. Then it extends its vacuum and sucks up the dirt from Mitch's feet.

Mitch slumps, flashing a sad indigo.

"Sorry, pal," I say, rubbing his head. "I think you speak a different language. Your software isn't compatible."

We start doing the homework Dad set us on making a time capsule. He never returned from going to see Mum, but he's probably using it as an excuse to get out of teaching us for the rest of the afternoon.

While we work, I dim the overhead lights and play a video on the big cinema screen. Shen and I can never agree on music choices – he likes classical music and I prefer rap – so when we're studying together, we usually put films on, as a compromise. Today it's the first episode of *Loch & Ness*, because Maya Waverley's love for the old TV show has made me curious. I'd never even heard of it until I found the purse.

I like Maya, even if she does seem like the kind of person who would have no idea how to work a flatbed planer. I keep wondering if she would have approved of me and the way I live my life, or if she'd think I'm wasting what little time we have left.

Reading her account makes my stomach twist up in knots. I'm suddenly grateful for the freedom I have, even if it does come with frequent safety talks.

I'm so glad the world isn't like that any more. People are

calmer now. I wonder what changed. I've never really thought about it before. I've just accepted things how they are.

I remember that I haven't told Shen about what I learnt in Maya's latest posts. When I tell him the kidnapping story, he's as shocked as me.

"I never knew that. How did no one tell us?" he asks.

"I *know*. Nobody ever mentions that there was such a bad reaction to the sterility." I forgot to ask Dad about the nosebleeds earlier too.

"I guess that people just want to live out their last few years in peace. If I'd been there during that kind of panic, I would probably want to forget about it and be happy too."

I nod, taking this in. It does make sense, but I still feel weird not knowing about any of this. "If things were as bad as her posts say, then we're not just lucky – we're completely blessed to get to live in such a safe, peaceful place."

"We definitely need to remember to discuss it with our parents," Shen says, determined. "They probably don't want us to worry about it, but it feels wrong to completely forget what it was like back then."

"There must be some way we can acknowledge it more," I agree, as a bot zooms into the room and deposits a tray of food on the sideboard. Efficient, as always.

Shen takes a toasted muffin dripping with golden butter from the tray and bites into it. I lean over and open my mouth. Courteously, he holds the muffin out so that I can take a bite.

He types something on his tablet, looking frustrated.

"What are you doing?" I ask, curiously.

"I'm trying to track down the blueprints for the Snowdon vaults online, but I can't find anything. I really wanted to see what they did there, for the time-capsule thing." He sighs, then shakes his head. "What are you going to do for yours?"

"I was thinking of burying mine," I say. "The stuff we find underground is always so well preserved."

"I like that idea!"

On the cinema screen, the main character is getting dressed for a party. There's a close-up as she applies dark red lipstick to plump lips. There are freckles on the bridge of her nose.

"She is so hot, wow," I say, awed. Sometimes I forget how attractive people can be.

Shen looks up to watch as the girl changes into a silk dress, pulling a thin strap over her shoulder. It clings to her skin, following a dip in her collarbone. "Her hair is gorgeous," he says.

She's blonde, with tiny curls of hair escaping her French plait and framing her face. She's so pretty that it almost hurts. There's never going to be anyone like her ever again. There's no one of her age left in the entire world, except me.

"Life goals or wife goals," I say, sighing.

I came out to Shen when I was fourteen and desperately in love with a woman in a TV show we were marathoning. She was also blonde and pretty, with extremely sharp cheekbones. In a break between episodes, Shen and I went to eat a pre-dinner snack of everything we could find in the fridge, to the disapproval of the cooking bots. Around a mouthful of Scotch egg, I had quietly admitted that I thought she was really cool and pretty, and that I might be maybe probably definitely bisexual.

Shen had been quiet for a few minutes. Then he had admitted that he liked her too, and he'd blushed bright red.

I had been panicking about coming out, and his reaction was such a relief that I laughed. Of course, then he turned even redder and refused to talk to me until Jia picked him up. The next day, while we were swimming lengths in the rooftop pool, he had said, "How do you know you like girls, if you've never kissed one?"

"I've never kissed a boy either. I don't need to do that to prove I like boys," I replied. "Why do I have to kiss a girl to know I like them?"

He had been quiet for a while, and then resurfaced from a tumble-turn and asked, "Do you like boys or girls more?"

I had shrugged and said, "I don't know. I don't fancy any boys. I don't know any, apart from you."

He had nodded thoughtfully and carried on doing breaststroke.

Shen and I watch the screen in silence for a while, captivated, as the girl in *Loch & Ness* delicately applies mascara, open-mouthed and intent.

"Do you think it's weird that we both have the same type?" I ask him.

"Blondes?" Shen tilts his head towards me, eyes only leaving the girl on the screen at the last second. "Why would that be weird?"

I'm blonde, I think, and my mouth goes dry. I can't remember what I was going to say.

"I think it's cool," he says. "Like having the same taste in music."

"Which we don't," I point out, trying to smile.

The show switches to a different character, and we both lose interest. But I can't stop thinking about the fact that I'm blonde, and so are the girls that he prefers, and that must mean that I'm Shen's type.

He's never asked me what type of boys I like since that day in the swimming pool. I'm not sure what I would tell him, if he did.

★ ★ ★

Maya Waverley
1 November 2024

Note to self: when the recipe says "mix by hand", it does not mean with your actual bare hands. I may have found this out the hard way. The first person to teach me to cook will honestly win my undying loyalty to the end of time, however long that may or may not take to arrive.

> **Riz Stevens** I make a mean lemon drizzle cake. Just saying.

> **Maya Waverley** How have we been friends for so long without me trying that? Rude.

> **Riz Stevens** Come over this weekend and I'll teach you?

> **Maya Waverley** I'll bring pizza!

Maya Waverley
7 November 2024

Today I was walking home from uni at lunchtime when a white van pulled up next to a woman with a pushchair. These two huge guys got out and tried to drag it away from her. Luckily there were a few of us around – me, an older couple, and a guy in his twenties from the corner shop – and we all ran over and got in their way, trying to stop them. Between us, we got the pram back, but the men got away before the police could arrive.

I haven't been able to stop shaking since I got home. If they'd had guns, that toddler would be theirs right now. I feel so sick, I can't even think. How can this be what we're reduced to now? How can humans be so cruel?

I read in the paper that there are companies that are claiming to have kids that need adopting. They charge a lot of money to match parents up with children, and a lot of the children are turning out to have been kidnapped – which is probably what nearly happened to that toddler.

I don't know how we can all go on living in a place where this kind of thing is happening every day. Why is nothing being done? Why aren't they fixing the sterility so these things stop happening?

Maya Waverley
10 November 2024

My aunt just found out that they're shutting down her son's school out of safety concerns. Thank god. Maybe this will end this kidnapping spree. 40 children have been taken now, just in Oxfordshire.

Maya Waverley
19 November 2024

Does anyone else ever feel like the time before the sterility was just a weird and incredibly boring dream? This version of reality feels normal now. That's horrible, but it's true. It feels bizarre that kids used to be able to walk around without an armed guard; that I used to take *birth control*, that there used to be whole aisles of the supermarket that just sold baby stuff.

I can't believe it's been nine months of this nightmare already. It's not even shocking any more. I've just started getting on with life again. For a long time I've been living day-to-day, while I get used to this new version of normal. But now small things, like traffic jams and broken mugs, have started annoying me again.

No women have been able to get pregnant since February, but I'm just like: "Urgh, I've got loads of coursework to do. I'm out of milk." Same old.

Our strange and adaptive human brains can get used to anything: plague or ice age or nuclear war or the end of children.

Riz Stevens How could you live, though, if you spent every day fully contemplating the real tragedy of it? How would it be possible to get up in the morning? The human brain has to protect itself somehow, even if it feels negligent to accept things the way they are without making even the smallest effort towards mourning it. It feels a little like we should all be wearing black crepe, wailing as we roam the halls of silent mansions, like rich Victorian widows.

Maya Waverley Do you think when this is all fixed and over and done with, we'll forget all about it? Will I one day tell my grandchildren about the whole thing as a horrible but exciting anecdote? Will it seem like a bizarre dream that lasted a few months, before normal broadcasting resumed? I'm not sure I'm the same person I was before this happened. I'm not sure any of us are. We've seen the desperate truth of how badly humans can behave when we're forced into a corner. If life went back to normal, how could we stand it?

TIME	DATE	LOCATION	OBJECT	NOTES
10.10	01/08/2108	50.095917, -5.125706	Plastic figurine of Star Wars character "Princess Leia", missing the head. Late twentieth century.	Found by LMBW lodged in the neck of a glass milk bottle from 1903. Victoria claimed the toy and chewed it up within an hour. The bottle is being used as a vase for flowers on my bedside table.

When Shen goes off to the bathroom, I read a few more of Maya's posts while *Loch & Ness* is paused. To my disappointment, she stopped using the account within a year of the virus. The long, chatty posts trail off and are replaced by a few birthday wishes from friends, interspersed with the odd link to an article. Nothing worth reading.

I sigh and close the website. I'd enjoyed reading about her, while it lasted. I really liked her. And she was *blonde*.

"I just overheard your mum and Baba talking," Shen says, coming back with new drinks. "They're going to watch the black-box footage in your mum's library."

I shoot up from where I was lounging in my seat. "What? Right now? We have to go and listen!"

"There's no way they'll let us."

"I didn't say we were going to ask permission!"

Shen grins at me. "I'm listening…"

"The mirror?"

"The mirror."

Mum's library is the kind of room that you'd willingly kill someone to inherit. I mean that in the most serious way possible. Not only is it filled with multiple first editions, including a Dickens and a Shakespeare first folio, but the dark rosewood bookcases are fitted with a mahogany ladder on rollers, which you can push around the shelves to access the upper levels. A spiral staircase leads up to a balcony with even more bookshelves, and there's a ceiling mural of angels and demons.

But more importantly, there's a secret passageway hidden behind one of the bookshelves that leads to a mirror-door in one of the third-floor corridors.

We go upstairs to the third floor and pull the door open. The mirror creaks, swinging noisily on its hinges, and then Shen climbs through. Mitch tries to follow, but I shake my head. "Your joints are too loud and rusty. You'll have to wait here. I mean it, Mitch." I hold eye contact with him, and for a moment he shifts like he's going to barge past me into the tunnel.

"It's OK, Mitch. We're not trying to run away from you. This is a dead end," Shen says, taking pity on him. "We can't go anywhere else without you. We'll be back out this way."

Mitch flashes a perturbed red light and sits on the ledge of a marble statue to wait for us, pulling a chain link out of his storage unit and threading it through his fingers. Honestly, the bot is like a magpie. Nothing shiny is safe around him.

I pull the mirror closed behind us and turn on my torch. Even tiptoeing, our footsteps echo on the cold marble slabs of the passageway. It leads to three different bedrooms and ends at the wooden library wall.

There's the muffled sound of talking coming from the other side of the panelling when I press my ear against it. I use a pair of pliers to remove the nails holding one of the slats in place, and twist it to the side, leaving a gap big enough to peek through. It reveals the back of a bookshelf, full of dusty leather-bound books.

We slide a few books out, blowing away dead spiders and cobwebs, and stack them on the floor until we can both see through. Mum, Dad, and Feng are sitting by the fireplace, talking. I can hear the low murmur of voices, but I can't make out any of the words. I watch the three of them talk for a while, trying to lip-read.

"Shadow, we can't even hear them," Shen says. His "judgement" crease appears between his eyebrows, like it always does when he thinks I'm being particularly ridiculous. He shifts, accidentally kicking over the books we've stacked on the floor.

I grimace and shush him.

Mum seems to be answering questions. When Dad says something, gesturing wildly, she holds up a hand to quiet him.

Shen shifts against me, tracing an idle pattern on the small of my back. When his hair brushes against my neck, I break out in goose bumps. There's a feeling between us then, like lightning. It happens sometimes. We'll be having a perfectly normal conversation, and suddenly the air will change and it's like we're caught in a thunderstorm. The hairs on my arms will stand on end and I'll freeze, locked into his gaze, waiting to see what happens next.

What usually happens is that I panic – because we can't do this. I won't let us. Our friendship is too important to possibly sabotage. So I'll turn away, or pretend to have a coughing fit or swat away an imaginary bee from his hair, or answer a fake call on my tablet. Then, quickly enough that I'll think I've imagined the whole thing, the tension will disappear again. We'll go back to our cosy, relaxed ways, bumping shoulders and teasing each other like nothing ever happened. But this time – and I don't know why – I'm filled with the urge to press my nose into the dark hollow under his ear. The desire is almost overwhelming.

I realise I'm leaning back into him, and I force myself to stand up and pay attention to what's happening in the library. I'm being ridiculous. I'm just hungry, or tired, or confused, or something. Shen and I are friends. Just friends.

In the library, Mum plays a video on the wall. It must be the footage from the black box, because it shows the inside of a helicopter cockpit. Alexei Wyatt sits at the controls, pulling on headphones and switching on the equipment. He flies for a few minutes, and then all at once, he shudders and begins to shake, almost uncontrollably.

Behind me, Shen gasps.

I don't know what we were expecting to see, but it wasn't this. Alexei's shoulders tremble and twist; his head is thrown back as though in pain. He tips forward again, still shaking, and his head knocks into the controls. There's a spray of blood.

My hand flies to my mouth.

Alexei's awful writhing seems to go on for ever, until he finally falls still, slumped over the helm. His head is pushing against the controls.

A message appears on the helicopter's screen: MANUAL CONTROL DETECTED. AUTO-CONTROL WILL BE DISABLED IN FIVE … FOUR … THREE … TWO … ONE.

The helicopter tips downwards so suddenly that I let out a little cry, as though I'm there with him.

The screen's message changes, glowing red and flashing.

DANGER! OBJECT COLLISION IS IMMINENT. PLEASE ADJUST CONTROLS OR RE-ENABLE AUTO-NAVIGATION.

Big Ben fills the window view, getting larger and larger as the helicopter flies towards it. Alarms flash, but Alexei is still slumped over the controls, and doesn't react.

The footage ends in an explosion of red and white flames.

I turn and bury my face in Shen's shoulder. He puts an arm around me. I'm dimly aware that Dad is shouting. Something about "this morning" and then I can't make out the rest.

"What was that?" I whisper to Shen.

"Some kind of fit. I don't know. I've never seen anything like it."

The video loops and plays again: Alexei Wyatt starting the flight, the convulsions, the red blast of the crash.

We stare at each other. We really shouldn't be watching this.

"We just need to stay calm," I hear Mum say loudly. Her voice makes me jump. Need to stay calm about what?

Shen is pale, biting at the knuckle of his hand. "Something is going on, Lowrie. Something they're not telling us."

We don't talk much for the rest of the evening. Our parents left the library soon after watching the footage, and we didn't hear any more of their conversation. I want to ask them what's going on, but Shen is reluctant.

"They'll know we spied on them, then. And they're clearly busy. We're only going to get in the way if we try and interfere."

I agree not to say anything, annoyed that he's probably right, even if he's being far too sensible.

After Feng takes Shen home, I sit in the theatre and watch the rest of the first episode of *Loch & Ness* in a daze, lost in thought. I'm startled when Mum comes in and turns on the lights. "Come for a walk around the grounds with me, will you?" she asks. "The dogs need their last wee, and I feel like I haven't seen you for days. I've been so busy."

It's drizzling, so we put on wellies and coats – and I pull on an old green felt hat, with a pheasant feather tucked into the ribbon, that I find on a hook in the boot room – and head out into the dark gardens with torches.

Victoria, Albert and Mitch sprint off into the bushes, the dogs yipping as they chase the scent trails of rabbits under the footings of the gazebo. I'm glad that even if Mitch can't make friends with the household bots, the dogs seem to like him.

The flock of alpacas near the lake are so used to the dogs that they don't even lift their heads. We keep them for their wool for clothing. We also have two dozen hens. There are little small-holdings scattered around central London, and everyone chips in to care for them. We all help out in summer with the harvesting of crops too.

I keep expecting Mum to bring up the footage from the black box, but after she talks about the dogs' latest antics for the tenth time, I lose patience. "Did you find out something about Alexei?" I ask. It comes out more bluntly than I'd meant it to.

She looks startled. "What do you mean?"

"Have you found out how he crashed yet?"

"It was just an accident," she says, but she can't quite meet my eye.

My heart sinks. She's not going to tell me anything. She's going to keep it a secret. Why? Why doesn't she trust me?

"Mum..." I say, trailing off and rubbing my hand across the moss-covered rim of a stone urn while I think. We walk down the steps in the centre of the lawn. "Mum – how come you never told me about what happened after the sterility? The riots, and kidnappings and stuff. I read something about it online and I couldn't believe I didn't know what had happened." If she won't talk about Alexei, maybe she'll talk about this.

Mum is silent for a long moment before she replies. Some-where in the bushes, Albert yips, paws scrambling at a rabbit hole.

"When I was born, the riots were still frequent." She pauses, looking at the moulting gutters on the summer house. Her mouth tightens. "I remember once, when I was *very* young, getting separated from my mum at the theatre. There was a protest happening outside – something to do with fertility research funding, I think – and the police had started using water cannons to control the crowds. A lot of people ran into the theatre to hide. In the chaos, I lost track of my mother."

I swing my torch, watching the beam light up moths and send the shadows of grasses and plants swelling across the damp lawn. There are bats fluttering overhead, amongst the sparkling stars. "What happened?" I ask, quietly.

She stares across the garden, searching for the words. A marble nymph stares back at us serenely. "I hid under a sofa in the theatre foyer until it was over. Your grandmother found me eventually. But for a while I thought that I was going to die, or get kidnapped. I didn't think I'd ever see her again."

"I'm sorry."

"It was a long time ago!" She tries to smile at me. "And that was during one of the last riots held anywhere in the country. Things settled down a lot after that, for many reasons. People accepted that this was what life was like now, and started living day-to-day instead of worrying about the future. I don't want you to think I had a terrible childhood, because I didn't, not at all. In a lot of ways, I was happier than many other children my age."

She winces, and rolls her eyes at herself. "Sorry. That sounds like something one of Mrs Maxwell's characters would say – but it's true. And I'm only telling you this so you understand why I haven't wanted to discuss it with you before. I prefer to just enjoy what time we have left. I don't like to dwell on the past, or on all the people we've lost. But I know that your father feels differently about that. We've argued about it before. There are things he feels that you should know about the time before you were born and he's wanted to tell you them for many years. But I thought it was best to wait."

My smile freezes. "What things? Tell me. Please. I'm ready. I'm old enough to know."

"I know you are. This conversation has proven that you're mature above and beyond what we were waiting for. But it's something we all need to discuss together – with the Zhangs too. It's not a conversation to rush. Can you wait a little longer? Can you do that, for me?"

There's nothing I can do but agree.

We're turning back towards the manor, passing the hen house where a bot is busy collecting eggs, when there's a large *boom* in the distance. There's a dust cloud rolling across the skyline. I squint at it, trying to work out what caused it.

"Another one's collapsed," Mum says wearily.

A tower block has fallen down in the suburbs. The blocks of flats out there have been crumbling to dust every couple of years for decades. First, the concrete slides off the sides in chunks then the building grows more and more decrepit over months until all of a sudden the whole thing crumbles to the ground in a pile of rubble.

TIME	DATE	LOCATION	OBJECT	NOTES
20.05	15/08/2108	51.504355 -0.148104	Art deco-style advertising poster, showing a girl in a nightgown at her dressing table, using a CHANEL-branded lipstick.	Found by LMBW. It was being used as cardboard backing for a picture frame displaying a Monet print and was held in place with masking tape.

That night, I lie in bed and mess around on my tablet, trying to stop myself thinking about everything that's happening. I wish I had more of Maya's posts to read, but as there aren't any left, I check my emails instead, and then the newsfeed, hoping for something about Alexei (there's nothing new, except for a nice compilation of interviews about him, which nearly makes me cry). I check my emails again, then the news, until I realise I've descended into an internet spiral and make myself snap out of it.

I should at least do something useful with my time, like sort through my old sandpaper, which is what Mitch is happily doing while I freak out. Instead, I message Shen, trying to distract my brain into switching off.

Lowrie MBW [22.55]:	Question for you
张申 [22.57]:	hit me.
Lowrie MBW [22.58]:	You know how we're super famous and amazing and everyone loves us?
张申 [23.00]:	with you so far.
Lowrie MBW [23.00]:	But it's not because of anything we've actually done, right? It's just because of our ages. Well, what if it was for something else, something we'd actually achieved? What would you want to be famous for?
张申 [23.02]	oh god
Lowrie MBW [23.06]:	I have no idea what mine would be. I know exactly what yours is, though.
张申[23.07]:	you do?
Lowrie MBW [23.08]:	Let's both say what you'd be famous for, on five.
张申 [23.09]:	OK.
Lowrie MBW [23.11]:	Ready?
张申 [23.12]:	ready.
Lowrie MBW [23.12]:	Finding alien life.
张申[23.12]:	being the first person to meet aliens
Lowrie MBW [23.13]:	YES! I KNEW IT!
Lowrie MBW [23.16]:	Do I know you well or WHAT
张申 [23.17]:	I mean, yes, but also, that was obvious to anyone who's spoken to me for five minutes
Lowrie MBW [23.18]:	Let me have this victory, Zhang
张申 [23.21]:	Yours would be discovering a casket of buried treasure
Lowrie MBW [23.22]:	OH, IT WOULD BE!!

I look at what I've written, our light-hearted conversation, and I realise I don't want a distraction. I want to discuss this – Maya, and Alexei, and everything Mum said in the garden.

In the past, I've walked over in the quiet of the night to see Shen, when neither of us can sleep. The Zhangs live in an eighteenth-century townhouse on the other side of Hyde Park, which is only a few minutes away. Shen's family could most accurately be described as nouveau riche, whereas mine is as old and traditional as a family can get.

I'm too comfortable in bed to walk to Shen's now, so instead I video call him. He answers immediately, lifting a finger to his lips – his parents must be asleep in the room next door. He's lying in bed too, on his side with the lights dimmed. For a while we stare at each other.

A warmth in my stomach reminds me of how good it had felt to have the long line of him leaning against me in the secret passageway. I clear my throat. I'm not thinking about it. I'm *not*. This is very much not the time.

"Did your baba mention Alexei and the black box tonight?" I whisper.

He shakes his head. "No, but he's clearly worried. I overheard him talking to Mama on the phone – she's staying at the hospital tonight, so she can keep an eye on Alexei."

"He's that bad?"

"It sounds like he's getting worse."

I sigh. "Did you hear anything about Mrs Maxwell? Is she still in hospital?"

"I don't know. Baba didn't mention her," Shen says. "He was really vague when I asked him."

"Yeah, Mum was the same. I asked her about the footage from the black box and she just waved it off, and said it was an accident – which it clearly wasn't. Alexei got sick and crashed. Why won't they just tell us that? I don't see what the big secret is. People get sick. It's terrible, but it's not..." I trail off. "I don't get the secrecy."

He huffs through his nose, and then says loudly, forgetting to keep his voice down, "Me neither. It's like the nosebleeds and kidnappings. They're keeping something from us, for some reason. *Why?*"

"I think – I think there's more to all of this than we thought. Mum said there was something about the time before I was born that she's going to tell me. She has to wait for your parents and my dad to agree to it first, though."

"What, really?" His brow furrows. "What does *that* mean?"

I shrug. "Who knows? I really wish Maya had carried on posting on her account. That told me more than our parents ever have!"

"Maybe we can find her on a different social network? Do some internet deep-diving."

We start with the obvious and run a search for her name plus *"Loch & Ness"* and a few other things mentioned in her profile.

"It doesn't look like she's got any other accounts under her real name," I say.

"Maybe there's one under a random username?" Shen suggests.

I go back to her original social media profile and find the name of the boy she was always talking to, Riz. I find his social media profile with the username *Rizzz* straightaway. From there, we work out that out of Rizzz's thirty mutual followers, he regularly spoke to five.

"What was Maya's date of birth again?" Shen asks.

"Um, I don't know exactly, but she was born in 2005, I think. Why?"

"This account is called MyWaves05. And they post about *Loch & Ness*."

"I bet that's her!"

We scroll down to the time when she stopped posting on the other site and read from there. It's a different kind of social media to the last one, which was centred around talking to family. This one seems to be more public. The posts are shorter and funnier. It's weird that the style of talking is so different, just because the website changed. I still don't understand social media. Reading Maya's new account is like having to learn a whole new language of memes and acronyms and slang and nuanced emojis.

MyWaves05

All right listen up, losers! You all need to sign this petition: <u>Make fertility tests compulsory for 16–55 year olds</u>. Scientists need more data and there might be one person out there who has the information they need in their cells. Thank you very much for signing (and I promise to stop calling you all losers now).

Posted on 28 Nov 2024

MyWaves05

At the risk of being an alarmist, apparently eggs that were frozen for fertility treatment are still fertile?! My friend Ashley just got offered twenty million (YES, POUNDS) for one of hers. Because that's a thing that's apparently happening now.

(She's not going to do it, obviously. She wants to try for a baby for herself.)

Posted on 13 Dec 2024

MyWaves05

I understand logically that the government needs to make sure the supply of eggs is protected, after that clinic in Toronto got robbed, but it's almost absurd to suggest that the donors of the ovum and sperm samples don't have a right to access their genetic material at any time. It's immoral – they should be able to choose for themselves when to conceive. It's not like any of the rest of us can.

Posted on 11 Jan 2025

> **Unhako_neko** on 11 Jan 2025
> Replying to **@MyWaves05**
> Hear, hear! Who cares if every person in the UK with frozen eggs chooses to have babies all at the same time? This whole thing will probably be fixed in a few months with a vaccine, anyway.

>> **MyWaves05** on 11 Jan 2025
>> Replying to **@Unhako_neko**
>> Besides, wouldn't scientists be able to learn a lot from the growth of those embryos? What do they gain from keeping them locked up in freezers and only releasing one ovum every three months? My friend Ashley's frozen eggs turned out not to be viable, but it was much better for her to actually know that for sure than to live for years in hope, while she waited for permission to access the sample. That's what they've started doing now. It feels so silly saying all of this, because at this point it just feels like it should be obvious.

MyWaves05

In what is almost certainly a slightly futile attempt at help, I just called my local MP to ask her to support increasing fertility funding again. I think I probably would have been better off cleaning my toilet for an hour instead.

Posted on 30 Sep 2025

> **Rizzz** on 30 Sep 2025
> Replying to **@MyWaves05**
> We have to keep fighting, even if it's not the most effective or realistic method of helping. I feel so useless, otherwise.

"I can't believe that…" I start to say, but when I look at Shen, he's fallen asleep.

His long eyelashes are spread over his cheeks, and he's

breathing steadily, in a small, barely audible snore. He's flipped over, so he's lying with his deaf ear facing upwards; his other ear is pressed into the pillow to block out all sound. Sometimes I'm jealous of how quickly he can fall asleep when he does that. He never gets woken up by loud noises.

It's probably good that I've got no way of waking him up, because I definitely would right now if I could. Seeing Maya talk to Riz and her other friends online makes me feel suddenly lonely. I'll never have a group of friends to chat to like that. I'm so grateful that I have Shen, at least. It's another reason why I can never, ever do anything to risk losing him as a friend – however much the sight of his dark hair curling under his ear makes me want to reach out through the screen and touch him.

After I hang up, I miss him even more than I did before the call, so I fetch the pillow from the room Shen sleeps in when he stops over. (It's called the blue room, but it hasn't actually been painted blue since 1878.) The pillow still smells of him, so after tucking it under the covers beside me, I wrap my arm and leg over it. I would never admit this to anyone, because I know it's weird, but sometimes doing this is the only sure-fire way I have of getting to sleep. It's just reassuring, having something of his around, that's all. It doesn't mean anything.

TIME	DATE	LOCATION	OBJECT	NOTES
12.22	12/03/2109	51.461235, 0.281735	Human skull missing two teeth on the lower left. Nineteenth century.	Found by SZ. "Yorick" was found on the foreshore. Possibly (hopefully) washed from an eroded graveyard upriver. Not retrieved.

The next day, Shen and I arrange to walk to the community gathering together. We're meeting our parents there. I have no idea what to expect from today's meeting, which has been rescheduled after Alexei's accident. Our parents have been so cagey about everything that I'm not sure what anyone else knows about what's happening. Have they told everyone apart from us that Alexei had some kind of fit before the helicopter crashed? They could be keeping that secret from everyone else too.

After showering, I have some time before Shen wakes up, so I sit cross-legged in front of my mirror, French plaiting my hair while it's wet. The plait reveals more of the grey patch above my temple, and I poke at it, wondering if it's getting bigger. I can't be sure. I quite like it, though. It looks dignified.

Mitch sits next to me, watching my reflection intently. He

extends a finger and pushes a stray curl back into the loop of the braid.

"You're a lot cleverer than everyone thinks, aren't you?" I ask, watching him carefully.

A blue light flashes on the top of his head.

I've never been friends with a robot before. I didn't know how *human* they could be, and how easy it might be to forget that they aren't human. It feels like Mitch has been around for ever. There must be dozens of other bots who are all alone like Mitch, quietly living by themselves in abandoned cities, getting on with their old jobs. I wonder if they miss human company. I wonder if being left running for so long has changed their original software, mutated it into a strange and unknown personality – oddball and silly, but even more interesting for it.

Mitch can't have been like this when he was first released on to the foreshore as a patrolling lifeguard. He made himself like this, over the years and years of isolation.

"You're part of the family now, you know," I say, tying off the end of the plait. "You can stay here as long as you want."

Mitch leans sideways and nudges me with his shoulder.

I take it as a thank you.

I apply red rouge to my lips (made by Mrs Singh by mixing beeswax from her hives with beetroot colouring), then put on a blue-and-white pin-striped shirt, which I stole from Dad, and a skirt in the same red as the lipstick.

Shen eyes me with an odd look when we meet. "You've done your hair like that girl from the TV show."

I touch the twisted strands, surprised. I hadn't realised that I was copying her. I'm wearing the same colour lipstick too. "So I have."

Whistling to himself, Shen squeezes my shoulder as we start walking. His thumb rubs against the side of my neck absently.

I shiver and stare at him, breathing open-mouthed. We touch each other like this all the time, but for some reason, today it hits me in the gut. Something changed in the secret passageway, and I can't seem to shake it off.

When he moves his hand, I rub my neck, tracing the place where he touched me, as I follow him and Mitch down the pavement.

We're nearly at City Hall when I catch sight of a car stopped in the road ahead of us. I tilt my head, squinting at it. Why is a car parked in the middle of the street? There's no one else around, except for us. The whole area is completely deserted.

We walk closer, and I realise with a jolt that there's a figure in the driver's seat. As we get even closer, I see that it's Mrs Bolton. She isn't moving.

"Shen." I grab his arm, coldness sinking through me. "What...?" I trail off as I tap on the window. It makes a loud noise, but Mrs Bolton doesn't react. She looks ... she almost looks like she's dead. My stomach twists over. "Are you OK? Mrs Bolton!" I bang harder on the glass.

Mrs Bolton's body jerks, shaking and seizing, like Alexei's did in the video. I fall back in shock.

Next to me, Mitch gives a long, mournful dark blue flash.

"Mrs Bolton!" Shen cries. He pulls desperately at the door handle. "It's locked!"

Mrs Bolton continues to shake on the other side of the glass.

"We need to get to her!" he says. He's sweating, panicked.

I nod. "You call your mama. Get help. I'll get us inside."

I don't want to hurt her by breaking the window and spraying her with broken glass. Luckily, I've had practice of breaking into cars before, when we've found intact ones in old garages that we wanted to restore.

I take a screwdriver out of my utility belt and jam it between the door and the body of the car, levering the door open enough to create a gap. Now I need something long and thin to push inside to press the "unlock" button. "Your metal detector," I say, holding out my hand to Shen.

He passes it to me, still talking to Jia. He stands stiff, speaking carefully. His expression is emotionless. I know that if I'd had to make that call, I would have ended up crying, but Shen doesn't even blink.

I turn the metal detector and push the end of the long handle through the gap. Mrs Bolton's body is still spasming. I try to ignore it as best I can and focus on what I'm doing. I press my forehead against the glass, staring down inside the car at the door as I direct the detector to the button. I push it down, and the door clicks open.

I kneel beside Mrs Bolton, holding her while she shakes. I don't want to move her until the emergency bots get here to take her to the hospital. Mitch crouches next to me, and I lean against him, shuddering, as Shen talks to Jia.

I managed to push away my panic while I was getting the car door open, but now I feel sick. First Alexei, then Mrs Maxwell, now Mrs Bolton. What is happening? Why are so many people getting sick?

"Thanks, Mama," Shen says. His voice is overly loud. He always talks too loudly on the phone, so you can hear him from a room away. I don't think he can judge the volume of his own speech on the phone because of his hearing. After he ends the call, Shen rests his hand on my back. "She's on her way. She's coming with the emergency bots. It's going to be OK."

He can't know that for sure. I lean back against him, trying not to think about how Mrs Bolton has gone still in my arms.

The four of us don't move until Jia arrives. She hugs Shen and me tightly then helps lift Mrs Bolton on to a stretcher and hurry her to the hospital. I stand and watch them leave, unable to look away.

TIME	DATE	LOCATION	OBJECT	NOTES
11.21	15/02/2108	51.479416, 0.191404	EREADER, WATERLOGGED AND IN A PLASTIC CASE COVERED IN ACRYLIC STICKERS OF JAPANESE ANIME TV SHOWS, CIRCA 2018.	FOUND BY LMBW. WE WATCHED ONE OF THE SHOWS. IT WAS PRETTY GOOD.

Soon after Jia leaves, Mum arrives to take us home. The meeting has been cancelled again, this time until we find out if Mrs Bolton is all right. Shen and I are ushered into the reading room, wrapped in blankets, and given mugs of tea. Mum and Dad come and sit with us.

"Lowrie, Shen," Mum says, "we've tried to protect you. I'm not sure if that was the right decision" – she glances at Dad – "but, well … there's something going around. An illness. We don't know what it is, but it seems to be – severe." She draws a deep breath. "Until it's sorted, we're putting everyone in quarantine."

Shen makes a muffled noise.

I drop my mug, tea splashing on to the carpet. I pick the mug up and put it down on the table and then focus on a gilt-framed oil painting on the wall, breathing carefully. I trace the brushstrokes with my eyes until I stop shaking. "Is it … is it life-threatening?"

"No!" Mum hurries to say. "No." She pauses. "We don't know. We hope not. But you two will be fine. We promise. This isn't about that. We're more worried that something will happen to us and you'll be alone, and—"

"This is really bad," Shen says. He leans forward to run his hands through his hair, sighing. The strands, usually slicked back neatly, slip down over his forehead. "This is so bad."

"We need to go over the emergency protocols again," Dad says. "As soon as possible."

"*What?*" Shen asks.

Ever since we were little, our parents have made us practice what we would do if something happened to them. It's routine things, like where to find the electricity generators and the water-distillation filters – everything we need to know to keep safe and healthy and well-fed in the aftermath of a crisis if Shen and I are left all on our own.

I've spent years rolling my eyes at the unnecessary health-and-safety routines. I used to complain that it was going to be decades before we were left on our own. But this doesn't feel like a practice. It feels real. They really think we're going to be alone. And *soon*.

"Is it that bad?" I ask, hoarsely.

"I'm just concerned that we haven't prepared you enough." Mum takes Dad's hand, looking at their interlinked fingers.

I sit back in my seat like I've been punched, all the air knocked from my lungs.

"I'm not ready," Shen says, and starts to sob.

★ ★ ★

MyWaves05

Today I downloaded a dating app for the
first time! It took me a full six minutes to
work out how to upload a picture –
so I'm off to a good start.

Posted on 15 May 2026

> **Rizzz** on 15 May 2026
> Replying to **@MyWaves05**
> Oh dear, good luck. My last experience
> with dating apps turned my hair white
> and transformed my vague dislike of
> the human race into a raging tower of
> fury. I've resigned myself to a long and
> productive bachelorhood.
>
> > **MyWaves05** on 15 May 2026
> > Replying to **@Rizzz**
> > Good LORD. This might have persuaded
> > me to delete it immediately. Though a
> > guy did tell me he'd bring his dog on
> > a date so: not entirely a lost cause?

MyWaves05

The app wants me to put in my
sexuality. Why isn't there an option
for "all girls and boys when they
are fictional, unrealistically perfect
or impossibly unattainable"?

Posted on 16 May 2026

MyWaves05

Anyone else see *Pride and Joy* yet?
I haven't cried so much at a film in
years. The CGI for the baby was so
good, it almost looked real. Definitely
go and see it if you get the chance.

Posted on 10 Jul 2026

MyWaves05

My date: systematically disparaging every
single one of my favourite things.

Me, listening furiously: yeah, totally, sure,
I see your point there, thanks, I hate this.

Anyway I left her there and got
cheesecake, no regrets.

Posted on 18 Aug 2026

> **Rizzz** on 18 Aug 2026
> Replying to **@MyWaves05**
> I hope the poor woman isn't still there?

>> **MyWaves05** on 18 Aug 2026
>> Replying to **@Rizzz**
>> She's probably busy negging the waiter about
>> the inadequacy of the wine, if I had to guess.

MyWaves05

Congratulations!

> RT **@Rizzz** I've been on hormones for 4 years
> this week. Best decision of my life. Now back
> to your regularly scheduled nonsense posts.

Posted on 4 Oct 2026

> **Rizzz** on 4 Oct 2026
> Replying to **@MyWaves05**
> Thank you so much for the rainbow cupcakes! They
> just arrived and everyone in my office let out a
> simultaneous gasp of amazement. They're stunning.

>> **MyWaves05** on 4 Oct 2026
>> Replying to **@Rizzz**
>> I hope you shared them, then.

>>> **Rizzz** on 4 Oct 2026
>>> Replying to **@MyWaves05**
>>> Don't be crazy. I made them watch
>>> as I ate all dozen, one by one.

>>>> **MyWaves05** on 4 Oct 2026
>>>> Replying to **@Rizzz**
>>>> How villainous.

Rizzz on 4 Oct 2026
Replying to **@MyWaves05**
Well, I heard you liked bad boys.

MyWaves05 on 4 Oct 2026
Replying to **@Rizzz**
Not really, actually.

Rizzz on 4 Oct 2026
Replying to **@MyWaves05**
Oh, thank God. I am
definitely not one.

CHAPTER 15

TIME	DATE	LOCATION	OBJECT	NOTES
14.20	17/08/2108	50.090557, -5.150173	Spanish doubloon coin, dated 1537, weighing 7 grams in 22-carat gold.	Found by SZ in an old basement behind a rusted iron trapdoor. Some kind of smuggler's den?

The next few hours are spent with Dad quizzing us on the emergency protocols. He makes sure that we know how to maintain the solar panels, where the backup power generators and canned food are stored, how to control the boiler and water supply, and how to care for the crops and animals on the estate.

Dad isn't satisfied until we've proved we can run the estate all on our own. He even checks that we know what to do when winter comes, which isn't for months and months.

"Dad – we're not going to need to know all this stuff, are we?" I whisper, barely able to say the words out loud. "You don't really think…?"

He shakes his head. "I don't know. But I'd never forgive myself if you two weren't ready, just in case."

Shen fiddles with his cufflink, frowning. It's his silver "Roswell Area 51" set, which I made for him for Christmas last year. I spent weeks hammering pieces of silver flat and soldering a design into the metal.

I meet Shen's eye, and his expression softens slightly.

"We really are just being cautious," Dad adds. "You don't need to worry. Everything will be fine."

Somehow, the more they try to reassure us, the worse I feel.

Finally, we're sent to bed. Shen is staying in the blue room tonight.

"I wish we'd been able to ask about Alexei," I say on the stairs, peering over the bannister to make sure that Dad isn't listening.

"There's no way we could have known about him having the same symptoms as Mrs Bolton and Mrs Maxwell unless we'd seen the footage from the black box. We couldn't bring it up."

"It has to be the same illness, though, right? It must be going around really fast – if we're in quarantine already."

This whole thing is making me think of Maya in the aftermath of the sterility virus. She must have gone through this same fear and panic. As soon as I've said good night to Shen and climbed into bed, I pull up Maya's account, and reread her posts about the day of the virus, seeing the same fear there that I'm feeling right now. I go to Riz's profile and read his too.

Rizzz

I used to have nosebleeds all the time when I was a kid, but I haven't had one for years. Then suddenly today my nose started bleeding and it won't stop. Give it to me straight, guys. Am I dying?

Posted on 21 Feb 2024

Rizzz

What's going on? Is this nosebleed thing
happening everywhere, or just in the UK?
Not to make any sweeping assumptions,
but is this the actual end of the world?

Posted on 21 Feb 2024

Rizzz

This is the end of the world. Shit.

Posted on 21 Feb 2024

Rizzz

My mum just called me to say goodbye.

Posted on 21 Feb 2024

Rizzz

I don't know what to do. I don't have
anyone here with me. What do I do?

Posted on 21 Feb 2024

Rizzz

Feeling a bit embarrassed by all my wild "farewell,
world" posts last week. Going back to work
after all that felt like a slight anticlimax.

Posted on 28 Feb 2024

Rizzz

As much as it might damage my flawless reputation,
I have to admit that I'm feeling kind of lonely
these days. Going through this whole thing
makes me realise the degree to which my life is
just worksleepworksleeprepeat. It's fine, but not
exactly the way I want to spend the apocalypse.

Posted on 1 Mar 2024

Rizzz

I never really assumed I'd have kids
(I'm a perpetual bachelor, for a start),
but it's a whole different thing to know
that I *can't* have kids. I'm not going to
cheerfully resign myself to a future without
something so essential to being alive.

Posted on 25 Sep 2024

Once I've read all of the posts about the virus, I go back to Maya's account, reading as quickly as possible in an attempt to distract myself – or at least pretend that this isn't happening to me.

I skim over years and years of Maya's life: posts about her daily routine and politics and uni work and relationships and family, until I can't keep my eyes open. I put on the audio description and listen to the mechanical voice read the posts while I bury myself under the duvet.

I can't remember feeling this overwhelmed since I was younger, when I helped Mr Kowalski to deliver Elizabeth's foal. It was exciting at the time, but perhaps a little traumatising for a nine-year-old.

At midnight, Mum pokes her head around my door to check if I'm sleeping. She's closing the door again when I sit up. "Hi."

"Are you doing OK, champ?"

"Not really," I mumble.

She comes and sits by me.

I roll over and press my head into her thigh. A dog hair pokes me in the cheek. Mitch, who is sprawled out in front of the fireplace, rolls over lazily to look at us.

"Mum, I'm scared."

"I know. So am I."

"What if we all die? What if this is the end?"

She rests a hand on top of my head, like I'm Victoria. "I don't think it is."

"What difference does it even make, if we all die now instead of in a few decades?" I frown, my expression unseen against her side. "What are we all doing here, anyway? What are we achieving?"

Mum smooths out a section of my hair, before twisting it around her finger. "There's no finish line you need to cross to have lived a worthy life, Lowrie. You don't need to achieve any-thing, if you don't want to."

"But if we're the last..." I sigh.

"Don't worry about making your ancestors proud. You don't need to be perfect, just on the off chance you're the last of your kind. Life is whatever you want it to be. With whoever you want to be with. Life is the people around you, the ones you love. You just need to be happy. That's all that matters."

I'm quiet for a moment, taking this in. "Are you happy?"

"I'm happier than I ever thought I'd be."

"What made you happy?"

"Having you."

I sigh, and sit up, rubbing my eyes. "Well, that doesn't help me. I can't have kids, can I?"

"I don't know about that. There's still time. I have hope."

"What about everyone else? They've never had kids. Does that mean they aren't happy?"

"It means that they're doing the best they can, in the hope that one day this will be fixed, and then there will be children again."

"And if it isn't?"

"We'll deal with that when it comes to it."

MyWaves05

shared the post "Scientists say they've made 'no real progress' on reversing the effects of the virus"

So the new infertility progress report says that they've still not got any leads for a cure, two years after they started looking. What are we going to do when the IVF eggs run out? This really might be the end of everything. A whole generation is just going to disappear if this isn't fixed soon.

Posted on 30 Nov 2026

> **Silentstar** on 30 Nov 2026
> Replying to **@MyWaves05**
> Oh, I hate this I hate it I hate it. What are they playing at?! How can they not know anything at all?

MyWaves05

Reasons my cat is mad at me: I didn't come home until two a.m. and then was too busy sleeping to feed him breakfast.

Reasons I'm mad at my cat: he didn't like the leftover steak my date kindly saved from his dinner.

Posted on 12 Feb 2027

> **Rizzz** on 12 Feb 2027
> Replying to **@MyWaves05**
> We get it, you went out last night –
> you're very cool.

MyWaves05 on 12 Feb 2027
Replying to **@Rizzz**
I knew you'd slip up and admit you were
jealous of my dates sooner or later. Good
work, everyone – we got him.

> **Rizzz** on 12 Feb 2027
> Replying to **@MyWaves05**
> Wow. Never have I been more
> exquisitely burned in public.

MyWaves05

I've donated to the fundraiser "Please help, the
Manchester riots destroyed our home". People
don't feel safe any more. They're rioting because
the government isn't doing enough to protect
children. They're trying to ride this out without
making any major policy changes, but it's gone
past that point. This isn't going to just go away
without every nation working together to fix
it, using every resource we have. More of the
budget needs to be dedicated to research.

Posted on 27 Apr 2027

MyWaves05

What's with **#Babygrow**? Why's everyone
so into an app game all of a sudden?

Posted on 4 May 2027

> **Blueburnedskies** on 4 May 2027
> Replying to **@MyWaves05**
> Maya, you have to download it! It's so amazing. You can
> create a baby! You put in descriptions of you and your
> partner, and it makes an embryo. It's in real time too, so it
> takes nine months before it's born. And while it's growing,
> it responds to sound and touch – so you can use the app
> to stroke the stomach, play classical music and speak
> to the baby, and even watch it kick. It's kind of sweet!

> > **MyWaves05** on 4 May 2027
> > Replying to **@Blueburnedskies**
> > Nine months? That's so long. Everyone will
> > have forgotten about it before any babies are
> > even born. What a weird idea for an app.

Unhako_neko on 4 May 2027
Replying to **@MyWaves05**
and **@Blueburnedskies**
I like that it's realistic! It feels like a real baby. Phil
and I are obsessed. We both have the app, and
we check up on ours constantly. I hope it's a boy.

CHAPTER 16

TIME	DATE	LOCATION	OBJECT	NOTES
13.57	04/08/2108	50.156859, -5.070932	Ivory walrus tusk, carved into the shape of a reindeer with antlers. Possibly Scandinavian. Twelfth century.	Found by LMBW. It was being used as part of a beaver's dam. We left it undisturbed.

After Mum leaves, I try my best to sleep, but my brain won't stop working. I drift off for a few minutes, only to wake up, gasping, from an anxious dream, to find Mitch towering over me, his head tilted to the side with a red light flashing in concern.

"Are you my own private therapy bot now?" I ask, pulling my pillow to my chest. My shoulders hurt with tension.

I check the time and realise it's only two a.m. There's no way I'm going to be able to get back to sleep. I flick through some old pictures, trying to calm myself down. We aren't gone yet. Everyone I know and love is still here, still alive.

I think over what Mum said about just being happy and enjoying life. It's nothing I've ever believed before. I've always felt like I have to carry on this legacy. I'm not sure I believe it now. Am I allowed that? A life that's just mine, that doesn't represent the whole of humanity? It sounds incredible.

As I'm scrolling through my tablet, I find an old video from when I was tiny. It's of me and Shen. I settle back to watch it.

L MBW   Mum, Dad, Aunty Jia and Uncle Feng,
         you all sit at the front. You're the judges.

M MBW   Who's going first, you or Shen?

S Z   Me!

J Z   What are you going to be performing,
         erzi?

S Z   I've written a play about aliens! It's
         amazing!

J Z   Introduce yourself first, for the camera.
         Everyone is going to want to see this at
         the next community meeting.

L MBW   Wait, wait, wait, we need a presenter to
         introduce us! Mum, you do it!

M MBW   OK. Welcome, ladies and gentlemen – and
         dogs – to the very first Zhang/Mountbatten-
         Windsor talent show! Featuring …
         actors! Rappers! Dancers! And maybe
         even a special guest slam poet! For as
         Shakespeare himself once said:
           "All the world's a stage,
           And all the men and women merely
             players;
           They have their—"

L MBW   OK, Mum. Sit down. That's enough.

M MBW	[quickly] Introducing our first act, wunderkind Shen Zhang, soon to be a famous screenwriter and performer!
ALL	[polite clapping]
S Z	My name is Shen Zhang and I'm ten years old and this is my new play ALIENS!
L MBW	[waving] I'm the alien!
S Z	Shh, Lowrie, not yet! Wait until I say! [in an exaggerated normal voice] "I am sitting outside my lovely home, drinking a cup of tea. I do not suspect a THING."
L MBW	"OH, HELLO, PALE-PINK SHINY CREATURE. I AM A NORMAL HUMAN BEING LIKE YOU."
S Z	"Oh whaaaat! It's an alien!"
L MBW	"WHAT? WHERE? THIS IS A NORMAL VOLUME TO SPEAK AT IN THIS TYPE OF ATMOSPHERE."
S Z	"Please don't kill me! How did you learn English? Will you take me to your planet?"
L MBW	"OH, ALL RIGHT. HOP ON MY SPACE MOTORBIKE."
S Z	"We are very high up! I nearly dropped my tea! Bye, Earth!"
ALL	[clapping, cheering]
M MBW	That was brilliant! Good work, Shen.

	Lowrie, what is your performance going to be?
L MBW	No, you have to give him feedback! Like we're on a proper talent show!
M MBW	Oh. Well, I've never seen anything so wonderful! I was in raptures. In fact, it reminds me of Emily Dickinson, when she said—
S Z	Thanks, Aunty Margaret!
F Z	It was beautifully performed, *bao bei*. It was very fast-paced and flowed really well. I think next time you could include more dialogue. The ending was also resolved quite quickly. If you send me the script, I can give you some more detailed notes.
S Z	Thanks, Baba! I'll email it to you later!
L MBW	Dad? Auntie Jia? Feedback?
H MBW	It was very concise. I enjoyed that.
J Z	I'm interested in how your alien survived in Earth's atmosphere. Does it respire aerobically? The green paint implies that its skin contains chlorophyll.
S Z	Well, I read this thing that said—
J Z	Maybe we can discuss that later, Shen. Let's give Lowrie her turn.
L MBW:	I'm Lowrie Mountbatten-Windsor and I'm going to do a rap next! I'm definitely

going to win; I'm really good at it. Shen is
gonna play the bass guitar for me. There's
swears in this bit, sorry. You ready, Shen?

The video suddenly makes me want Shen. He'll still be awake
this late, reading something in bed in the blue room. I know that
I won't feel so sick and lost if I'm with him.

I send him a message: *you awake? roof?*

He immediately sends back a thumbs-up emoji.

"Come on," I tell Mitch. "You're good at climbing, right?"

He nods his head.

I pull a jumper on over my pyjamas and then push up the
sash window, before climbing out on to the balcony. The moon is
bright and the air is warm, but I still shiver. It's cold compared to
the warmth of my bed.

I grab on to the gold wrought-iron barrier and pull myself
over the edge. The window frames are all coated in gold leaf
because – according to Mum – it's more practical than paint. I'm
not sure I believe her.

The gravel drive is far, far below me, but I've had a lot of practice at climbing. I mastered the art of outer-wall navigation by the
time I was ten. There are so many bronze statues and ornaments
and gargoyles and carved stone windowsills on the outside of the
building that you can travel the entire circumference of the manor
without ever stepping foot inside. It's extremely handy for late-
night rendezvous, midnight snacking and secret excursions when
you're grounded.

I grab the lower foot of the angelic figure that guards the left side of my bedroom window, so that I can pull myself into the deep alcove where the statue stands.

"Come on, then," I tell Mitch, twisting to lean back into my bedroom window.

He looks at the ground far below us, flashing a nervous red.

"It's not that bad. Here, put your feet on this bit and then twist, like that, see?"

Mitch doesn't seem convinced.

I smirk, and carry on climbing, leaving him to muddle it out on his own. He'll catch up once he gets over his nerves.

Standing in the statue's alcove, I secure a foot on the angel's elbow and push myself up. The alcoves on the outside of the building are brilliant for hiding things, as well as climbing. There's a climbing wall in the basement, next to the bowling lanes, but the outside of the building is so much more fun that I barely use it.

Grabbing on to the sandstone jutting out above the alcove, I use the framework to inch to the left until I can reach out with my foot and boost myself up using the bolts of the drainpipe. Then it's just a simple matter of kicking off the sandstone, grabbing on to the edge of the tiles and twisting on to the roof.

I'm still catching my breath when Mitch throws himself up beside me in one lightning-fast, slightly panicked motion. He bounces, leaping forward a step or two as he tries to catch his balance. Finally, he comes to a stop ahead of me, legs spread and braced wide.

"Not so bad, right?" I ask.

There is a careful, judgemental silence.

"It'll be easier on the way back," I say, confidently. I ignore his quiet, indignant orange light and make my way to the centre of the roof.

Mitch follows me, picking his way around chimneys, raised sections of brickwork, shallow trenches and skylights. It's approximately the size of a football pitch up here. The rooftop pool is on the far left, on a lower section of the roof that is inaccessible from this high up, unless you're willing to dive in from a great height – which, of course, Shen and I are experts at doing.

Shen is already here, leaning against a red-brick buttress and watching video-game walkthroughs on his tablet. He's lounging on a blanket as if he's been waiting for me to arrive for hours, instead of a maximum of about three minutes. Shen made it here the same way Mitch and I did – by climbing out of the blue room's window on the opposite side of the east wing.

I go over to the storage shed and retrieve something I stashed here last time we did this: an incredibly rare bottle of sherry, taken from Dad's wine cellar. It's for "emergencies", and I think today counts. Then I settle on the blanket, pulling it up around my shoulders. He does the same so that we're sitting facing each other in a little cave of blanket, the sides lifted between us.

"You OK?" Shen asks me.

"I keep worrying about everything. This is all so weird, and I just – it just—"

"Ah. Come here, then." He holds out his arms for a hug.

I let myself tip forward, pressing my head into the crook of his neck.

"I didn't want to go to sleep either," he admits.

"I'm so glad you're here tonight."

"Me too." He squeezes the nape of my neck. "It's going to be OK, you know."

"Is it? I can't see how."

He doesn't need to say anything to tell me that he doesn't either.

We pass the bottle of sherry back and forth while Mitch meanders around the roof, shining his small blue light across the bricks and gutters. My brain seems to be in overdrive. Every time I remember the seizures, I can't believe what's been going on.

I used to sometimes yearn for something to happen. I think that's another reason I like exploring and hunting for treasure so much. But now that something terrible is actually happening, I don't want it. I want to go back to our soft, gentle life. None of this should be real. We were supposed to miss out on this kind of thing and have a dignified farewell to the end of civilization, not convulsions and panic and seizures. It's all *wrong*.

Above us, the Union Jack flutters in the cool breeze. We're sitting so quietly that a bird trills somewhere, long and calm.

"I need a distraction," I say briskly, rubbing my arms. "I can't think about this any more."

"OK," Shen says, and tilts his head thoughtfully. "What do you want to talk about instead?"

"I read more of Maya's posts before I went to sleep. She was talking about these things called Babygrows." I tell him about the baby-simulation software.

"I've never heard of anything like that," Shen says, frowning.

"I know. It's weird, right? Kind of creepy."

"I wish we could just – go back in time and see what life was actually like back then. I think I've got a grasp on it, and then I learn something new like that and realise I don't know even one per cent of the truth."

"If you got one turn in a time machine, what time period would you visit?" I ask. "The time just before the infertility?"

"Oh no. Definitely not."

"The future? There might be aliens there."

He seems swayed by that, but he still shakes his head. "Not then, either. Before you messaged me tonight, I was reading about species extinction. It said that way before dinosaurs existed, there was this period called the Cambrian explosion. Basically, about five hundred million years ago, when there was no life on land yet, things in the sea were just starting to evolve from single-celled organisms to proper creatures.

"When the first versions of eyes appeared, it meant that the animals could hunt each other properly for the first time, instead of drifting around underwater randomly. So suddenly everything had to try and find a way to fight off predators. There was this huge burst of lots of different species all evolving different defensive features, like enormous flat shells covered in spikes and slugs with massive armour-plated claw arms." He raises his hands to the sides of his mouth, miming pincers with his fingers.

"Wait, you'd want to visit *there* in a time machine? It sounds like they'd eat you!"

"Probably. But it would be worth it, to see it for real!"

I lean over and pinch him with my own finger claws.

He squirms out of my reach, laughing.

"So what made them all go extinct in the end?"

"No one really knows. That's what's so interesting. It's like what's happened to us. All of sudden, *bam*, they were all dead and gone. Our best guess is that there was an ice age."

I sigh. "I suppose that's a bit more exciting than a measly virus wiping out your species. It makes us humans seem a bit pathetic, really."

Sometimes I wonder if this kind of thing has happened before. How do we know there wasn't a fertility problem in the ice ages, or in ancient hunter-gathering times? There aren't any records from back then. How do we know humanity doesn't go through cycles of birth in high numbers, then die off to reduce the population?

Maybe this is just the first time that humanity has been in communication with the whole planet, so it's been noticed and recorded. Maybe one day Shen and I will find out that we can have a baby – even the thought of how we'd accidentally discover that makes my stomach squirm – and then that'll be that: people will start having babies again. Like the sterility never happened at all.

This time it would actually be remembered, though. With the internet, it will never be forgotten.

Shen grimaces. "We aren't going extinct. Doctor Ahmed and Mama and the other scientists will work out a solution for the fertility one day, I know they will. I'm not going to accept a life where I can't have kids."

I think of a baby with Shen's features, all dark hair and careful observation and stacks of books on every surface. My heart clenches. "If you do have one, you've got to call her Eve. Or Adam, if it's a boy. 'Cause, you know, they'll be the first."

Shen looks horrified. "We can't do that! It would be way too much pressure!"

The "we" burns hot and long in my chest. I bite away a smile on the inside of my cheek. "It's weird to think that if a single other one of those creatures had survived the Cambrian explosion, animals today would be totally different," I say. "By random chance, this bonkers creature got eaten and this one lived – so animals have spines and legs instead of armour plating and spikes."

"Spiky humans might have survived a bit longer than we seem to be doing," he agrees. "What about you? What time period would you go to, if you could?"

"I dunno. Until this started, I quite liked living right now, actually. We've got such a unique perspective on life. If we'd been born ninety years ago, there's no way we'd be discussing things like Cardassian—"

"Cambrian."

"Cambrian explosions, or the future of intelligent octopuses. I love learning about that stuff, even if it is tragic. I just wish we had – had more time." The words crack as they come out.

When I imagined us going extinct, it wasn't now, while I was still a teenager. I always thought I'd be an old lady. How can this be happening?

Shen looks at me with wide, dark eyes. I see his throat bob as he swallows.

I clear my throat and look away, embarrassed.

He wraps me in a tight hug, pressing a kiss to my temple. I tuck my head into his shoulder, breathing in deeply, and I immediately feel safer. Shen always feels like home.

"I'm OK," I say, and this time I mean it.

He pulls back a little, and suddenly his face is close to mine and he's staring at me, pupils wide. For a second I'm convinced he's going to lean in and kiss me. But he doesn't move and we just stare at each other, his arms hooked around my shoulders. His chest expands against mine as he takes a slow, deep breath.

And because I'm a coward, I pull back, casually tugging my hair out of its ponytail as though that's the reason I'm moving. "Well, I'm not going to sleep any time soon." I force my voice to be light and steady. "Shall we move this party to the pool?"

CHAPTER 17

TIME	DATE	LOCATION	OBJECT	NOTES
16.17	05/12/2108	51.519817, -0.129017	IRON NAIL, SECOND CENTURY.	FOUND by SZ WRAPPED UP IN SEAWEED ON THE bEACH. SHEN thinks it CAME fROM A PIECE of CHAINMAIL, but I think he just likes knights IN ARMOUR. IT'S fROM A WALL, OR SOMEThing.

"ALIENS," Shen declares some time later, leaning over the edge of the hot tub to unsteadily pour us both another drink. Alcohol pools on the marble, shining silver against the dove grey. "They definitely caught a disease from aliens."

We've been sharing increasingly unlikely explanations for the seizures over the course of the night, both of us steadily getting more and more useless as we get drunker.

"YOU ALWAYS THINK IT'S ALIENS!" I yell, loud enough to make Mitch lift his head from where he is draped on a sun lounger. He stares at us in disapproval. "You'd lose your shoes and think that aliens had taken them!"

"THEY DID, LOWRIE."

I throw my head back, groaning in disgust. I'm pretty sure Shen would marry an alien, if one came along.

I help myself to some of Mr Flocks' stilton, surreptitiously stolen from the kitchen on a midnight snack raid without the bots noticing, as Shen pours me a glass of wine: cool and crisp and golden yellow. I drink it in two gulps, then gesture for more, while filling my mouth with cheese.

"If this is being caused by aliens…" I say, seriously, as Shen sits upright, looking over at me. "But the aliens said you had to marry one of them before they would—"

"Yes," Shen replies instantly and without hesitation.

"I didn't even tell you what they were offering!"

He shrugs. "I mean, I would marry an alien anyway. Regardless of the scientific advances they offered humanity."

I wince. "Even if it was a gross sticky green one? Or, like, a butterfly?"

"Stop kink-shaming me, Lowrie."

I snort. Despite everything, I'm surprised to find that I'm enjoying myself. It's such a relief to have a distraction. "I would too, I guess. I mean, maybe."

"Kink-same," Shen says, beyond delighted.

I push his shoulder in disgust, sending him splashing into the water. "This hot tub is a pun-free zone. You've seen the sign. No singing, no swearing, no puns." The sign is another one of mine and Feng's creations. Feng is very against puns.

Shen nudges me back, slipping on the tiles. For a moment our sides are pressed together, until he corrects his balance. Then, as I take another sip of wine, he asks out of nowhere: "Does it feel different? Having a crush on a girl, compared to a boy?"

"What, like the hot blonde from *Loch & Ness*?" I ask, pretending to swoon.

He shrugs. "Sure."

I consider it. I want to say that girls are soft and smooth and warm, and make me want to be gentle and soft in return. Boys make me feel delicate, protected, confident. They make me want to go out late and party and roam the streets, whereas girls make me want to curl inside under a blanket and watch TV. Hypothetically and theoretically, anyway.

That all feels too revealing, so instead I say, "It's like comparing your favourite foods, or sweet and savoury. They both taste delicious, but for completely different reasons."

Shen nods. "Makes sense. It's like fancying a blonde compared to a redhead. Totally different."

I snort. Shen is totally, unbelievably, impossibly straight.

"What about you?" I ask. "What are you…? Well, what does it feel like when you like someone? An actor, or something?"

"It makes me want things. Nothing sexual, not really. Just … intimacy, you know? Brushing hands, catching their eye and knowing what they're thinking. Simple, quiet things. Someone to lean against, wrap my arms around, for no reason but because I want to be close to them." The tips of Shen's ears have gone a little pink.

My mouth is dry. How can I reply to something like that when it's so obvious that *I give him that* and I have for as long as I can remember?

I clear my throat. We're just friends. I have to keep things the way they've always been.

"Kink-same?" I say, weakly, and giggle.

He rolls his eyes. "I'm cutting you off. You're hysterical." He pulls the glass out of my hand.

"I am not! Can we go treasure-hunting? I want to go treasure-hunting."

"It's three a.m. and we're drunk! We are *not* leaving the grounds."

I roll my eyes. Even drunk, Shen is sensible and mature. "We can look for treasure here," I say. "Let's explore the attics. There's always stuff up there."

Shen stares at the sky, then heaves himself up. "Yeah, OK."

Sometimes if it's raining we go up to the attics and do a kind of lazy version of mudlarking. The attics stretch along the full length of the building and contain several generations' worth of accumulated junk. The winding series of rooms and crawl spaces are packed with old portraits, collapsing antique furniture and stacks and stacks of records, household accounts, broadsides, manuscripts, maps and correspondence dating back to the eighteenth century. More recently, the rooms have been filled with a hundred years' worth of broken phones, tablets and laptops.

There's even a ghost – the legendary Marchioness of Lansdowne, who Mum swears she saw when she was a teenager. I have my doubts.

Bats flutter away when we clamber over boxes and sofas, shushing each other when we make too much noise, giggling all the while. Mum and Dad would not appreciate being woken up this late.

Mitch follows us as we poke through the crates of silk scarves and linen suits, look through stacks of *Tatler* and *The Lady*, and try on helmets from suits of armour.

"I love it up here," Shen says, trailing a finger through the dust.

I find myself eyeing his forearms, yet again.

I thought I could ignore my feelings for Shen, but it's becoming obvious that I can't, and that however hard I try to make them go away, it's not going to work. I've always said that I just know him far too well to see him as anything other than the little boy who always had food crusted around his mouth after lunch, because he couldn't use chopsticks properly yet – or the grumpy teenager with spots and a fury to rival Hades' if he thought someone was making fun of him. But that isn't true.

I like him. I like the way he laughs with his whole body, head tilted back and teeth flashing, and I like the solid warmth of his hands when he touches my arm. And I love that when we hug, it presses our whole bodies together, from head to toe.

But what can I do about it? I can't start anything with Shen, not when it might end with me losing him completely.

Feeling hot and overwhelmed all of a sudden, I wipe the dusty glass of an oval skylight with the flesh of my palm so I can peer out of it. Between the branches of a five-hundred-year-old yew tree tapping on the window, I can make out the bones of the old abbey in the lawn below. The stone walls loom out of the darkness, their crumbling buttresses disappearing into hollow dips just below the grass.

A single pane of stained glass remains in the lower right corner of a vaulted window. I can't make it out in the darkness, but I can picture from memory the image etched on to the yellow glass of a snail fighting a medieval knight.

"Ahh!" Shen shouts, and I turn to see him standing on top of an old tapestry footstool, stitched with the family crest. He's rubbing a hand through his hair sheepishly. "Mouse," he explains.

At that Mitch jumps forward, pouncing like a cat. There's a scurry of tiny feet and a flourish of dust, but the robot returns from underneath a four-poster bed empty-handed.

"Good effort, Mitch," I say.

The roaming household bots have been engaged in a decades-long war with the mouse populations of our home. Each spring, the bots win a minor battle and clear them all out. Then every winter, the mice flood back in, and the war starts up again.

We move on to the next room, where half of the roof has collapsed, covering cupboards in tiles, plaster, rafters and dirt, and blocking the doorway into the next room completely. It must have happened months ago and gone unnoticed. It's a mess of rotting and thoroughly damp wood.

"Noooo!" Shen cries. "There's no way we're going to be able to get through there!"

I grin. "Don't give up so fast."

"Tools?"

"Tools! You do know the way to a girl's heart," I say.

"Why do you think I get you screwdrivers for Christmas every year?"

"Really?" I ask. He wants to get into my heart? "I didn't...
I mean..."

We stare at each other for a moment. Maybe Shen and
me together is not such a scary idea after all. Maybe we could
work...

Then he giggles and says, "Maybe tools aren't a good idea
right now. You're very drunk." And he's just Shen again.

"Yeah. Maybe not. We should probably call it a night," I say,
sighing and trying not to feel disappointed. I'm not ready for this
night to end, so I make one last attempt to search for interesting
stuff by pulling open the doors of a bureau.

A few books slide off the shelves on to the floor. I try to grab
them and get a splinter in my arm from the wooden panelling.
I bite at it with my teeth, trying to pull it free, but it sinks more
deeply under the skin. I'm still poking at it when Shen pulls
something pale out of the cabinet.

It's a doll about the size of a small baby. Its eyes open and
close and its joints move. It would be cute, if it wasn't for the
completely blank features – white eyeballs with no irises, a flat
space where the nose should be, and a mouth with no lips.

"What is that?" I ask.

"I have no idea. Is it creepy or what?"

He passes it to me, and I flip it over, so I don't have to stare
into its blank eyes. At the base of the back there's an embossed
seal in the latex, saying, MADE IN CHINA © PATENT PENDING.

Shen shakes its hand. "It looks like a fake body an alien would
use to blend in with humans."

I squint at it and then at him. "Why would an alien want to pretend to be a human baby?"

He shrugs. "Assimilation into the local population? Guaranteed protection from human parents? If they are from a small and weak alien species, they wouldn't want to risk being killed as soon as they made themselves known."

"Sometimes I wonder if you're an alien," I tell him solemnly.

He beams. *"Thanks."*

"I wonder who it belonged to," I say, gesturing at the doll.

"Your grandmother, maybe?"

"Maybe." I never met her, so I don't know anything about her, really.

It's strange to think of a child walking around my home, cradling this doll in their arms. I've never seen a child in real life, just in recordings.

When we go downstairs, I bring the doll with me, still manipulating the joints and inspecting the features. It feels a little sad that it was forgotten about and dumped it in a cupboard up here.

In the hallway, we bump into Mum going for a midnight wee.

She jumps, raising a hand to her chest. "Lowrie, Shen – you gave me a heart attack. What are you doing creeping about?"

I keep silent and let Shen answer, knowing that I'm not going to be able to hide my tipsiness.

"We couldn't sleep," he says, running a hand through his hair.

Mum smiles sympathetically. "No, me neither." She hesitates and says, "There have been more seizures. Jia rang. Mr Flocks passed out a few hours ago."

I draw in a breath. "Is Mrs Bolton any better?"

"There's been no... *What is that?*" She stares at the doll in my hands, a look of dawning horror crossing her face.

"We, er – we found it in the loft," I say.

Mum takes it off me. Her hands are shaking a little.

"Should I not have taken it?" I ask, unsure why she's so upset. She usually has no problem with me playing with anything, even the oldest, most priceless of the heirlooms, like the emerald tiara that is kept in a cabinet in the smoking room. She let me wear *that* to go trick-or-treating a few years ago. Why would this doll be any different?

"It's fine," she says tightly. "It just took me by surprise, that's all." She pulls off her cardigan and folds the doll up in the fabric, then stares down at the bundle. I've never seen her so shaken.

"Who did it belong to?" Shen asks. "Do you know?"

The corner of her eye twitches. "Get to sleep, both of you. You've had a really long day. You need your rest." Then she marches back down the corridor, holding the doll out in front of her like it's on fire.

Shen and I stare at each other, baffled.

"Do you think it belonged to her?" I ask.

"Maybe. But that doesn't explain why she'd be so weird about it."

Shen and I watch her retreating back in silence.

CHAPTER 18

TIME	DATE	LOCATION	OBJECT	NOTES
03.33	07/04/2109	51.500375, -0.141975	Latex doll, around the size of a ten-month-old baby. Twenty-first century.	Found by SZ. Taken away by Mum. Hers?

The next morning, I wake up with an awful headache. My last memory is of yelling to Shen through the bathroom door to get me a new loo-roll, angry at him for not replacing the old one. I wince as I sit up and stabbing pains ripple through my head.

Shen is sleeping in my armchair, head tilted back, snoring. I stumble out of bed, untangling myself from the four fluffy blankets that Drunk Lowrie cocooned herself in. I tiptoe to the bathroom, where I spend an hour napping in the bath.

When I surface, I notice that my toes are messily painted a pastel purple. I have a vague memory of demanding that Shen paint them for me while we were watching a film, after our attic exploration. We'd started having an argument about something dumb. He'd pulled my toes into his lap while we bickered, attempting to carefully apply the varnish, despite his drunkenness and the heat of our debate. I'm amazed that he managed to paint them at all, although the varnish has dripped all over the skin of my feet.

When I emerge from the bath, Shen has gone and there's a message on my tablet: GONE TO FIND BACON.

I turn on the newsfeed and immediately feel guilty that we were getting drunk while people might be dying. I try not to let myself hope that the seizures have stopped and were due to something as simple as fungi-contaminated flour. I've heard stories about those kind of things happening in small settlements in the past.

The presenter – it's Ms Fikry today – says, "I'm afraid that after the terrible incident with Mrs Bolton yesterday, we've had another four people fall ill during the night. Prisha – sorry, Doctor Ahmed – has asked that everyone stay at home and not use any heavy equipment until this has all been sorted out. I'd like to extend my best wishes to everyone who's caught this awful bug, and hope you all get well soon."

I slump on my bed. The panic hits me again like a tidal wave. I can't believe how dangerous such a small thing has become. Life becomes so fragile when the population is small. A single disease like this might wipe humanity out for good within a single day.

Shen is sitting by the window when I come into the morning room. He's listening to something with one earphone and staring out over the garden, where drizzle is coating Dad's plants in a silver sheen of water. Early morning light plays on his face.

He takes a sip of green tea from a bone china teacup, holding it in his mouth for a long moment before he swallows.

I touch his arm, and he jumps and pulls out his earbud. "Did you say something?" he asks.

"Morning."

Shen nods hello.

"Are you hungover?" I ask.

"Not yet. I took a tablet." He passes one to me, and says, "I'm listening to this thing about global warming. It says that as climate change melted the permafrost back in the twenty-fifties, it released dormant bacteria, which have been extinct for thousands of years, into the soil. They got into the water table and then people or animals caught the diseases. There were outbreaks of anthrax and the black plague. Maybe these seizures are—"

I draw in a tight breath. There's an uneasy prickle of panic threatening to blossom in the back of my mind. "Shen, can we not discuss it? I'm trying my best not to think about it too much. It freaks me out."

He looks contrite. "Sorry, Shadow. Would you like a cup of tea?"

"Coffee, please."

I stir cream into my coffee and take a sip, wincing. It's always too bitter for me, but I'm hoping that if I keep trying it, I'll develop a taste for it eventually. "Is Jia back yet?" I twist my rose-gold stud earring back and forth in my lobe. My brain feels slow and gloopy.

"No." His voice is tight, foot tapping repetitively against the wooden floor with a soft clicking noise. "Your mum's gone with Baba to take a few more people who had seizures this morning to the hospital."

"It's still spreading, then."

Dad comes in with the dogs at his heels. He startles when we both swing around to look at him, dreading bad news. "You both seem very… Look, I don't want you two worrying about everything. It'll most likely all be fine. It's just a small bug; it's all going to blow over in time."

"But what if you and Mum catch it?" I say desperately.

"We won't, Lowrie," he says gently. "I'm sure of it. We didn't mean to scare you yesterday with all that talk about emergency protocols. Really. It'll be fine."

I bite my lip and nod.

He grabs a toasted teacake and slathers it with butter and marmalade, before eating it standing up. "I don't suppose I can persuade either of you two to come and dig the herbaceous border with me?"

"Dad, it's raining," I say, appalled.

"Thought not," he says glumly and whistles for the dogs. They suffer through the indignity of having tartan fleece coats put on in stiff silence, then follow him out into the garden to supervise the digging of the herbaceous border. Mum's family have owned the manor for generations, but as soon as Dad married her, and took her last name, the gardens became his masterpiece.

"Don't look at me like that – it's not that cold, old boy," I hear Dad say to Albert as they walk away.

I don't know how Dad can garden given everything that's going on. But maybe it's no different to me and Shen getting drunk. Just another distraction technique.

MyWaves05

I'm going to give the hellscape of a dating app one last chance to redeem itself for every terrible human being who it has claimed is my 98%-matched soulmate. Then it's going wherever it is that apps go when they are sent to recycle bin hell.

Posted on 11 Jun 2027

> **Rizzz** on 11 Jun 2027
> Replying to **@MyWaves05**
> I don't want to say "I told you so", but...

>> **MyWaves05** on 11 Jun 2027
>> Replying to **@Rizzz**
>> Tell me again why didn't I make an account when you were still on there.

>>> **Rizzz** on 11 Jun 2027
>>> Replying to **@MyWaves05**
>>> Be right back, reactivating my profile now.

>>>> **MyWaves05** on 11 Jun 2027
>>>> Replying to **@Rizzz**
>>>> Wait, are you serious?

>>>>> **Rizzz** on 11 Jun 2027
>>>>> Replying to **@MyWaves05**
>>>>> Deadly.

MyWaves05

Sometimes life pleasantly surprises me, because there are sometimes good things as well as bad. Just when I'd given up hope of anything but mediocrity and despair too.

Posted on 12 Jun 2027

MyWaves05

I donated a uterine sample to the fertility research today. It was a bit like a smear test – kind of scary, but I felt comfortable and safe, and it was so fast! If you're been thinking about donating, I highly recommend it – they need all the data they can get.

Posted on 13 Jun 2027

171

Unhako_neko on 13 Jun 2027
Replying to **@MyWaves05**
Oh damn, I've been meaning to book
mine. Thanks for the push, Maya!

MyWaves05

@Rizzz TOMORROW

Posted on 14 Jun 2027

Rizzz on 14 Jun 2027
Replying to **@MyWaves05**
Tomorrow!!

MyWaves05

So **@Rizzz** and I went on a date today
and he brought me flowers and chocolate.
Straight off the bat. Honestly, this boy.

Posted on 15 Jun 2027

Rizzz on 15 Jun 2027
Replying to **@MyWaves05**
This is my one opportunity, I'm not going to
squander it.

MyWaves05 on 15 Jun 2027
Replying to **@Rizzz**
Today was pretty much the best day of my
life, so I think you did an OK job of it.

MyWaves05

Third date report: **@Rizzz** is so charming,
it's suspicious, and never fails to
render me completely immobile.

Posted on 24 Jun 2027

Rizzz on 24 Jun 2027
Replying to **@MyWaves05**
Yikes. I think we need to get date #4
started immediately, times a-wastin'.

MyWaves05 on 24 Jun 2027
Replying to **@Rizzz**
If you feel we must.

MyWaves05

I am honestly so stunned that I've actually
graduated. I'm a qualified nurse! I feel like I've
been living in a grey cloud of fear since the
sterility started. But I did it! And I'm so excited
to get into a hospital and start helping people.

Posted on 8 Jul 2027

> **Rizzz** on 8 Jul 2027
> Replying to **@MyWaves05**
> I am so proud of you. You've worked so hard for this.

>> **MyWaves05** on 8 Jul 2027
>> Replying to **@Rizzz**
>> Chinese tonight to celebrate?

>>> **Rizzz** on 8 Jul 2027
>>> Replying to **@MyWaves05**
>>> I guess we could ... if there wasn't this
>>> pesky surprise party planned for you...

>>>> **MyWaves05** on 8 Jul 2027
>>>> Replying to **@Rizzz**
>>>> EVEN BETTER

MyWaves05

I was in London visiting **@Rizzz** when the Oxford
bomb went off, so I'm OK. Everyone in my family
is safe too. Thinking of everyone who was at the
fertility clinic at the time of the attack. <3

Posted on 26 Aug 2027

MyWaves05

There's still no news on who is behind these
fertility clinic attacks, but I hope you all call
your MP and encourage them to support the
bill to move all IVF stocks to a secure, secret
facility immediately. It's not worth putting lives
at risk by advertising the locations of embryos.
This is too political now. There is more at stake
than just the loss of possible babies. A hundred
people were killed in the Oxford attack. The

population is dropping quickly enough as it is —
we need to stop doing this to ourselves too.

Posted on 28 Aug 2027

MyWaves05

OK, these Babygrow things are really cute,
I admit. Look at that little leg kicking!

> RT **@Blueburnedskies #Babygrow** update!
> The baby is doing well. We decided to find out the
> gender — we're having a boy! <u>Here</u> are some of our
> favourite app screenshots from the last week.

Posted on 4 Sep 2027

TIME	DATE	LOCATION	OBJECT	NOTES
16.17	05/12/2108	51.519817, -0.129017	Egyptian shopping list, written in hieroglyphics on a papyrus scroll and wrapped in linen. 1100 BCE.	Found by LMBW, inside an ibis mummy that had never been opened, and which was buried under rubble in the collapsed basement of a museum. We ran an X-ray to see what was inside.

Shen and I are still sitting at the breakfast table, trying not to talk about the terrible sense of dread we're both feeling, when we hear a car pull up.

"That's Baba's car!" Shen says, and jumps up.

He must be back from helping Mum at the hospital. He'll have news. We run to the front door in time to see Feng climbing out of the car. Victoria and Albert jump up his legs in delight, as Dad greets him, wiping compost off his hands.

"Margaret is still at the hospital," I hear Feng tell Dad, as we walk up. "Three people were gone before we got to them."

"No," I breathe, freezing in my tracks.

Feng turns, surprised to see us. He looks pale. "Lowrie, Shen," he says, and then stops. He puts a hand to his head. "I feel a bit..." He leans back against the car door.

"Baba!" Shen cries just as Feng slips forward on to the ground, his body starting to judder uncontrollably. Shen leaps for him, catching him as he shakes and convulses. *"No."* His voice, usually solid, has splintered into broken glass.

The journey to the hospital disappears in a blurring rush of movement and panic. All I can focus on are the logistics – carefully stretching Feng out in the back seat, keeping him still as he shakes, bracing when the car turns corners, scrambling out to open the gates – while Dad drives faster and faster, turning back every now and then to look at Feng over his shoulder.

When we pull to a stop in front of the hospital, Jia and Mum are waiting for us with a stretcher, and they rush Feng inside. Jia pushes Shen gently out into the waiting room when we try to follow them on to the ward. "Stay here, *bao bei*." The doors bang shut, and Shen, my parents and I are left staring at the closed door. My heart pounds in my ears.

Shen makes a small, helpless noise. He's crying, tears pooling at the corners of his eyes. He wipes them away with the side of his hand in annoyance.

"It's going to be OK," Dad says, but his voice is weak. He rattles his car keys in his palm, a jangling frenetic beat that matches the quivering of my muscles. "Let's go and sit down."

His deep, steady voice calms me, and I press my fingertips to Shen's arm to guide him over to the waiting-room area. I don't know whether I should touch him. Every muscle in his body is tense. He won't look at me.

Shen folds himself into a chair and ducks his head, shoulder blades drawing up, pulling at his hair like he wants to use it to extract the thoughts from his brain.

I sit next to him and carefully slip my arms around his waist. I hesitate, then press my forehead into the space between his shoulder blades.

Mum comes to sit with us while I hold him tightly. I let my parents' reassurances blunt and drop away. I can't think of anything to say that might help, but that's OK. I just need to be here, holding him the way that he would hold me, if this was my father. There's nothing else I can do except be here for him.

Feng can't die. It can't happen. I refuse to accept it.

We sit together for hours, waiting for news. As the day goes on, more and more patients are brought in on stretchers or in wheelchairs. I feel sick myself, just at seeing everyone I know looking weak and pale like this.

At around midday, Mrs Jackson comes in, pushing Mrs Fletcher in a wheelchair. The tight lines of panic on Mrs Jackson's face are carefully hidden behind a blank expression. Ms Bard is carried in by Mr Fields, who looks terrified. More and more people come in. Each new patient disappears behind the swinging doors of the ward, one after the other. Nobody comes out again.

The whole time, I hold on to Shen's hand. His grip never loosens on mine. He never speaks. I wish desperately that there was something I could do to fix this. I've only seen Shen look this soul-broken once before – when he begged and begged his parents to give him a baby brother for Christmas, and they explained to us both for the first time that no children would be born ever again.

Shen's tablet *dings*, and he moves quickly to answer it. "Mama."

I listen, holding my breath, as they speak for a moment in rapid Chinese. Shen looks over and sees how carefully I'm listening. He switches into English. Jia follows suit. "He's going to be all right, Mama, isn't he? Has he woken up?" Shen asks, his voice cracking.

"… Not yet. But it's very early. We're doing everything we can. I don't want you to worry. We don't think that the disease is contagious to you or Lowrie. You don't have to worry about catching it."

"I wasn't worried about that," Shen insists, voice thick. "Can I come and see him?"

Jia is silent for a moment, then she says, "It's best if you wait until later, I think. For now, you should stay with Lowrie and her parents. I'll talk to you soon. I love you."

The call ends, and Shen's shoulders drop. I hook my fingers over his palm, pulling his hand into my lap, and rub my thumb over his lifeline, waiting for him to say something. Such a long time passes that I compose whole speeches in my head, revising every word to make it as reassuring as I can. I don't say any of it out loud.

When I go to the toilet a while later, I see Mum and Dad standing close together in the hallway, their heads ducked towards each other. I slow down, listening.

"What are we going to do?" Mum whispers. She wipes at her eyes, and I realise with a horrified shock that she's crying. "If there's no way to stop it…"

"They'll be fine," Dad says, tugging her under his arm and kissing the top of her head. "We've prepared them for this. They have each other. They won't be alone." He squeezes his eyes tightly shut.

"I'm so scared for them," Mum says.

I take a step back, and another, and quietly go back to the waiting room before they notice me. I don't want them to know I've heard. I don't know why, but somehow that would make it all real. My throat is full of something thick and terrible. I drop into the chair next to Shen, closing my eyes. What is happening? Why are they so – so certain that we're going to be left on our own? Do they really think they're all going to die from this illness?

I've always known that my parents will die one day. It has been a disconcerting, uncomfortable fact in the back of my mind since I was a child. Our parents were already old when we were born – it's extremely unlikely they will still be alive by the time we're thirty. They are going to die. Soon. But is it going to happen right now? I thought it would be years, hopefully decades. Is this the end? Is this what destroys us all?

Beside me, Shen stirs, waking me. I hadn't realised I'd fallen asleep. "Lowrie?" he says. The words are hoarse.

"Yes? Are you…" I twist to inspect his face. "Are you OK?"

"No one's come in for ages."

Mitch turns to look at us, flashing purple.

Shaking myself, I glance down at my watch – one p.m. – and then I look around. Somehow, we're completely on our own.

Mum and Dad didn't come back from the drinks machine. Only Mitch is left, pacing backwards and forwards across the waiting room impatiently as he guards us.

Everywhere is still and silent. I swallow. "Do you think we should go and see what's happening?"

Shen nods and stands up. He sticks his hands in his trouser pockets, then removes them and wraps his arms around his chest as he follows me on to the ward.

The corridor is bright and clean but eerily empty of the dozens of people who've come here in the last few hours.

"Hello?" I call. No reply. My breath starts coming fast and quick.

Finally, we turn a corner and find Mrs Wheeler, the nurse. She's unconscious on the floor. Shuddering, I kneel to roll her over. She isn't breathing. I put my fingers against her wrist. There's no pulse.

Dead.

She's dead.

I snatch my hand away. Suddenly I'm unable to support my legs, and they crumple beneath me as I slide to the floor. I think I'm going to be sick. I gasp, shuddering and trying to draw in air.

This is happening. This is actually—

"Shadow, stop." Shen's voice is strained at the edges. "Please, stop. I can't do this if you're…" He breaks off, trembling.

I take a deep breath, and nod. I straighten my shoulders. "Let's look in there," I say, nodding my head to the next room. "I think they're in there."

★ ★ ★

MyWaves05

Um, cliff-hanger or what?! If Lyra is
actually pregnant, I might cry.

Posted on 30 Sep 2027

MyWaves05

So I keep trying to make **@Rizzz** read Harry Potter
because I want to know what house he's in – but he won't.
How am I supposed to decide whether we're a suitable
match now? Everyone, please bust his chops about it.

Posted on 19 Nov 2027

> **Rizzz** on 19 Nov 2027
> Replying to **@MyWaves05**
> It's not that culturally important. I think you're
> making far too much of a big deal about this.

>> **MyWaves05** on 19 Nov 2027
>> Replying to **@Rizzz**
>> Honestly, Riz, stop pitching such a fit
>> and just download the audiobook.

>>> **Rizzz** on 19 Nov 2027
>>> Replying to **@MyWaves05**
>>> I am NOT pitching a FIT. I have
>>> NEVER pitched a fit in my LIFE.

>>>> **MyWaves05** on 19 Nov 2027
>>>> Replying to **@Rizzz**
>>>> Yet again, you weasel out of agreeing
>>>> by pitching another fit.

>>>>> **Rizzz** on 19 Nov 2027
>>>>> Replying to **@MyWaves05**
>>>>> I don't know what you're talking about and
>>>>> frankly I refuse to address your madness.

> **Rizzz** on 3 Jan 2028
> Replying to **@MyWaves05**
> Harry called his son ALBUS SEVERUS? What about Hagrid?!
> He deserves to be a namesake so much more than SNAPE.

>> **MyWaves05** on 3 Jan 2028
>> Replying to **@Rizzz**
>> For someone who had no interest in HP,
>> you read them all mighty fast, huh?

Rizzz on 3 Jan 2028
Replying to **@MyWaves05**
I don't know what you're talking about. They were
fine, but the books didn't change my life or anything.

> **MyWaves05** on 3 Jan 2028
> Replying to **@Rizzz**
> Suurrree, Riz "listen to my feelings
> about my son, Draco" Stevens.

MyWaves05

TWO BILLION? Wow.

Posted on 4 Feb 2028

NEWSBREAKING.COM

BABYGROW APP CONTINUES TO TAKE WORLD BY STORM

The Babygrow app passed two billion downloads this week – just as the first wave of simulated babies are starting to be "born" on the child-raising simulation app.

Designed by a team in San Francisco, USA, the app only launched ten months ago and is now downloaded by millions of people every day.

The app works in real time, meaning that early adopters are only just "giving birth" to their simulated offspring this month. The app is fully personalizable to the user, and before a baby is "conceived", the user is asked to program in their height, weight, skin, eye and hair colour, as well as that of any other parents of the baby (up to three are allowed). This has resulted in a delightfully diverse range of CGI babies, as seen online – the happy new parents are all uploading pictures and videos of their offspring under the hashtag "Babygrow".

The newborns currently have a limited range of movement, but can respond to sound, light and touch by wriggling their heads and opening and closing their eyes.

The creators of the app have been tight-lipped about how the model will develop as the babies grow up into childhood, but the developers will have plenty of time to code the software, as they will age in real time.

Congratulations to all the new Babygrow "parents", and good luck to everyone watching jealously as you wait for your baby to be born.

MyWaves05

The thing about this new IVF research budget is that it's all too little, too late. This should have been pushed through parliament as soon as they realised everyone was infertile, not four years later.

Posted on 17 Mar 2028

> **Rizzz** on 17 Mar 2028
> Replying to **@MyWaves05**
> Stop reading the news! It's date night and you are NOT discussing the current global reproductive crisis while I'm trying to woo you. We will have a perfectly lovely evening and I will not stand for anything less.
>
> > **MyWaves05** on 17 Mar 2028
> > Replying to **@Rizzz**
> > Not another word about it will pass between my lips, light of my life, angel of my soul, etc. etc.

CHAPTER 20

TIME	DATE	LOCATION	OBJECT	NOTES
12.17	04/04/2108	50.124430, -5.090172	GREEN glass bottle, containing a piece of paper with the message, "If you find this, please forward it to my wife and do a favour for a British soldier on his way to the front. To Lucy – I told you I would write. TA-RA, sweetheart. Your hubby. Signed Able SEAMAN LAWRENCE, 63rd Royal Naval Division, 20 August 1914."	Found by SZ. We looked Able LAWRENCE up, and he died two days after sending the message.

Inside the ward, every bed is occupied. There are endless rows of lifeless people, hooked up to beeping machines. Dr Ahmed is collapsed over the end of the nearest bed. I let out a rasping, rough breath that hurts the back of my throat, as I pull her on to the bed properly.

Shen runs across the room, crying out, "Mama!"

Jia is seated in the chair next to Feng's bed, her head tilted back. I catch sight of Mum and Dad slumped on the floor next to her. Darkness curls around me. Leaving Dr Ahmed, I fall to the ground in front of them. Trying to keep my touch gentle, I lift them upright, pressing my ear to their chests. There's no sound of a heartbeat. I can't think, can't move without my hands curling into trembling claws.

Do I need to restart their hearts? With a defibrillator? Or do they need oxygen first, so they can breathe? How do I do this? What do I do?

I twist to look at Feng. He's sleeping on his back, eyes closed. There's an IV running from his arm to a piece of medical equipment in the wall. The machine beeps, and something inside me clenches and then releases. If it's beeping, it must be doing something to keep him alive. Maybe if we hook Mum and Dad and Jia up to the machines, they'll be OK too; they'll stay alive while we find a way to fix this. I won't let them die. I can't survive if they die.

"Help me," I say to Shen, fumbling through the mass of plastic tubes spilling out from the equipment by the side of Feng's bed. I find a spare mask and pull it over Mum's head.

But Shen isn't moving. When he turns to me, I see that his eyes are glossed over. He looks slightly feverish.

"Shen! Come on!"

He starts and runs to the next bed, pulling the equipment closer and carefully adjusting Jia and Dad so they're breathing into masks too. Mitch watches us, then does the same for the other patients and Dr Ahmed.

I look back at Feng, trying to work out what to do. Hands shaking, I try to remember what we were taught in first aid. What comes next? I think I need to set up an IV drip. Dad showed us what to do, but we never had anyone to practise on. I'm not sure I can do it.

There is a tube running along Feng's arm, so I peel away the tape to see where it's connected. I need to find out what kind of needle we need. They should be sterilized – there must be a supply cupboard somewhere, or something I can…

I stare down at Feng's arm.

There is no needle under the bandage. Instead, the IV tube carries on, up the length of Feng's arm. It's been hidden under the folds of his pillow. Frowning, I brush aside his hair, searching to see where it ends. Shen says, "What are you—?" just as I expose Feng's scalp.

We both suck in a breath at the same time. I blink, trying to take in what I'm seeing.

Beneath Feng's black hair, where there should be skin, is a huge hole in his scalp. Instead of blood and skull, there's – there's a *circuit board*.

The IV cable is plugged into a port in the circuit board. In Feng's head.

MyWaves05

@Blueburnedskies Congratulations on the birth of Hailey, Ash! She's a cute little thing. I admit it: I feel kind of left out – everyone's babies are being born on the app at the minute! **#Babygrow**

Posted on 11 Feb 2028

> **@Unhako_neko** on 12 Feb 2028
> Replying to **@MyWaves05** and **@Blueburnedskies**
> Congratulations! I'm due in May, we can't wait!

@Blueburnedskies on 12 Feb 2028
Replying to **@MyWaves05** and **@Unhako_neko**
You should download it now, Maya. Loads of
people are starting late. You and Riz would
make the most adorable baby in the world!

I know everyone thought it was weird at
first, but it really does help. I've always been
broody and this just ... I can't describe it. It
feels real. I love Hailey already, and I don't
feel sad about never being able to have a
biological baby any more. The app has honestly
changed my life. Give it a try. You can always
delete it if it doesn't do anything for you.

> **MyWaves05** on 13 Feb 2028
> Replying to **@Blueburnedskies** and **@Unhako_neko**
> Maybe. I'm just not sure what I'd
> do with it? I've seen the videos of
> people singing to theirs and stuff,
> and I don't know ... it feels strange.
> I guess it's not realistic enough
> yet for me to connect to it.

>> **@Blueburnedskies** on 14 Feb 2028
>> Replying to **@MyWaves05** and **@Unhako_neko**
>> I get that. You should look here, though:
>> Babygrow modifications. People are uploading
>> add-ons and mods to make the graphics
>> and movements of their babies more
>> realistic. There's an adorable "peekaboo"
>> mod that we've installed for Hailey.

MyWaves05

Happy trans day of visibility! I am dating the
greatest and most underrated trans boy in the
world and I couldn't be more proud of him.

Posted on 31 Mar 2028

> **Rizzz** on 31 Mar 2028
> Replying to **@MyWaves05**
> This post has rendered me immobile and stunned.
> Please delete it in case someone attempts to
> woo you away from me before I have a chance
> to propose and lock you down for good.

>> **MyWaves05** on 31 Mar 2028
>> Replying to **@Rizzz**
>> I just let out a squeal like a rat trapped
>> in a fully stocked fridge.

187

MyWaves05

Just found out that they're making one of those doomsday storage vaults in the UK – in Snowdon! It sounds like something from a film!

Posted on 10 Jun 2028

> **Redcello1** on 10 Jun 2028
> Replying to **@MyWaves05**
> Is this a vault for seeds, like the one in Norway?

> > **MyWaves05** on 10 Jun 2028
> > Replying to **@Redcello1**
> > No, it's for everything, I think! It's for future generations, in case there's a war or something, so they can get supplies and internet data and stuff afterwards.

> > > **Redcello1** on 10 Jun 2028
> > > Replying to **@MyWaves05**
> > > I'm not sure I see much point in that. There aren't going to be any future generations to find it at this rate.

> > > > **MyWaves05** on 10 Jun 2028
> > > > Replying to **@Redcello1**
> > > > They are going to solve the sterility, I know they are.

> > > > > **Redcello1** on 10 Jun 2028
> > > > > Replying to **@MyWaves05**
> > > > > Agree to disagree xx

MyWaves05

So **@Rizzz** is having a sweaty meltdown because he forgot my birthday. Jokes on him! I never told him when my birthday was.

Posted on 29 Aug 2028

> **Rizzz** on 29 Aug 2028
> Replying to **@MyWaves05**
> I vowed to love and protect you, and a vow is a sacred thing for a gentleman like me. Ignorance is no defence for such unfeeling treatment.

> > **MyWaves05** on 29 Aug 2028
> > Replying to **@Rizzz**
> > I refuse to engage in this shameless bid for attention.

MyWaves05

Me at myself: oh do you have a boyfriend maya, I hadn't realised because you haven't mentioned it lately

Posted on 29 Aug 2028

MyWaves05

@Unhako_neko It was so great to see you yesterday!

Posted on 9 Sep 2028

> **Unhako_neko** on 9 Sep 2028
> Replying to **@MyWaves05**
> You too! Riz dropped me off after you went home. A right good one, he is.
>
> > **MyWaves05** on 9 Sep 2028
> > Replying to **@Unhako_neko**
> > Trust me, I know. I won't be letting him go any time soon. I aim to be a millstone around his neck for decades to come.
> >
> > > **Rizzz** on 9 Sep 2028
> > > Replying to **@MyWaves05** and **@Unhako_neko**
> > > I don't see any problem with that.

MyWaves05

@Rizzz Good morning! I woke up wanting to kiss you.

Posted on 6 Mar 2029

> **Rizzz** on 6 Mar 2029
> Replying to **@MyWaves05**
> I'm leaving work right this very moment and I will fight and kill anyone who tries to stop me.

MyWaves05

Oh dear...

> RT **@Rizzz** My car just broke down on the way to see **@MyWaves05**'s parents. It's taking every ounce of my over-inflated self-confidence not to take that as some sort of sign.

Posted on 2 Oct 2029

MyWaves05

Everyone put on something comfortable, because I
have a story to tell you!! So this weekend **@Rizzz** and
I went to Prague, and he was acting kind of strange.
Then I realised he was NERVOUS. I cleverly deduced
this because while we were eating dinner on a river
cruise, he got down on one knee and proposed. With
a ring and everything! So, surprise – we're engaged!

Posted on 18 Nov 2029

> **Rizzz** on 18 Nov 2029
> Replying to **@MyWaves05**
> Now you'll have to stop replying "just lucky, I guess"
> when people ask you why you aren't married yet.

>> **MyWaves05** on 18 Nov 2029
>> Replying to **@Rizzz**
>> Now that can be my answer for why I am married!!!

MyWaves05

So when I took **@Rizzz** home to see my
parents last month he apparently ASKED MY
DAD FOR PERMISSION TO MARRY ME (!!!!)
and my dad said, "You'd need my permission
not to." So now I'm going to spend the next
week in tears. Thanks a lot, Father dearest.

Posted on 19 Nov 2029

TIME	DATE	LOCATION	OBJECT	NOTES
16.33	13/11/2105	51.473131, -0.312075	Section of wooden panelling from a medieval church, painted with a gold gilt stag. Tenth century.	Found by Albert, who thought it was a stick to be thrown for him.

We stare at the circuit board in Feng's head in shock. *"Baba?"* Shen says, lost.

I'm just as confused. I can't understand why Feng would have this inside his head. Have they done something to him, to try to stop the seizures?

What is it? I reach out and touch it, feeling the cool smooth surface of the silicon chip. It looks so natural, like it's always been there. What could it possibly be for?

"What...?" Shen asks.

"It must be some kind of pacemaker, or something," I say, but as I'm speaking, my eyes drift to Mr Fisher, the patient in the bed next to Feng. He's also hooked up to an IV and when I look more closely, I see that it is going into the gap underneath his hair as well. Has he got a circuit board too? How can they both have the same thing in their heads? What is this?

I go over to Mum and push aside her grey hair, fingers

scraping at the skin. My nail catches on a latch and I tug it open. Circuit boards. Inside Mum's head, where her brain should be. She's – there's…

I scramble over her lap and claw at Dad, scratching until I find the latch. He's…

I stare at their unconscious bodies, twisting my bottom lip between my fingers. My head buzzes with improbable and unlikely explanations, but even the unlikeliest and most improbable one doesn't seem unlikely or improbable enough.

Mum and Dad haven't been treated for the seizures, so whatever this is, it wasn't put there today. It's always been there. They've all got computer parts inside their heads.

How can they all – how can every single one of them…?

"What is this?" Shen asks, sounding sickly and small.

"I think – I don't…"

I look around the ward, at the rows and rows of people I know and love, and then at Mitch, who is standing near by, red lights flashing at our distress. The metal sheen of the robot's head glints in the yellow light.

Robots.

They're – they're robots.

They aren't real.

None of them are real.

They're all—

Our parents are robots.

Time seems to stop.

"They're robots." The words come out small and unsure.

Shen's eyes are wild, so I say it again, repeating it until I see it sink in.

My parents are robots. Mum. Dad. Jia. Feng. But how? How can they be *artificial*? How can they not be real? How can any of this be happening to us?

I pinch the skin of my throat, worrying at it until it hurts.

Shen is clearly struggling with this as much as I am, because it's only now that he says: "No. *No*. What? I don't believe it."

I make a weak noise of agreement. It's almost too impossible to believe, even when I'm staring right at the evidence.

How can we not have noticed?

I am human, right? How do I know for sure? Maybe Mum and Dad don't even know about this themselves.

"Are we robots too?" I ask, panic weaving through the words. How can we tell? How is it possible to know for sure? There's suddenly far too much saliva in my mouth. I swallow, but I can't seem to make my throat work.

I must be human. I must be. I have *periods*. Who would make a robot with period pains? Or ear wax? Or curving toenails which press into the skin? Or *bacne*? Nothing about my body is designed to be neat and tidy. It's the result of nature, not design. I'm human. I am.

Still, I scrabble at my scalp, searching for a panel, scratching at the skin. Surely I would have felt it before, if there was something there? I keep looking. I've never noticed anything before, but maybe I missed it. I need to be sure. I need to know, I need to—

"Hey, hey," Shen says, holding out his hands. "Stop." He

takes hold of my head. His eyes are glassy.

I tighten my jaw, making myself hold still while he gently tilts my head to the side. His fingers work over the skin of my scalp, pressing along the edges of the bone in search of a panel. For the first time, I notice his bloodshot eyes and the sunken depths of the circles under them. "Anything?" I ask between my teeth, keeping my mouth still.

"Nothing. You're human."

I let out a breath of relief.

Shen tilts his head so that I can check his scalp too. When I don't find any sign of a panel, something dense and cold inside my stomach eases slightly. We're human. Right?

I drop my hand from his neck. But when he steps back, I reach out and take his hand to keep him close. I need the warmth of his skin against mine right now. I need human contact.

I turn back to the rows of patients, and it strikes me how much they look like a line of corpses waiting to be taken to a morgue. They are so motionless and sterile that I can't look directly at them. It makes horror crawl up my spine, at how completely wrong they are.

"It doesn't change anything," I say at last. "They're still our parents." Do I mean that? Yes. Yes, of course I do.

"I *know* that," Shen says. He sounds angry, but I know it's not at me.

"Is it everyone, then?" I ask, the realisation hitting me, all at once. "Everyone in London? So many of them are sick … and does that mean they're all … robots? I mean, all of them…?"

I swipe at my tablet, checking the newsfeed to see if anyone is awake. There haven't been any new posts in hours, and even those before that were just automated emergency warnings telling people not to leave their homes in case of infection. I do a head-count, looking in all of the wards. Everyone in London is here. The entire community. *But does that mean they are all robots?* I walk from person to person, checking their scalps. All of them have the panel, the circuit board, the cables. It's everyone. Shen and I are the only ones still awake. More than that, we're the only humans left in the whole world right now.

"At least we're together," Shen says, his voice trembling like he's realising this at the same time as me. "We always knew this might happen eventually, that we'd be the only people left. It's just happened sooner than expected. Right?"

"Right." Except this is nothing like we expected, because our parents, *everyone*, is a robot. Aloud, I say, "This is nothing we can't handle." I hope.

Incredibly, there's a part of me that still believes this is all a terrible, dramatic and tormented dream of some sort. My brain insists on being an optimist, even when the evidence is undeniable.

I brace my arms on the bar at the end of Mum's bed, looking at her closed eyes and calm expression. I can feel tears forming again, even as I try to blink them away. "Why would a bunch of robots want to pretend to be humans? Why would they want to raise the two of us? What's the *point*?" I wipe the tears away from my eyes, trying to control myself.

Shen isn't crying. Shen is stronger than me. He knows that

this isn't the time or the place for tears. He knows that we have to control ourselves.

"Lowrie, you know what this means? The seizures – they aren't caused by a disease at all. They can't be, if no one is human. It's something different altogether. Maybe it's, I don't know, a malware or something."

A malware? That doesn't sound too bad. We can fix that, surely.

That's when it hits me. "They aren't dead!" I shout, sobbing with relief. "Shen, they aren't dead! They're not really dead! They *can't* die, because they *aren't alive*!"

"They aren't dead," he says to himself. "They can't die?"

"They can't die," I say.

Our parents are robots. They can't die. They can't ever leave us. They're ours, for ever – if only we can get rid of the malware. No wonder our parents weren't worried about us catching it. It's a computer virus, and we're human.

And then the panic sets in again. "A malware? But how – how are we *possibly* going to fix that?" I find my voice has gone high and anxious, stretching and morphing without my permission. "I don't even know what a malware is!"

Shen makes a noise low in his throat, a kind of anxious *tsk*. He folds his arms around his chest, curling in on himself. "Mama and Doctor Ahmed were working on a cure. They must have been. Maybe we can find it and try and use it. Or we can learn. Can we learn? I might be able to learn."

"Shen! You might be able to do little things on a computer, but you aren't a programmer. This is way beyond anything we can do. Our parents will be stuck in this ward for years while we try. *Decades*. What if they never wake up?" The words circle back to loop around my throat, tightening.

I know I've been preparing for this moment for my whole life. But now it's here, I don't feel at all ready. There are still so many things I don't know how to do, and so many things I have to say to my parents. What if this is it? What if we can't fix this, and they're gone for ever? We'll have to do everything on our own. Can we really handle that?

Shen's expression crumples. "We don't have any other choice, Lowrie!" he spits. "I'm not going to give up and let them – and let them…" He bites at his knuckle.

"I know we can't give up! That's not what I'm saying." I swallow, again and again, trying to push away everything I'm feeling.

"How is being so negative going to help? We need to do something, and this is the only idea I've got. Do you have any better ones?"

"I – I…" I stare at him, trying not to cry. My mind is blank. "We just need time to think."

The corners of his eyes tighten. "We don't have any time! We have no idea what this thing is doing to them. It might be erasing their minds right now. I can fix this, I know I can."

"We're just *kids*, Shen. Your mama and Doctor Ahmed have been working day and night to try and stop this, and they got nowhere. They're unconscious right now, because they couldn't stop it. There's nothing we can do that they won't have thought of, that they won't have tried dozens of times. What do you want to do, get a *Dummies Guide to Programming* and start at page one?"

"Shut *up*, Lowrie!"

"You shut up! Stop being so obtuse!"

Suddenly we're fighting, in a way we haven't since we were ten-year-olds, all spit and indignant fury.

"*I'm* obtuse?" he hisses, getting right in my face. "You're the one being negative. We just need to work on this, and we'll find an answer!"

I throw my hands in the air and growl, too frustrated to think straight. He has a way of making me angry in seconds, like he just flicks a switch and gouges straight into my nerves. When we're friends, we're the best of friends, and when we're not, I hate him to the depths of his bones.

"This isn't my fault!" I say. "I'm just trying to be sensible here."

Shen's face goes blank. He turns and walks away, only stopping when he reaches the wall. He braces his hands on it, and I watch his shoulders rise and fall. "I know it's not your fault! I just wish…" He slumps. "I wish – I wish this wasn't happening."

"Me too. I'm sorry. Of course we need to try to fix this."

"I'm sorry too." Shen holds out his arms.

I step into them, more relieved than I can say that we're not fighting any more. "We're going to be fine. Whatever happens, we're going to be fine," I whisper, not brave enough to say it any louder. "We've got each other, and that's never, ever going to change. We're always going to be together, OK?"

He huffs. "I know, Lowrie. Trust me, I would be freaking out a lot more if you weren't here."

I press my ear to his chest, listening to the steady thump of his heartbeat. That sound, at least, is real.

MyWaves05

It's strange to think that the anniversary of the day the last human dies is already fixed, even if we don't know it yet. The anniversary of our future extinction passes every year. How soon is it going to be? Is it today?

Posted on 19 Aug 2030

> **Rizzz** on 19 Aug 2030
> Replying to **@MyWaves05**
> How long do you think it'll be before the last human dies?
>
>> **MyWaves05** on 19 Aug 2030
>> Replying to **@Rizzz**
>> I think if they never solve the sterility, then ... 2179, give or take a few years.
>>
>>> **Rizzz** on 19 Aug 2030
>>> Replying to **@MyWaves05**
>>> I reckon more like 2167.
>>>
>>>> **MyWaves05** on 19 Aug 2030
>>>> Replying to **@Rizzz**
>>>> Always with the glass half empty. But it's a bet.
>>>>
>>>>> **MyWaves05** on 19 Aug 2030
>>>>> Replying to **@Rizzz**
>>>>> Winner inherits the Earth. Literally.

MyWaves05

It's moving day for us newlyweds!!!

Posted on 15 Sep 2030

> **Unhako_neko** on 15 Sep 2030
> Replying to **@MyWaves05** and **@Rizzz**
> I can't wait to see your new house (and the puppy! Only you would pick up a new dog on the same day you get the keys.)

Rizzz on 15 Sep 2030
Replying to **@Unhako_neko** and **@MyWaves05**
Come over at your own risk. Things we have bought
for the house: the entire contents of Ikea, including,
absurdly, 4 toasters (4!). Things we have not bought
for our house: any FOOD. It's 11 p.m. and we are
on our way to fading away from desperate hunger.

MyWaves05

@Unhako_neko @Blueburnedskies
Look at this. It's so cool!

Posted on 8 May 2031

TECHNEWS.COM

COMPUTER PROGRAMMER HOOKS HIS BABYGROW "SON" UP TO AN ELECTRICAL DOLL TO BRING HIM INTO THE FAMILY FOR REAL

The Babygrow app has taken the world by storm
since it was launched four years ago on Apple
and Android systems. It recently reached nearly
four billion downloads, far outranking its nearest
competitor. This is no surprise, as the simple
program gives would-be parents one last chance to
have the child they've always wanted, at a time when
scientists admit they still see no hope of a cure for
the sterility in the immediate future.

Recently, one man took his love for his simulated
offspring to the next level. Yuri Oni, an engineer,
designed and built a doll of his Babygrow son. A
projector takes the code from the app and converts
the simple CGI display into a three-dimensional
model, which is then transmitted to a mechanical
doll, providing instructions for it to move and open
and close its eyes.

The model does not yet respond to physical stimuli,
and users currently still requires the app interface to
feed and speak to the babies. But Oni has already

revolutionized the app's future, and the company who developed Babygrow have reached out to offer him a job. They have already licenced his hardware, which is currently patent-pending. Plans are well underway for the hardware to be developed for public manufacture, with Oni as the lead developer and shareholder.

Blueburnedskies on 10 May 2031
Replying to **@MyWaves05** and **@Unhako_neko**
The tech is very cool, but the dolls cost five hundred grand! Are they serious? So millionaires are the only ones allowed to have kids now?

> **MyWaves05** on 10 May 2031
> Replying to **@Unhako_neko** and **@Blueburnedskies**
> Who would even spend that much on some dodgy tech? They probably don't even work.

MyWaves05

My favourite brand of sweets has stopped being made!! Can the company really be making that little money nowadays?! Wow. I genuinely thought that adults bought just as many sweets as kids used to do. Am I eating too many sweets? Don't answer that.

Posted on 26 Aug 2031

MyWaves05

I have some big news. Riz and I have decided to have a baby. We're pregnant! I was really sceptical about the Babygrows at first, but I love my friends' kids, and I can't wait for one of my own.

I'm going to be using one of those brand-new fake pregnancy wombs that connects to the Babygrow app and transmits the baby's motions. I've posted a picture of it strapped on to my stomach <u>here</u> and a picture of it off <u>here</u>, so you can see how the device works. It's surprisingly comfortable. I can't wait until the baby starts kicking. Apparently, it's quite an experience.

Has anyone else got one of these yet? I know they're expensive. If you have any tips, please let me know! **#Babygrow**

Posted on 27 Dec 2032

Blueburnedskies on 27 Dec 2032
Replying to **@MyWaves05**
CONGRATULATIONS!! Hailey and I are so excited to meet them! What a wonderful Christmas present!

MyWaves05 on 28 Dec 2032
Replying to **@Blueburnedskies**
I'm so excited too!! We don't know the gender yet.

(I love Hailey's new haircut, by the way! In the screenshots from the app it looks like she's got super curly hair now!)

Blueburnedskies on 28 Dec 2032
Replying to **@MyWaves05**
She really has, just like her papa! We're trying to save up to get one of the body kits now they've released the new model that actually works. They're so expensive, though. Do you think you're going to get one?

MyWaves05 on 28 Dec 2032
Replying to **@Blueburnedskies**
Honesty, we haven't discussed it yet. Maybe? They are soooo pricey, though, and you'd need to get a new one so often as they grow. I'm not sure.

TIME	DATE	LOCATION	OBJECT	NOTES
15.06	19/03/2108	51.509732, −0.075873	ROMAN MOSAIC OF A CRAB, MADE FROM SQUARES OF MARBLE AND GLASS SET INTO MORTAR. THIRD CENTURY.	FOUND by SZ UNDER THE SAND OF THE ERODING BANK OF THE RIVERBED, SO WE DUG AWAY THE SAND TO REVEAL IT FULLY. WORTH THE EFFORT.

Shen and I stand together for a long time, unable to decide what to do. Finally, we make ourselves get up and go through the hospital, making sure that everyone is in a bed and hooked up to the equipment with a cable-IV thing, like Feng was when we found him. The whole community fills an entire floor of wards.

The machines beep reassuringly, even if I'm not quite sure what they are doing. With Mitch's help, we fetch Mrs Wheeler, the nurse from the corridor, and get her into a bed too. She must not be dead at all, just in the same kind of unconscious state as the other robots.

"What do we do now?" Shen asks, staring at them all.

"You were right. We need to see if we can fix this. Let's see if this actually is a malware. Like you said, Jia must have research in the lab." There's an odd calmness in my mind now. If I just focus on the next step, then this all starts to seem less impossible.

If I think about everything that comes after that, I'll have to give up and collapse on the floor in a puddle. One step at a time. That's the only way to get through this.

Jia's lab is just across the hall. We used to come and visit her at work when we were little. Shen would try to help with her research while I attempted to fix a perpetually broken cupboard bracket. I haven't been in years, though.

It's immaculately clean, with grey benches stretching the length of the room. To my surprise, the counters are empty. Whenever I pictured Jia working on fixing the virus, I saw her surrounded by batches of blood samples, or bacteria cultures in petri dishes. But there's only a long computer screen embedded into the counter, displaying a single medical record. It's Feng's, I realise – just as Shen makes a small noise of distress in the back of his throat.

CONFIDENTIAL MEDICAL RECORD OF FENG ZHANG (封张)

```
ADMITTANCE DATE:     07/04/2509
ADMITTANCE TIME:     11:14

------------------------------------------------
SYMPTOMS:
Unconscious episode occurred at 10:46. No visible
after-effects. Analysis in process.

------------------------------------------------
DIAGNOSIS:
Patient appears to be infected with a malware, as
suggested by symptoms which match previous cases.
This has overridden the motion controller in the
hardware.
N.B. Check again about getting inside Snowdon?
```

TREATMENT:
System has been rebooted offline and short-term
memory has been erased to remove malware, which
seems to be running in the form:

```
ToInfect.CodeModule.AddFromString.Lines(BGN, 1)
    <>"" ("Document_Close.exe( )*)
; Invoke StartProcessKiller
IFN DisablePK target[]= void usage \n\n
EncryptEnd ""$$""
;Create admin synchro mutex
Printf("usage:killoperatingmemory")
RESTORE_REDIRECTION_STATE.SECS_BETWEEN_RUNS
    [151secs]
End If = [NextRequestTime -> [432000secs]]
```

Page 1 of 102

One hundred and two pages of code! I grimace. It's even worse than I'd imagined. I still don't see how we've got a chance of fixing this on our own, but, like Shen said, we need to at least try.

"Do you think you can do this?" I ask carefully. "Because I have no idea where to even start." I scroll through the code. I don't recognize any of it. This looks impossible.

"I can try," he says, sitting in Jia's chair and rolling up his sleeves. "I suppose we'd better get reading."

I keep examining my memory, trying to work out how I never guessed my parents were robots. I wonder if there's a part of me that has always known. Surely, I must have suspected that something was not quite normal? But there's nothing. I can't say with any honesty that I ever suspected a thing.

MyWaves05

Well, this is a bit of perfect timing, huh? Government
announces plans to extend paid maternity
and paternity cover to Babygrow parents.

Posted on 22 Aug 2033

> **Rizzz** on 22 Aug 2033
> Replying to **@MyWaves05**
> One month to go!!!! We're having a BABY, Maya!

MyWaves05

Urgh.

> RT **@Rizzz** We are on minute fifteen of
> **@MyWaves05** explaining why the birth is going
> to be more scary for her than for me, and I'm
> 100% confident it's the funniest things I've heard
> in my entire life. It's a simulation of a baby!
> She doesn't actually give birth! But you would
> not know that based on her hormone levels.

Posted on 18 Sep 2033

> **Blueburnedskies** on 18 Sep 2033
> Replying to **@Rizzz**
> Ask her to tell you about the time she was
> convinced her arm hurt with sympathy pains
> after I broke mine when we were 6.
>
> > **Rizzz** on 18 Sep 2033
> > Replying to **@Blueburnedskies**
> > Her response was essentially "I swear I will
> > start a riot if you don't unfollow her right
> > this instant", in a kind of raspy screech.

MyWaves05

EVERYBODY STAY CALM, BUT OUR BABY IS
BEING BORN. Nobody panic! I'm certainly not!

Posted on 19 Sep 2033

> **Unhako_neko** on 19 Sep 2033
> Replying to **@MyWaves05**
> They're impatient, they're two weeks
> early! I'm on my way over! Wheeee!

206

MyWaves05

I am over the moon to present our daughter, Darcy
Cynthia Stevens. She was born at 14.11 on 19 Sep
2033, weighing 7 pounds 3 ounces. We are both
exhausted but so, so happy. We're parents!

Posted on 19 Sep 2033

> **Silentstar** on 19 Sep 2033
> Replying to **@MyWaves05**
> Oh, she's gorgeous. Congratulations to you and the
> new dad. Is that one of the new body kit models?
>
> > **MyWaves05** on 19 Sep 2033
> > Replying to **@Silentstar**
> > It is! Riz's parents treated us – they wanted the
> > best for their first grandchild! Isn't it gorgeous?
> > Her movements are so smooth and realistic.

MyWaves05

OK, so not to feel like a failure of a mum or anything,
but I'm struggling a bit to get to grips with the
Babygrow software. Can anyone recommend any
good Babygrow vloggers I should follow for tips?

Posted on 28 Sep 2033

> **Silentstar** on 28 Sep 2033
> Replying to **@MyWaves05**
> Ahhhh, this is my guilty pleasure. I'm kind of
> obsessed with mummy bloggers. Try **@mamagrow**,
> **@BGblogger05** and **@GlitterGoldandBabyGrow**.
>
> > **MyWaves05** on 28 Sep 2033
> > Replying to **@Silentstar**
> > Thank you! There are so many mods being
> > made – how is anyone supposed to keep up? It's
> > like every programmer in the world has started
> > making improvements to the BG software.
> > It's great, but it's going to be a full-time job
> > trying to stay up with the latest updates!
> >
> > > **Silentstar** on 28 Sep 2033
> > > Replying to **@MyWaves05**
> > > Agreed. There must be an easier way to organise it.
> > > But it's so worth having trawled through the mods
> > > when you find one that makes a huge difference.
> > >
> > > The biggest one for me was when the intelligence
> > > became skills- and learning-based, as opposed

to the old ultra-high artificial IQ that just felt completely fake and robotic. The learning-based one makes it feel like the time I spend teaching my son is really useful – I'm actually imparting wisdom to him, as it were.

> **MyWaves05** on 28 Sep 2033
> Replying to **@Silentstar**
> That update sounds amazing – like the muscle memory one from a while back. That made a huge difference, even to the tiny babies. Their learned movements, like sucking their thumbs, became so much smoother. I'll make a note of the IQ one!

CHAPTER 23

TIME	DATE	LOCATION	OBJECT	NOTES
09.22	07/11/2107	51.510697, -0.115654	Plastic Ganesh religious votive offering. Twentieth century.	Found by SZ, washed up on shore of the Thames. Not retrieved.

Shen studies the code in the lab, while I sit with him, trying to be helpful but mostly being distracting. I don't know anything about software. Even now, when I desperately want to contribute something useful, my mind goes blank. Why can I never make myself study like Shen can? Why am I so absolutely *useless*?

I check the time, surprised to find that it's only three p.m. It feels like we've been here for days, not just four hours.

There's a picture of baby Shen on Jia's desk. He's smiling at the camera, face covered in mashed banana and seeming very pleased with himself. I can't stop staring at him. The photo reminds me of one we have back at home, hanging on the wall of the library. It's a picture of me that was taken in the growlery. Goggles are pushed up on to my forehead, with blonde hair tangled around the strap. There's a smudge of grease on my cheek and a wrench is teetering on the brink of falling out of the pocket of my sawdust-covered overalls.

I used to wonder why Mum kept that picture on display,

rather than one of the others where I'm dressed up in a pretty ball-gown. I thought it was embarrassing, in the same way Shen must hate this one of him, covered in banana. But I see why Mum likes it now – there's a big grin on my face, and I'm flushed pink with excitement at whatever I'm working on.

Mum keeps that picture of me for the same reason that Jia keeps this one of Shen. It's also why I have a secret folder on my tablet full of pictures of Shen curled up under a blanket with a book, or lounging half out of the pool scribbling Chinese characters on his tablet.

You don't remember the perfect things when you think about the people you love. You think of the *them* things. The little habits or guilty pleasures or secret flaws that only they have. Those are the things that make them unique. Those things make us all human. That's why I could never have guessed that Mum and Dad are robots. They have flaws and obsessions too. Dad's passion for lichen and Mum's love of dogs make them who they are. It's what makes me care about them, no matter who – or what – they are.

They are real, and human, and nothing is going to stop me from making sure they stay that way. They are my family. I don't care if they're made of code.

MyWaves05

OK, but why didn't anyone tell me how *hard* motherhood is? My lofty plans to get work done at home were hopelessly optimistic.

Posted on 17 Feb 2034

Unhako_neko on 17 Feb 2034
Replying to **@MyWaves05**
We all told you this.
Every single one of us told you this.

> **MyWaves05** on 17 Feb 2034
> Replying to **@Unhako_neko**
> Ah, see, the problem here is
> that I wasn't listening.

> > **Unhako_neko** on 17 Feb 2034
> > Replying to **@MyWaves05**
> > Just wait until Darcy grows into the
> > next body kit and starts walking. You'll
> > never have a moment's peace.

MyWaves05

@Blueburnedskies I can't believe
how big Hailey is in all your latest pics!
How is she six already? She's going
through those body kits like water!

Posted on 19 Aug 2034

> **Blueburnedskies** on 19 Aug 2034
> Replying to **@MyWaves05**
> I know, she's costing a fortune. Thank
> God the kit upgrades will be on the NHS
> from October, because I'm not sure
> how we'd have kept affording the yearly
> upgrades as she grows up otherwise.

MyWaves05

Darcy went in for her upgrade today!
She's grown up into the 2–4 years body
kit. She's so big now. I can't believe
she's really my tiny baby daughter.

Posted on 18 Oct 2035

MyWaves05

Good one, Labour! This is exactly what was needed.

Posted on 29 Nov 2035

NHS TO OPEN SPECIALIST BABYGROW TECH SUPPORT CLINICS AT SELECT MEDICAL SURGERIES

In this year's budget, the Labour party announced plans to open new BG clinics at surgeries around the UK within the next six months.

The NHS is hiring programmers and software developers to run the clinics, which will be available free of charge for people registered at the medical surgery.

In the press release, the national medical director of NHS England anticipated that the service's main function would be to "help patients repair general wear and tear to their children's body kits, such as replacing damaged limbs".

Tech-wary parents will also be able to get assistance in installing body kit upgrades, as well as dealing with software malfunctions and malware infections. A recent report suggested that there has been a sudden surge in malware and computer virus attacks aimed specifically at Babygrow systems.

The first NHS clinic will open in February, with the rest to follow in late April, once an operational protocol has been established. Until then, people will have to take their sick Babygrows to computer repair shops for servicing, where a charge will apply. A directory of shops which deal with Babygrow medical issues can be found here.

The announcement coincides with the ninth birthday of the first Babygrow child, who was born when the software was still in beta-mode, before the public launch in May 2027.

MyWaves05

Today **@Rizzz** downloaded a new social interactions
mod made by someone in China. The software's
language is a bit odd, but when it's installed it works
great. Darcy's behaviour was noticeably different
almost immediately. It makes Darcy a lot more aware
of body language and subtle facial expressions now.
She picks up hints a lot more quickly when we're
not happy with her – which is amazing considering
she's so young. She also laughs at funny faces a lot
more and comes up and asks for hugs all the time.

I dust off the picture of Shen as a baby, placing it back on Jia's
desk. Our parents loved us, just as much as we love them. There's
no doubt about that, even if they are robots.

And Maya loved Darcy in the same way that I love my parents.

The fake babies seemed creepy when I first learned about them, but now that I know about my parents, I can understand it a bit more. It's no wonder that Maya could love a computer program. I love my mum and dad, even knowing what they really are. It seems impossible that I could stop loving them just because they're made of silicon instead of cells. They are like us in every way that matters. Just like Darcy.

That makes me think.

"Shen, is there anything in Jia's notes about Babygrows?"

Shen looks up from the computer. His eyes are bloodshot and tired. He hasn't stopped working for hours. "What do you...?"

I realise that I haven't told him much about how the Babygrow app was developed. I don't have time to go into that now, though. "Just have a look!" I say and make a *hurry-up* gesture at him, jumping up to lean over his shoulder.

He runs a search, and a result pops up:

```
. . . as is standard, Alexei Wyatt was running on the
Babygrow 12.4 operating system. There doesn't seem to
be any faults in his coding, but . . .
```

Babygrow. Alexei was using the Babygrow operating system.

"Oh my God. *Shen.* They're – they're the Babygrows! Maya's Babygrows!"

"Are you sure?" he asks. "Those things were just *apps*. How can they be – how can they have – no way."

"It might have started as an app, but it didn't stay that way." I quickly fill him in on the Babygrows' development, including how Maya and Riz had a baby of their own via the app.

"How did they get from this Darcy to our parents, though?" he asks, skimming through Jia's notes.

"I don't know. I haven't had a chance to read any more of Maya's posts. Let me look."

I run a search for all her posts about the Babygrows, quickly reading about their development over the years. Shen peers over my shoulder.

"Oh my God," I gasp, when I read about the body kits. "The doll. In the attic. That was—"

His eyes widen. "That was one of them! One of the babies!"

"That wasn't Mum's toy at all," I say, stunned. "That *was her*. When she was a baby."

"*Tamade,*" he swears, in an overwrought tremble.

We sit in stunned silence as a hundred moments shift and take on new meaning. Then Shen bursts out, "Wait, this could help us!" He looks at me, eyes bright. "If we know that they're Babygrows, then there must be some information out there about how to get rid of malware infections in their operating system. There was a mention of something about malware in one of the articles Maya posted." He scrolls back through her entries. "Here, this one." He points at the piece about the NHS opening tech clinics at local GP surgeries. "Can you see if Maya mentioned anything else like this? Or maybe even anything about viruses in general."

I nod. I can do that. This is something I can actually understand. "We'll fix this. I know we will," I say, to convince us both.

The sliver of wood from the bureau in the loft is still embedded in the flesh of my arm. It's thrumming with a low-level pain, so I press on it to make it hurt in a less quiet way that's easier to ignore.

"Do you have a splinter?" Shen asks, noticing my movement. "You need to remove it."

I grimace. "It'll come out on its own."

"It'll get worse if you leave it."

I shake my head. "It'll be fine."

He rolls his eyes and leaves the room, coming back with a sterilized needle from a hospital supply cupboard.

"No! Shen!" I hide my arm behind my back, grimacing.

"Lowrie, come on. It'll go septic. I can do it for you if that makes it easier. Your..." He draws in a breath and stops talking, looking sad.

"What? What were you going to say?"

"I was going to say that your parents will be mad at you if you don't get it out. But I guess we're on our own now."

I swallow. "You can remove it. But I hope you appreciate the full extent of my bravery here." I hold out my arm for him to take.

He nods in fake solemnity and then carefully tugs the skin around the splinter taut. I squeeze my eyes shut and breathe in, trying to ignore the jerking sensation happening under the surface of my skin.

"Done," he says. He holds up the needle. On the end is a minuscule sliver of wood, so small that it's almost embarrassing.

"Thanks." I shudder, trying to release the tension. "Day one of isolation: Lowrie nearly succumbs to splinter."

"Let's hope neither of us gets a paper cut tomorrow." He smiles at me. Lines crinkling around his mouth, but his eyes are still sad.

MyWaves05

Today I was walking with Darcy in the park and she had some kind of ... seizure? We were feeding the ducks when her hand started twitching and her eyes fluttered. It was really scary. If she was biological, I'd have sworn she had epilepsy. **@Rizzz** took her to the GP, but they couldn't see any software errors. Does anyone know of anything like this happening before?

Posted on 16 Apr 2036

> **Silentstar** on 16 Apr 2036
> Replying to **@MyWaves05**
> Shit, that sounds awful. Is she OK now?
> I've never heard of anything like that.

MyWaves05

Darcy has been having her little seizures every few days. She says the pain goes away after a few minutes, but it's making her forget things, like where we are or what we had for lunch. Obviously we're quite concerned. Does anyone have any recommendations for specialist private BG doctors? We're losing patience with the NHS GPs. They've not been able to offer any kind of helpful support.

Posted on 9 May 2036

> **Blueburnedskies** on 9 May 2036
> Replying to **@MyWaves05**
> I'm sorry, Maya. We've been lucky, and Hailey has been very healthy. I've asked around but no one in my mums group has had any issues either.

>> **MyWaves05** on 9 May 2036
>> Replying to **@Blueburnedskies**
>> Yeah, that seems to be the general reaction we're getting everywhere. Everyone is completely baffled. It's so frustrating. We all work so hard to make the BGs seem human, but the minute they start getting illnesses, it's suddenly *too* human and no one knows what to do.

UK PARENTS TOLD THEIR BG DAUGHTER IS TERMINALLY ILL, FACING REBOOT

In the first case of advanced Babygrow illness in the UK, an Oxford couple, who wish to remain anonymous, are facing a difficult decision. Their two-year-old daughter has suffered from increasingly painful and frequent seizures for the last month. Efforts to diagnose and fix the problem have left doctors baffled.

After multiple treatments, the distraught parents were told this week that the only chance of curing their daughter's illness is to reboot her system, in the hope that the malware or coding error which is causing the seizures will be removed. However, there is a risk that this may remove all personality traits which have been developed since the child's birth. Effectively, she might revert to the original Babygrow newborn program.

The parents don't have long to make a decision, as if she isn't turned back on within the next forty-eight hours then her body kit will automatically deactivate and all memory files will be lost.

Follow @newsbreaking for more updates as the story develops.

CHAPTER 24

TIME	DATE	LOCATION	OBJECT	NOTES
10.17	04/04/2108	51.453130, 0.362473	Laminated red tag with the Beanie Baby "TY" symbol, and text saying, "Millennium, Date of birth: JANUARY 1, 1999". Twentieth century.	Found by LMBW, caught in the drain outside Westminster Abbey.

Since I found out that our parents are Babygrows, I've been reading Maya's posts as fast as I can, seeing Darcy with new eyes. When Maya and Riz stop posting, I have to do a search to find out what happened. The news articles about Darcy's illness make me blanch in horror. My heart breaks for Maya and Riz, even as my mind is racing.

"*Shen!*" I shout.

He jumps at my exclamation. He's slumped over the computer, reading internet archive results about Babygrow malwares between half-closed eyes.

I explain what happened to Darcy, then say, "The posts say that if the body kits are turned off for more than forty-eight hours, they will deactivate. If we don't solve this today, then their memories are going to be lost. They'll forget who we are!"

Mum and Dad passed out around one p.m., which means

they've already been turned off for three hours. We've barely even started trying to find a way to fix them yet. The thought of Mum and Dad waking up, only for them to stare at me with blank, unrecognizing eyes makes me want to throw up. We are so close to losing them completely.

"I can't fix this in *a few hours*!" Shen says. There are deep circles under his eyes. "I can barely understand the code yet – even knowing they're Babygrows doesn't help much, as I don't know anything about that system either. I'll keep trying, but I don't think I'll have time before it's too late." He's been chewing on his knuckles again, and they're red and swollen. When he lifts one to his mouth, I push his hand away.

"There must be *something* we can try," I say.

"I don't know what to do, Lowrie. I really don't. You were right, there's nothing I'm going to be able to come up with that Mama won't have already tried. I just – I need more time. A *lot* more time. And we don't have it." He rests his chin on his knees, curling around himself protectively, and stares at the screen in deep contemplation.

I bite at the inside of my cheek, trying to hide my fear.

All I can see is the countdown playing in my mind, marking out the hours we've got left until our parents' minds are wiped. Forty-*three* hours. That's it, before they're gone for ever.

Silentstar

@Blueburnedskies Have you heard from M at all?

Blueburnedskies on 15 May 2036
Replying to **@Silentstar**
The last I heard they were in London seeking a second opinion. I don't think they've made any decisions yet.

> **Silentstar** on 15 May 2036
> Replying to **@Blueburnedskies**
> Shit. Calling you now.

Unhako_neko

There is a farewell dinner at the Stevens' house tomorrow at six. If you'd like to see Darcy before the treatment, please feel free to come along. If you'd like to pass on a message, let me know.

Posted on 16 May 2036

> **Silentstar** on 16 May 2036
> Replying to **@Unhako_neko**
> I still can't believe this is happening.

> > **Unhako_neko** on 16 May 2036
> > Replying to **@Silentstar**
> > I don't think any of us can.

Unhako_neko

YES!!!

Posted on 17 May 2036

NEWSBREAKING.COM

TERMINALLY ILL BG SAVED AT LAST MINUTE BY PARENTS' QUICK THINKING

The sick two-year-old Babygrow child who faced rebooting this week to stop her seizures has instead been cured of her illness by her parents' quick thinking.

Only hours before the procedure to wipe her memory was due to take place, the parents, who have yet to be named, suspected that a small part in their daughter's body kit might be broken. A specialist clinic in London confirmed their theory, when they discovered that the component that controls motor function had malfunctioned, causing disconnected movements in the body kit's limbs, which appeared like "seizures".

"We're thrilled," the mother said in a statement released by the hospital this morning. "We thought we'd lost our daughter completely. This has saved her life, and ours too."

MyWaves05

Thank you to everyone who has reached out in the last few days, since Darcy woke up. Riz and I appreciate your support, even if we haven't been able to reply individually. Darcy was discharged from hospital yesterday and she seems to be in a stable condition. We're all tired but relieved.

Posted on 25 May 2036

CHAPTER 25

TIME	DATE	LOCATION	OBJECT	NOTES
11.36	05/02/2109	51.491455, -0.088470	Glass jar of miscellaneous buttons.	Found by SZ in the rubble of a collapsed tower block.

I reread Maya's posts about Darcy's seizures several times, thinking over what happened. What if Jia was approaching the malware all wrong? What if a broken part has caused this? What if this can be fixed by replacing the malfunctioning bit of kit, like with Darcy?

I don't want to get Shen's hopes up until I'm sure, so I leave him in Jia's lab and sneak back on to the ward. I look through the supply cupboard until I've found what I need: a magnifying lens, some tiny screwdrivers designed to fit the smallest of screws and an antistatic cloth.

I decide to start with Alexei Wyatt, since he's been here the longest. If the Babygrow systems get erased after forty-eight hours, then there's a chance he's gone anyway. He crashed his helicopter three days ago. If I break something, it will be less awful.

I clench my hands into fists and flatten them against my sides. What if I've got this wrong? My stomach is twisting like I'm about to take an exam.

Telling myself to stay calm, I direct the light from a table

223

lamp at the bed. I don't know exactly what I'm looking for, but I've spent enough time fixing bots to know that there has to be some way inside the system, to repair damage. If I can get inside, I'll be able to find any broken parts.

Feeling incredibly weird, I take off Alexei's shirt. I close my eyes and try to see him as a bot to fix, instead of my friend. I shudder slightly as I search his chest for a panel, like the one in the side of his scalp. It takes a while, but eventually my fingertips run over a small bump in the side of his fifth rib. I run my fingernail under it, working it open.

I pause for a moment, collecting myself. He's a robot. This isn't going to hurt him. Mitch is watching me work with interest, and I look at him. "You'd tell me if I was doing something wrong, right?" I ask.

He flashes green at me. Somehow, I find that reassuring. Summoning my courage, I tug at the seal and the entire surface of skin over Alexei's chest peels away in one complete layer of silicone coating. Seeing the skin come away still makes me feel sick, even though I know it's not real. I can't even handle removing a *splinter*, let alone skinning a human male.

To my relief, his insides aren't as realistic as his skin. Instead of fake organs and bones, there's a clear plastic casing protecting computer components. Suddenly, this isn't gross at all. It's just engineering. I shine the light through the plastic to see the innards. There's something dark tucked underneath a circuit board where the heart should be. It's a charred and twisted chip, blackened from overheating.

I let out a hum of satisfaction. Just what I'd been hoping for.

I put down the magnifying glass and go and fetch Shen.

"Come with me. I've got something to show you."

At the sound of my voice, he looks up from the code, rubbing his eyes. It takes him a moment to focus on me, then he stands and follows me on to the ward. He stops walking in shock when he sees what I've done to Alexei. "Lowrie… What?" Then he leans in to look at the charred component. "What *is* that?"

"I think they've all stopped moving because this part broke. When Darcy had these seizures, they thought they were going to have to shut her down to fix the problem in her coding. But it turned out to have been a malfunctioning part in her body kit."

"I can't believe Maya and Riz went through all that. It's annoying enough when my tablet breaks. I can't imagine nearly losing my *child* just because of some broken software."

"I know," I say. "It must have been a constant worry, mustn't it? Life is so fragile, whether it's software or biology." The thought of a whole world full of Mayas, all worrying about their Babygrow children, makes me feel ill.

Shen rubs his brow. "So you think the same thing is happening here?"

I nod. "Look!" I point out the tiny charred chip in Alexei's chest. "That can't be normal, can it? If it's the same in all of them, maybe we can fix it."

Shen is quiet for a moment. "Maybe, but … it seems very unlikely that the same piece of hardware would break in all of them at the same time. I'm not sure, Lowrie…"

"But what if it was a virus, like your mama thought? Some sort of malware that affected that bit of kit specifically in everyone. That's possible, right?"

"Maybe," Shen says slowly, and then more confidently, "Yes. That used to happen all the time: viruses destroying laptops and stuff. One of those old ones could have done this." Shen's face slowly clears. "Lowrie! This might just work! You're a genius!" He grabs my arms, delighted, and spins me in a circle, before tugging me in close.

Mitch nudges my hand insistently, so I add, "Well, Mitch helped too. A bit."

Shen turns to look at him, still keeping his arm around me. "You're a true hero, Mitch of the Thames."

Mitch dips his head, noble and dignified.

I lean into Shen's side, enjoying the weight of his arm around me. "Do you really think it could work?"

"It's worth a try! As you say, replacing a broken part is a lot easier than destroying the malware. And we have so little time – we need to try anything." Shen abruptly sits on the end of Alexei's bed, thinking hard. "But" – his face falls again – "this doesn't make any sense. Why wouldn't Mama replace the chip herself if that's what the problem was? She must have noticed the part had broken."

"Did she not mention anything about broken parts in her notes?" I ask.

He shakes his head. "Not that I saw, but there's pages and pages of notes. I've only read the section on the coding so far. I haven't even looked at anything about circuit boards or processors. I was just trying to focus on what might help fix them."

"Run a search for it in her notes," I suggest.

I suddenly feel so much more confident that we'll fix this. There was nothing I could do to help with the malware. But this – broken equipment? Replacing parts? – is my specialty. I can do this. We can save them.

We go back to the lab, and Shen runs the search for "processor" in Jia's notes.

```
. . . The malware seems to be attacking a motion-
controlling processor, located in the chest, causing
it to overheat. There are no replacements available
for this type of chip. The last replacement Babygrow
body kit we have access to was used sixty years ago,
so it is not possible to take the part from any pre-
existing kits. All body kits are currently in use by
other people. It therefore seems unlikely that there
is a way to bring back the patients whose processors
have broken.

We will have to focus instead on using the effects
of the malware to program a defence in the code, to
ensure that no one else is infected, before more body
kits are damaged. . .
```

"What?" I ask. "No! How can there be no spare parts? Can't we make more? How can she give up like that?"

"She must be wrong. She must be." Shen has gone white and is chewing on his knuckle again. "We'll make more processors. We'll find replacements. There must be more *somewhere*."

"We can't just accept they're dead because of a *broken part*." I nod decisively. "We'll fix it. We have to." I rub my hand up and down my trouser leg, smoothing and re-smoothing the fabric, focusing on the rough texture against my palm while I try to think.

I want to read more of Maya's posts, to see if she wrote anything which might help us. She must have bought Darcy's part from somewhere. Maybe we can track down the factory where the Babygrows were made. They might have spare processors in storage. But we have so little time, and even if we can find the factory, who is to say that we'll even be able to get there? It might be thousands of miles away. It might no longer exist.

I wonder for a moment if we could build our own processors, but then I start imagining all the complicated machinery I'd have to assemble first and the types of silicon and metal I'd need to find. It would take too long. Even with careful instructions – which we don't have – there's no way we'll be able to learn how to make the processor in time. Making our candyfloss bot took weeks and weeks of solid work from three of us, including Feng, who had done it before. We can't possibly do that in just a day by ourselves – if we could ever manage it at all.

Still, there is something niggling in the back of my mind. "Can you pull up Feng's medical record again?" I ask.

Once Shen has found it, I reread it, wondering what part of it stood out to me.

"There," I say, pointing to the last line. It says, *'N.B. Check again about getting inside Snowdon?'* "Could she be talking about looking for spare parts there?"

"Maybe. But why there?"

I tilt my head. "Wasn't that the place Dad told us about?

The bunker for supplies? I think I remember reading something about it in Maya's posts too. Hang on." I pull up her account and search for the word "Snowdon". There are two mentions of it. The first one is very brief, so I skip over it, but the next one is more promising.

MyWaves05

I find this place so fascinating. I wish I could visit before it gets sealed up.

Posted on 17 April 2035

NEWSBREAKING.COM

SNOWDON VAULTS NEAR COMPLETION

Construction of the Snowdon vaults finished this week. The tunnel system is excavated deep into Mount Snowdon in Wales and is designed to store and preserve supplies for thousands of years.

The long-term storage facility has been filled with millions of pounds' worth of supplies of every type, all stored in optimum condition to preserve them for the future. A number of tech firms have donated products, including Babygrow Labs, which has given a significant quantity of its latest body kits.

Seed samples of every type have also been preserved in specially built solar-powered freezers. DNA samples from all agricultural animals have also been included.

In addition, several internet companies have installed memory banks containing copies of significant cultural data from the last thousand years.

Taxpayers initially raised objections to the project, which many considered to be a waste of money at a time when it is unlikely that another generation of humans will ever be born. However, the latest fertility report was optimistic that a solution to the sterility might still be found, so it was decided last year that the Snowdon vaults project should proceed as planned.

Currently, discussions are in progress about how to mark the entrance to the tunnels. The entrance has to protect the supplies against time and weather, whilst also signposting what is inside to any future discoverers who may not speak or read language as we know it.

Possible designs include picture hieroglyphics and motion-activated holograms of people demonstrating how to open the vaults.

"The vaults?" Shen says, reading over my shoulder. "Wait, the vaults! Lowrie, that's it! Surely they'll have spare processors there!"

"But why would your mama not have gone to Snowdon, if she thought some parts might be there?" I ask, although my mind is already racing with excitement. This could be the solution. I wonder how easy it would be to get to Wales.

"It's only been a few days since the outbreak, and it's all happened so quickly. Maybe she didn't have time. What do you think? Should we give it a go?"

"We have to!" I say.

"How are we even going to get to Wales?"

"The hospital has a rescue helicopter on the roof." The idea of getting in a helicopter is scary, as I can remember Alexei's crash in vivid detail. But I don't see any other option, and the thought of losing our parents is even scarier.

Shen nods. "Even if we don't find anything, we'd be back here in a few hours anyway. Let's do it." He looks animated for the first time since Feng collapsed. He grabs my hand. "Lowrie, can you imagine if this works? We might actually be able to save them."

I hold him tightly, a broad smile breaking out on my face.

We walk up to the roof of the building, where there's a bright yellow helicopter, covered in a tarpaulin. The inside is fitted out like an ambulance, with a stretcher and boxes of medical equipment for the paramedics.

"Don't do that!" I say, when Mitch picks up a defibrillator, poking the end.

He flashes a sullen purple at me.

When Shen turns on the computer in the cockpit, it displays a warning: POWER ALLOWS OPERATION FOR NINETY MINUTES BEFORE RECHARGE NEEDED.

"That's not enough time," I say. My heart sinks. This had all seemed too good to be true. "We won't have enough power to get there and back."

"I guess it is designed for short trips around London, not cross-country hauls. What does it run off?"

I click on the screen, searching for information on the power source. "Lithium-ion battery packs. They're stored in the back. I guess…" I frown.

Shen nods encouragingly at me, giving me a moment to consider.

"We have some of those at home," I say, at last. "They're the same kind as we use to store the excess energy from the solar panels, I think."

"So could we go home and get some more? Would we have enough?"

"Well, I don't know. The batteries are heavy. The more weight there is, the more power it takes to lift the helicopter. But maybe..." I check the weight capacity of the helicopter on the system and scribble a few numbers on my tablet, checking the maths. "I think if we took out the stretcher and paramedics' equipment, we could carry enough batteries to get there and back."

"OK." Shen brushes off his hands, already eyeing up the stretcher. "I'll clear everything I can out of here, and you go home and get the batteries."

"I'll pack our rucksacks with clothes and supplies and some food too. It's nearly dinner time, and we'll need provisions." Before I leave, I pull him into a hug. It feels wrong to leave him, when he's all I've got left.

MyWaves05

We're slowly getting back to life as normal. I keep catching myself watching Darcy for any sign of a seizure, but so far there's been nothing. She seems completely fine again now.

Posted on 16 June 2036

MyWaves05

I feel so lucky to have a Babygrow daughter. If
she had been biological, she might be dead by
now. At least with Darcy, it's possible to replace
parts when she gets sick. She's much, much safer.
The likelihood of losing her is so much smaller.
I don't need to hold my breath all the time.

Posted on 9 July 2036

CHAPTER 26

TIME	DATE	LOCATION	OBJECT	NOTES
07.37	12/10/2104	51.497335, -0.124587	Yellow-gold Celtic bracelet in the shape of a curled snake, with a ruby for an eye. 400 BC.	Found by HMBW. Picked up by Dad while walking the dogs. Unbelievable.

The streets are quiet and deserted as I walk home. Not deserted like they usually are, but *dead*. There's no sign of life at all, except the wind in the trees. We really are completely and utterly alone.

I've always known that I'm one of the last humans. I thought I understood it. But now that it is just us, alone, possibly for ever … I'm terrified. This isn't tragic. This is beyond that.

I can't see this ending in a way that doesn't destroy everything. There is no happy ending, no satisfying outcome that lets us go back to life the way it used to be. Even if our parents do wake up and come home, I'm not going to be able to fold this all into a box and hide it in the back of my mind. Everything has changed. Everything about our lives is a lie.

I don't even know any more what it means to be alive. I thought I understood what *living* meant. It seems such a basic, essential concept. If it moves, if it breathes, if it thinks, if it feels – then it's alive. That seemed obvious; barely even worth stating. But now, that definition seems to have slipped from my grasp.

Does being alive mean that you grow and develop, learn and change? The Babygrows do that too, just like any other child. To Maya, her daughter was a real, living person, even though she was made of circuits and programming. The idea of Maya losing Darcy hurts just like the death of a human child. And I feel the same way about my parents.

Maybe that's what matters. Maybe that's what being "alive" is. It's not some trick. There's no magic chemical that gives something a soul. It's about being loved and loving in return. Everything else "human" can be manufactured. These robots were brought into the world by people who loved them more than anything – who invested their time and love and energy into raising them like children, to replace the ones they could never have.

Everything that it means to be a human was written and taught to the Babygrows. In some ways, they're probably more human than I am. They grew up in the time before human society collapsed completely. They have seen more of the real way that humans lived than Shen and me. We've only ever been here, in the last dying days of civilization.

There's nothing recognizable here, not any more. Our world is filled with relics of a lost time. The things we find are interesting but impossible to truly understand without context.

However much Shen and I might think we understand the past – however many films we watch or social media posts we read – we can never really *live* it. We've been studying the history of our world for years, but even we had no idea that the Babygrows existed. Yet here they are, all around us.

Records can be changed and erased in an instant. Something as important to society as *an entire generation of children* can be forgotten for ever. Here on the outskirts of civilization, we're just archaeologists trying desperately to understand the echoes of long-lost objects, which we don't have the context to properly imagine. We can use shards of tiles and screenshots of articles to assemble a picture, but there will always be pieces missing.

By the time I get home it's nearly six p.m. Victoria and Albert greet me, whining and upset at being left alone all day. I wish I didn't have to leave them again, but there's no way we can take them with us. It's too dangerous.

The bots have fed them as Mum's not here to do it. I wonder if the dogs miss her as much as I do.

Once I've taken the fully charged lithium-ion batteries from the power generator, I pack my rucksack with tools, food and supplies, including sanitary towels. It'd be just my luck to start my period while we're up a mountain or something. Once I've put some stuff in a bag for Shen too, I quickly search online for any other mention of Snowdon, but there's barely anything about the vaults that might be useful.

I spend ten minutes trying to choose between two pickaxes, and only make a decision when Shen calls to ask if I have fallen into an abandoned well somewhere. When I tell him what I'm doing, he yells that the two tools are "exactly the same, Shadow, come on".

Shen meets me in the hospital reception and grabs his rucksack and two of the batteries off me.

We walk back up to the roof, walking past the discarded tarpaulin, which Shen has used to cover the medical equipment from the helicopter. The fabric flutters in the wind on the shale rooftop. Mitch is sitting in the pilot's seat of the helicopter, pushing the controls back and forth in delight.

"Wait – he's flying us?" I ask in disbelief. "I thought we were going to use the autopilot."

"He wanted to help. This is an air ambulance, right? Mitch is an emergency rescue bot."

I wipe sweat off my upper lip. "Our *lives* are at stake. You think he knows what he's doing?" The robot is thirty per cent rust and seventy per cent moss.

"Well, I wouldn't go that far." Shen eyes him.

Mitch swivels his head back to front and flashes indigo at Shen, offended.

"I guess, if he manages to get us off the ground…" I grimace then as something occurs to me. "If the processors are being damaged by a computer virus, how come Mitch hasn't caught it?"

Shen shrugs. "He's ancient, right? Maybe his software is incompatible with the malware."

"Lucky you," I say to Mitch.

He prods me with one long finger.

"Did you bring food? I'm starving," Shen asks.

"Ham sandwiches."

"Brilliant."

Shen is clearly not as bothered as me about the flight, because he has already pulled a sandwich out of his rucksack and started eating it. He holds another out to me.

My stomach twists, and I push it away. "How are you so chill right now?"

He shrugs. "It's not like it can get much worse, right? Our parents are unconscious, our whole community was a lie, and we're probably the only real humans left in the world. I'm long past the point of freaking out."

I sigh. "I'm not. Nor is my stomach."

He makes a sympathetic face and shoves a home-brewed ginger beer into my hands. "Drink up. We've got a species to save." He pulls the door closed, tugs on his headphones and says, "Let's get going, Mitch."

To my surprise, the drink actually does calm my stomach as we lift upwards in a roar of air. I pull on my glasses, peering out of the window. London comes into view before us: the hospital, and the familiar streets, and my house in the distance, with the beige curve of the drive and the lush green of the garden. Then we're high enough to see across Hyde Park to Shen's house and, all the way in the distance, the brown expanse of the Thames.

Seeing London from above really makes me notice the decay. Every street is a wreck of collapsed buildings. It gets worse and worse as we fly out of the centre. The houses out here are overwhelmed with green: nettles and brambles and elder trees growing out of rooftops.

Seeing it all like this makes me realise how carefully the

Babygrows have maintained the streets in the centre of London. Our houses are a small museum to the past. The life we live, full of pristine, gilded furniture and endless recreational facilities, has all been kept in the middle of a lost ruin.

I never used to think about it like that. I only saw what I wanted to see: my home. I used to think of London as a small but strong community, fighting to survive. Now it looks pathetic: a few scattered houses full of people refusing to accept that humanity isn't needed any more, that the world has moved on.

None of it really matters anyway. It's all just – stuff. We're living in an entertainment circus designed to keep us from hurting over the real state of the world. With every silk throw, every gold ornament, every expensive piece of tech, our parents were avoiding having to face the truth.

We leave London quickly, crossing countryside as we fly towards Wales. I try to focus on feeling less sick, watching the shadows of clouds as they drift across the land below. The old agricultural fields are now meadows and forests, full of wildlife. The patchwork pattern of hedges between fields is still visible, overgrown but clinging on. How long will it be before even those medieval human structures are gone?

If anything, the near-extinction of humanity has improved the world. Without billions of humans creating carbon emissions, the Earth is healthier and cleaner than ever. Hard-working armies of bots have restored the planet's ecosystem after it was left in a wreck of rising seas and nuclear waste.

Maybe we should just accept that our time has come. *Homo*

sapiens have reached the end of our branch in the genealogical family tree. For the first time, I don't fear the thought. This might be for the best, after all. It's evolution.

All that's left to do now is bide our time until the end. My existence is just a token gesture, one final attempt to show history that humanity isn't extinct yet.

MyWaves05

Darcy looks just like a little version of **@Rizzz**. She even sits with him and draws now, and she's getting quite good because she's been practising so much. (Of course, her tantrums are all from him too.)

Posted on 18 Sep 2036

> **Rizzz** on 18 Sep 2036
> Replying to **@MyWaves05**
> I will not stand to have my name slandered in this fashion. Her sass comes from you and only you.
>
> > **Blueburnedskies** on 18 Sep 2036
> > Replying to **@MyWaves05**
> > This is so cute! Are you going to teach her dressmaking when she's a bit older, so she has one of your hobbies too?
> >
> > > **MyWaves05** on 18 Sep 2036
> > > Replying to **@Blueburnedskies**
> > > Definitely! She's already helping me choose fabrics for her dresses and dungarees.

MyWaves05

I left my bag on the Tube today, with my purse and Darcy's teddy in it. She's distraught. If any of you are on the Circle line, can you keep an eye out for it, please? You'll make her day. Here's a pic.

Posted on 31 Oct 2036

MyWaves05

If they try to shut this boy down, I swear I will drive to Yorkshire and adopt that child myself. Poor kid.

Posted on 21 Nov 2036

NEWSBREAKING.COM

SINGLE DAD DIES, LEAVES BEHIND BABYGROW SON

The Yorkshire Authorities are in chaos this week after Anthony Potdar, a local father, died leaving behind no legal guardian for his eight-year-old Babygrow son, who he has raised alone since his birth.

As there is no structure in place to deal with an orphaned Babygrow child, the boy has been placed with an ex-foster parent in the local area.

The future of the boy is currently being discussed, as the father left no will with instructions for his son's care. Some are suggesting that the boy should be put up for adoption, while others believe that, without a living guardian, the Babygrow should be shut down.

This debate ties into a global ethical conversation which has been taking place for many years now at the Equality and Human Rights Commission: what is the status of a Babygrow? If they are to be classed as living beings, then shutting down a Babygrow child is akin to murder.

Meanwhile, the Yorkshire Adoption Agency is seeking any friends or relations of Anthony Potdar who may be living in the local area. If you know someone, you can contact the YAA here.

Blueburnedskies on 21 Nov 2036
Replying to **@MyWaves05**
I'm always so worried about this happening to my daughter. My mum is really prejudiced against Babygrows and doesn't see the point of them. I genuinely think if I died she'd just shut her down. Under current laws, there's nothing I can do to stop her.

MyWaves05

Since Darcy's illness, **@Rizzz** and I have become increasingly involved in campaigning for Babygrow rights. Our children deserve to have a future. They deserve birth certificates. They deserve full equality under the Human Rights Act. They deserve to inherit our estates after we die. They deserve a future beyond us. How long after our deaths will they survive? We have no way of knowing unless we change the laws. Please sign this petition to help get these issues debated in parliament.

Posted on 18 Dec 2036

MyWaves05

This just made me cry.

Posted on 4 Feb 2037

NEWSBREAKING.COM

COUPLE CHOSEN TO RECEIVE IVF FROZEN EMBRYO DECIDE TO RAISE CHILD ALONGSIDE THEIR BABYGROW SON

When Derek and John Trentham received the letter of a lifetime, telling them that they had been chosen to adopt one of the last UK-owned fertile embryos, they were faced with a dilemma. The embryos, which came from donors who are no longer living, are only available to those couples without any existing children, and the Trenthams have a nine-year-old Babygrow son, Stefan.

"It took about a millisecond to make our decision," Derek said. "We told the NHS that we had a son already."

"We had no idea whether they'd give the embryo to someone else when they found out about Stefan," John added. "There was no precedent for this that we could find. But Stefan has been our first priority since he was born. There was just no way we would choose any child over him, even a biological one. If the NHS decided to offer the chance of adoption to someone else, then that was a risk we just had to take."

Luckily the fertility council was understanding, and Derek and John were allowed to adopt the baby, Oliva Trentham, who was born last month in their hometown of Norwich. She is only the third biological baby born in the UK this year, and it seems unlikely that another embryo will be released until 2039.

"Knowing that Olivia is one of the few biological babies to be born this year, and that we get to raise her – well, we feel very lucky," Derek said.

Stefan, meanwhile, is ecstatic about the birth of his new baby sister. "She's got blue eyes like mine!" he told this paper, when asked for a comment. "I love her!"

There are now fewer than a hundred fertile ovum left, and a recent global fertility report announced that there has been no progress on solving the fertility crisis. By contrast, the rate of Babygrow births continues to rise each year. In 2036, there were over 450,000 BG births.

Blueburnedskies on 4 Feb 2037
Replying to **@MyWaves05**
Oh, this made me cry too. Of course, I'd do the same.

> **MyWaves05** on 4 Feb 2037
> Replying to **@Blueburnedskies**
> It does make you wonder, though, doesn't it? What is the world going to be like in the future, when the fertility crisis is fixed and people can really have babies again without needing BGs? Do you think anyone will still use the app, for convenience? How many BG children are going to have biological siblings in a few years?

MyWaves05

I've never seen the coding of the Babygrow
software before! This is really cool.

Posted on 22 Jul 2037

NEWSBREAKING.COM

BABYGROW SOFTWARE TO INCORPORATE ALL ONLINE USER MODIFICATIONS

**All Babygrow users will be aware of the online
community focused on creating modifications
to the Babygrow software, in an attempt by
tech-savvy parents to make their children more
human. It was recently declared to be the largest
collaborative project in human history. Some think
that the creation of an artificial intelligence as
complex as our own is as important as the moment
humans discovered fire or invented the wheel.**

It has seemed inevitable for a long time that the
most popular Babygrow-user mods would be
folded into the official software. From this week, all
Babygrows will run using the modifications created
by programmers around the globe.

If you're interested, you can see some of the latest
changes below:

Index: Babygrow 18.0.2 OS – file notes

```
path: root/babygrow-os/scripts/notes-script.php
// 21/06/2037 – Software has been updated with
    all online crowd-sourced modifications. All
    future mods will be fed into this centralized
    system and updated worldwide every Wednesday
    at 00.01 GMT
// 25/06/2037 – Update – BGs now have a
    randomized probability of being ticklish
// 05/07/2037 – Update – BGs with food-processing
    hardware installed will have automated hunger
    pangs if energy levels are running low.
    Battery-operated BGs can continue to only eat
    for pleasure when desired
```

```
// 19/07/2037 - Update - BGs now dream using all
    footage saved in their memory files
// 21/07/2037 - Update - Accent update - BGs start
    to pick up the accents of anyone they spend
    over 10 hours a day with

Require_once("MT/babygrow-OS.php");
```

CHAPTER 27

TIME	DATE	LOCATION	OBJECT	NOTES
12.17	11/07/2108	54.375307, -0.619591	Domed iron shield plate, engraved with Valkyries on horseback. Viking, tenth century.	Found by Alexei Wyatt on a supply trip to the abandoned city of York, and given to Shen for his sixteenth birthday.

By the time we reach North Wales, I've worked myself into a state of anxious vibration. Mitch, in what is presumably an attempt to drive me to distraction, has started making origami swans out of pages from the helicopter's instruction manual. His long, dexterous fingers flash back and forth with a disconcerting clicking noise as he manipulates the paper into elegant shapes, while also keeping an eye on the controls.

"Could you – use something else to make those, if you insist on doing that instead of focusing on flying?" I ask tartly, through gritted teeth. "We might need the manual."

Mitch shifts a few centimetres away from me and slowly rips another page out of the booklet.

Shen bends a glare in my direction. "Stop antagonizing the pilot."

I huff. "Fine. You've got us this far without incident. Carry on."

"If you need a distraction, try and find the vaults," Shen says.

"Their location isn't listed on the mapping software, because it was a secret when it was built. We're going to have to try and track them down the old-fashioned way." He leaves Mitch in charge of flying and comes to sit by me in the back, unfolding the yellowing pages of an old paper Ordnance Survey map of Wales, which I found in the library when I was packing.

I blink at it. The colours and lines are all a bit overwhelming. I've never used an actual map in my entire life, just the navigator on my tablet. We've used maps to Geotag the locations of our mudlarking finds for years, though, so maybe it's not that different.

When we were especially bored, we used to make up scavenger hunts using the maps of London. We would start by giving each other a set of longitude and latitude coordinates to somewhere in the city, where a clue would be hidden. Sometimes the clue was a paper scroll tied to the branch of a tree, or a data chip thrown in a gutter, or – on one memorable occasion – an imitation duck with a message written on its underside in permanent marker. Shen had to wade into a pond to retrieve it. It was amazing. That message would then give another set of coordinates leading to the next clue, and so on. Finally, the Geotagged locations would link up to form a shape on the map. At the very centre, there would be a hidden prize.

It was basically a treasure-hunter's dream – but it takes for ever to come up with the clues. Mum was always the best at it, because she writes them in rhyming couplets, with lots of book references. Feng once made one with chemistry reactivity equations as clues – which was far too hard for me. Shen loved that one, though. One of the clues was "Tungsten reacts with two carbon molecules and one hydrogen molecule to make oxygen and helium. Darwin would disapprove." The answer to that was "$WC^2H = OHe$", and "WC2H OHE" is the postcode for the National Portrait Gallery. The next clue was hidden behind a painting of Charles Darwin.

"Snowdon is…" Shen pauses to unfold three more concertina layers of the map so it stretches across the full width of the helicopter's cabin. "This general area. The vaults could be anywhere here."

"Well," I say, unimpressed, "I guess it's a good job that we're treasure-hunters, then."

Shen grins widely, flashing white teeth. "On the bright side, it is a mountain. We're not likely to fly past it and miss it, even if the entrance is hidden."

I snort.

We start marking places on the mountain where the vaults could be. We decide that it's likely to be somewhere there's a clear access route to a road, and it will probably be placed in a higher section of the mountain, so that they could excavate lots of tunnels.

As we're poring over the map, a question swells up inside me, until it bursts free. "If … if we can't wake them up, what do you want to do?" The idea of not having our families is terrible, but the thought of the long, long future stretching out ahead of me is almost worse. Eighty, ninety, maybe a hundred years where Shen and I are all on our own. With nothing to do. Just time to spare. An endless century before the end.

"What do you mean, do?"

"With … the rest of our lives, I guess."

Shen doesn't reply.

"Shen?" I ask, softly.

"I've thought about it a lot, actually. Over the years. I don't want to just waste my life. I want to feel like I've done something worthwhile." He gives a long sigh. I squeeze his hand, and he gives me a sad smile.

His answer surprises me, though – the idea that he wants to do something worthwhile. I'm not a person of ambitions. Not at all. I live from moment to moment and enjoy the pleasures of life. I don't have lofty goals. But Shen… Of course he wants to make a difference. I should have known that.

"Like what?" I ask.

"I'd like to travel. See all the places that nature has taken over. I'm sure people have left messages all over Earth, in all the old cities and landmarks. I'd like to find them and document them."

Something yanks at my gut. "Would you come back and visit me?"

Shen looks confused and then shocked. "Lowrie, you'd be coming with me!" He laughs, disbelievingly. "Of course you'd be there for everything! What would be the point without you?"

Warmth rushes through me, until I feel like I'm glowing from the inside. "Right. Yeah. Of course."

"Did you really think…?"

"No. Not – not really."

I consider exploring the world with Shen and leaving an empty London behind for years and years until we've seen everything there is to see. It sounds like a good way to deal with losing our family. It might very well be the only way to cope with so complete a loss. Much better than living alone, the last two people in an empty city. We could keep moving for ever, not settling down until we're old and fragile. If there's no other option, that might be a kind of life I could cope with – a tour of the world, to say goodbye on behalf of the human race.

"Could we go to Africa first?" I ask. "To see where the first humans lived?"

"We could start there and work outwards," he suggests. "Retrace the migration path of the first tribes of *homo sapiens* as they left Africa and spread across Europe into Asia."

"It would be like a victory lap." The last humans following the journey of the first.

"We could find the old cities. The first place where language was created, and writing, and maths, and farming. We'd be able to follow humanity's creations across the planet."

"We could even do what they did: plant crops on the same land the first humans did; find a wolf and train it, where they first bred dogs."

Shen sighs, then reaches and twists his little finger around mine. "Let's do it. Let's pinky swear right now. If we can't wake our parents up, we won't sit around moping and crying. We'll pack up our things and fly this helicopter away from here."

"I promise." It would be so bittersweet, that life. I can see how happy I would be, doing those things with Shen. We would see so many incredible, unimaginable sights, but, if our parents never wake up, we would be alone for all of them. I will one day have to watch him die, or him me. And I don't want that. I want family, and safety, and the comfort of knowing I have people to rely on when I'm weak and in need of support. We would never have that out there in the deserted world. Humans weren't built to live alone. We need community.

"What next?" Shen asks, interrupting my thoughts. "After our tour. What do you want to do, Lowrie?"

"I just want to be with you," I say. "And our parents."

"Oh," he says, winded. "No matter what, you've got me. All right?"

"Good. That's sorted, then," I say, grinning widely.

"Nothing else? Really?"

"I suppose a global scavenger hunt sounds pretty great," I say, trying to lighten the mood a bit.

"A global scavenger hunt?"

"Yeah, going around the world finding all the last messages that people have left. We could copy them all and put them in our time capsule. It would be something – something worth doing with our lives, don't you think?" The thought of the time capsule reminds me of Dad's last homework assignment, and I swallow hard. I had no idea back then what was coming. I wish I could return to that oblivious happiness: sitting in the green-house with no more worries than having to pay attention to the lesson. Even if we fix this, that naïve Lowrie is gone for ever.

"Whatever makes you happy, we'll do," Shen says. "Whether it's worthwhile or not."

Tears well up in my eyes because Mum said something similar to me, about the importance of happiness and being with the people you love. Life is the people around you, the ones you love. You just need to be happy. That's all that matters. I didn't realise then that it would be the last piece of advice she'd ever give me.

"It's a plan," I choke out, and Shen pulls me into a tight, long hug. I feel weak and tired, and more prepared, all at once. It's like something inside me has looked directly at the future, faced the worst that could happen to us and accepted it. It's made this all seem so much more feasible.

I can do this. I can save my family. And if I can't, I will make the most of it and carry on being happy anyway.

Finally, we pass through a cloud and enter a curtain of grey rain, and the mountain appears before us: a jagged burst of brown rock and green trees, rising into the sky. The dips of the valleys and peaks of the mountain range stretch out into the distance. It's a sparse alien terrain, draped in mist.

I scan the incline for any sign of a man-made building that might be the vaults. I spot a glimpse of something shining, but it's just a pool of water, reflecting the white clouds.

We fly the helicopter in low circles around the mountain range until finally, deep in a shadow where the cliff face folds in on itself and blocks out the sun, I catch sight of a carved rectangle etched into the rock. "There!" I say, pointing. "That's a door, right?"

Mitch lands on a perfectly flat valley near by – one-handed whilst making a paper crane, which nearly gives me a heart attack.

We hike up the incline with our rucksacks and kit. Even with the light of my headlamp, I still trip up in the dark. Steps have been carved into the rock, with metal rails on either side that must have been used to crank crates up.

"Do you think that valley used to be a helicopter pad?" Shen asks, pointing back at where we landed.

"Would it be that overgrown? Surely it's only been a few decades since it was built."

He shrugs, looking like he wants to say something but doesn't know how to start. I'm too out of breath to try and get it out of him. I packed our scuba gear as well as a fair selection of my tools, and it's making climbing really hard work.

Finally, we reach the doorway to the vaults. It's big enough for a car to pass through and made of heavy concrete painted in camo paint to blend into the rock. There are security cameras on either side of it. I squint up at them. "Is it just me, or does this look ominous?"

"It's not just you. There's a solid chance we may never come back out."

"We're still going in, though, right?"

He grins. "Oh, totally."

As we approach, a hologram flickers into life, making me jump. A fuzzy figure waves at us. His legs are missing, and half his head is in black-and-white. He gestures towards the doorway,

253

stepping closer at the same time. Then the hologram breaks up completely and disappears into a cloud of random light beams.

"Not the most impressive thing I've ever seen," Shen says. He leans back, rolling on to his heels to look up at the projector. "Looks like a tree branch smashed it up. I'm impressed it worked at all."

"Do you think that was going to tell us how to open the door?" I ask, heart sinking.

"We can work it out without the instructions. Probably. You can break into any door in the world, right?"

"Challenge accepted, Zhang."

This is exactly the kind of problem I love. I tie up my hair and then, after a moment's thought, pull on gloves, a face mask and breathing visor. Dad would kill me if I didn't put safety first, even in an emergency. "Put your kit on too," I tell Shen. "This is about to get messy."

The door has been sealed with cement that has been pushed into the gap between it and the frame. Using a chisel and hammer, I chip away enough of it to see where the cement ends and the door begins. This is the first time I've done anything like this without an adult supervising. I think I know what I'm doing – I've done it hundreds of times before – but it's weird, not having someone there to warn me if I forget a step.

I decide to power up my portable angle grinder. It'll be quicker to open up the door using the rotating circular blade than tapping away at it by hand with a chisel. Shen holds his torch up so I can see what I'm doing in the dark.

Dust shoots downwards when I press the blade against the cement seal. It slices through the stone easily, and I work my way around the edge, moving upwards. I'm turning the blade at the top right-hand corner of the door, standing on tiptoes to reach, when I stumble on a loose pebble.

The angle grinder slips in my grasp and the blade skates across the surface of rock in a sparking arc of white light. I fight to catch it, but it's too heavy. It jerks my shoulder, twisting my arm back, and before I can process what's happening, the grinder is tipping back and falling.

I leap out of the way. The grinder narrowly misses Shen, hitting the ground with a crack, sharp blade still spinning.

I breathe heavily through my mouth, unable to believe what just happened. The blade came so close to shearing into Shen's side.

"Shadow—" Shen starts, but I shake my head.

Trembling, I crouch and press the *off* switch on the saw. The whirring blade comes to a stop. "I can't do this."

I walk down the path, kicking at mulch and leaves, furious with myself and terrified of what might have happened. This is the only thing, the *one single thing*, that I can do well, and I'm messing it all up. What is wrong with me? Why am I so useless?

I keep walking until I'm out of sight of Shen, then I twist into an outcropping of rock in the side of the cliff face. I press my hands to my eyes to wipe away hot tears.

I should have found something to stand on, rather than holding a heavy tool over my head. Why am I forgetting basic safety guidelines? I've had them drilled into me since I could speak. None of this is difficult.

What are we doing here? Why are we risking our lives for this? We should be following the emergency procedures that Mum and Dad taught us, not racing off across the country on a wild-goose chase.

"Lowrie," Shen says. I feel a hand on the flat of my back.

"I nearly killed you," I sob.

"I'm fine, look at me," he whispers. "I'm totally fine. You just need to take a breath. Think this through. You can handle this. You do this kind of stuff all the time."

"Yeah, but not on my own," I snap. "Usually someone is here to stop me when I mess up. I could kill us both! I'm not good enough at any of this to be trusted, Shen. Not without supervision. I make stupid mistakes all the time, and I'm not letting you die because of me."

"I trust you."

"Well – I don't!"

Maybe I only ever thought I was good at this stuff because I was practising in an environment designed specifically to make it easy for me. What if I only thought I could do things like scuba diving because everyone made it easy for me?

Everything about my life has made me think I'm special: the youngest girl in the world with parents and friends that love me. It has made me overconfident and tricked me into thinking I can handle anything. But nothing I can do is actually useful, not really. I'm just a pampered brat, totally unprepared for the real world.

"Just tell me what to do," Shen says. "I can help. We can do this together."

"No!" I say immediately. Somehow, needing his help would be worse than admitting I can't do this at all. This is *my thing*, not Shen's, who can do anything he puts his mind to. This is the only thing I have that I'm good at and he isn't. If he takes over and does this without me, then I have nothing at all.

"Leave me alone," I say. "I just – I need you to not be here to distract me. I can do this if you just *go away*."

Shen jerks back, looking hurt. He opens his mouth to speak but bites off a reply. "Fine. I'll walk around the cliff face with Mitch – see if I can find another entrance. Message me if you – if you change your mind, I guess."

I scowl at his back, not wanting him to leave but not willing to call him back either. *Let him go. I can do this on my own. I don't need him.*

I aim a kick at the trunk of a tree and tug a leaf off one of the low-hanging branches, tearing it in half, then in half again. I keep tearing it along the veins until it's too small to grasp, then I use a fingernail to separate the tiny section left into two. When I bring it up to my eye, I can see more veins, on and on and on, smaller than my eye can discern. It calms me down enough that I can think again.

I can't waste time like this. The clock is ticking: we need to get moving if we're going to wake everyone up before their memories are wiped.

I walk back to the door, which is battered and ravaged from

my futile attempts to get inside, and I think carefully about my next step. Maybe Jia and the others couldn't get through the door either. Maybe they tried, and that was why they weren't able to get the parts.

I direct a torch into the gap I've created between the door and the cement. Metal locks at the top and bottom of the door shine in the light. If I cut through the locks with bolt croppers, then I might be able to get the door open without using the angle grinder again. My stomach twists just at the thought of turning it back on.

I wish I'd never sent Shen away. I turn around, determined to find him and apologize, when I see him standing on the path. I rush to hug him, squeezing tightly. "I'm sorry. I do need you. I'm *sorry*. Don't be mad at me, please."

He laughs. "Come on. Let's try again."

We walk back to the door. "I think we need to try cutting through the locks next." It's starting to snow now, and small, white flakes drift past in the wind. Despite this, I'm boiling hot. I peel off my gloves and wipe sweat away from my forehead, leaning against the door as I catch my breath. To my surprise, the door lets out a quiet *beep*.

I spin around, looking at it and then at Shen in surprise. "Did I imagine that?"

He frowns. "No. I heard it too." He looks at my bare hand and takes off his own glove, before pressing his skin to the door.

It beeps again.

"Oh my God…"

"Is that—?"

We both laugh, and press our hands to the door at the same time and hold them in place. The door rings out in a series of high-pitched tones. There's a green flash, and the lock clicks open.

"It recognized our touch," Shen says, awed. "It knew we were here and opened for us."

"It must – do you think it's made that way? To let humans in?"

"That might make sense," he agrees, tilting his head. "A DNA lock maybe? If this place was designed to be found by humans living thousands of years in the future, then they might not understand written or spoken language. The door would need to be able to open on its own – to show them that there was something inside even worth looking at. Otherwise they'd have no idea there was anything here."

"So the lock opens when it recognizes human DNA but not when an animal touches it or a tree falls against it." I say, impressed. I should never have put my gloves on. My safety precautions worked against us.

"This is why Mama couldn't get any spare parts," Shen says suddenly. "They had no way of getting into the vaults! If only people with human DNA can unlock it, then even if they had known it was here, the door would never have let the Babygrows inside."

I blow out a breath. "Do you think – does that mean that for years the Babygrows have been shutting down – *dying* – because they couldn't get at the spare parts?"

I think of the older people in the community who've died over the last few years: Martha, in our choir; Etta, who kept chickens.

Could they have been saved, if only we'd come here earlier?

"Why didn't they bring us here?" I ask. "Didn't they trust us enough to tell us the truth? Did they think we wouldn't love them any more if we knew they were robots?"

"No!" Shen says. "Surely not. No. They must not have known that a human would have been able to get in," he adds, but he doesn't sound that convinced.

Despair creeps up inside me. Why didn't they just tell us? Why didn't they let us help?

I sigh. "I don't understand why the Babygrows weren't also given access. They were their children, right? Surely their parents would have wanted them to be able to fix themselves."

I think of Maya, who had been desperate to make sure that her daughter had equal rights with biological humans. Did that never happen? Were Babygrows always considered second-class citizens? The thought makes me angry and incredibly sad. I am going to have so many questions for Mum and Dad when they wake up.

"Come on," I say. "Let's go inside." I push against the door, but it doesn't budge. "It's stuck. I think we could lever it open with a crowbar," I add, running a finger along the gap between the door and its frame. "It's worth a try."

This time, I make Shen stand ten metres away. "Stay there," I say, glaring at him. "You're not getting hurt this time. Mitch, watch him."

Mitch moves to stand in front of Shen, arms folded over his chest, tapping one finger on his arm. Shen raises his eyebrows but doesn't move when I pick up my tools. Satisfied that he's safe, I start working.

The metal squeals and grinds as I lever the crowbar, but finally the door opens to reveal a long, wide tunnel carved out of the rock and stretching into the dark of the mountain.

"Thank God," Shen says, sagging against Mitch's back. "I thought we'd have to stand out here in the snow for ever."

I roll my eyes at him. "A thank you would be nice."

"I did all the emotional labour, and that's the hardest part," he says, as we strap on our equipment: kneepads, gloves, helmets and rappelling harnesses.

Despite the awful reason we're here, this is the coolest place we've ever explored, without a doubt. I pack my tools back up, wincing at the sight of the angle grinder. I'm going to feel a wave of shame and guilt whenever I see one of those for the rest of my life, I just know it.

I loop the end of my longest rope through the metal delivery rails set into the sides of the steps in the mountainside, before tying the other end to my harness with a bowline knot. If we get lost, this will help to guide us back to the entrance.

"Ready?" I ask Shen. "We need to hurry. It's nearly nine p.m. – your baba has already been turned off for ten hours."

"Let's do this," he says, determined. He adjusts his helmet and rolls up the sleeves of his khaki shirt.

"You look like Indiana Jones," I say, grinning.

"In a good way?"

"In an excellent way."

Shen preens. "You don't look so bad yourself."

I realise I'm leaning into him, one hand on his arm. I shake myself, straightening up. "Let's go over the plan one more time before we go in."

"We find the storeroom, track down the processors," Shen says, marking items off on his fingers. "Get the hell out of there. Then fly home, wake up our parents and demand they tell us the truth about what's going on with them *not being human*, and stuff."

"We've got this! We've been practising for this all our lives!" I hold out my hand, and Shen takes it.

Beside us, Mitch twists in a circle and flashes yellow.

We take one last look at the landscape around us. It's hard to believe that only today we found our parents unconscious. It seems so long ago.

Together, we step into the flooded tunnel.

TIME	DATE	LOCATION	OBJECT	NOTES
15.36	9/07/2108	51.51117, -0.106151	Iron ring of skeleton keys. Nineteenth century.	Found by LMWB, hanging from a hook on a beam in the guardhouse attic. We had hoped it would help us open the mysterious secret passageway but no such luck.

The light from the waterproof torches on our helmets lends an eerie glow to everything, casting shadows over the smooth, machine-carved walls. Motion-activated lights set into the walls turn a pale blue as we walk past, but one by one they flicker and die.

The only sound is the swish of water around our ankles and the rope spooling out behind us. It occurs to me that this is the first time we've ever gone underground without my dad. I'd been desperate for permission to go into the Tube lines without him, but now that we're finally independent, I just miss him terribly.

At first the tunnel roof is covered with layers of white cobwebs, but they disappear after we've been walking for a few minutes.

"This is definitely not a few decades old," I say, thinking of how overgrown the helicopter pad was and how broken the holographic projector had been. Something isn't adding up here. I don't know how, or why, but this place is a lot older than we thought.

We pause at a split in the path, looking between the two routes. Both are smooth and man-made and equally interesting. There's a low howl of wind coming from further inside one of them. Shen turns his head from side to side, cupping one hand around his hearing ear to work out where the noise is coming from. "Shall we split up?" he jokes.

I roll my eyes. "Like either of us are that stupid."

In the end, we choose the left-hand route at random. After a few minutes, we reach a lift that is set into the rock. When we press the *down* button, nothing happens.

"You'd think they'd have realised how quickly a lift would become unusable," Shen says.

"Even if it did still work, I'm not sure I'd trust ropes and pulleys this old," I say. "The lights don't even work any more."

We carry on walking instead. The tunnel slopes downwards, slow and steady, with doors on either side. We stop to open each one along the way. One is full of building supplies, with tools still covered in dirt from constructing the tunnels. There's a giant digger covered in a faded tarpaulin, neatly parked in a chamber barely big enough to hold it. There's a bathroom, full of portable toilets which have long since dried up.

Another room is an old office, full of filing cabinets and desks with trays of faded papers and old computer monitors. The printed text on the documents discussing builders' wages and architectural plans has faded into brown.

It's like an Egyptian pyramid, perfectly preserved just as it was left. I can imagine these rooms being discovered by future archaeologists trying to work out what kind of ancient ritual the computer monitors represented. The god of glowing screens, as Shen would say.

We keep going, passing through the general work area and going into the real storage rooms. The tunnel doubles back on itself occasionally as it zigzags down the mountain. Sand and sludge have formed a soft and shifting floor beneath our feet. I reach out to Shen, and we hold hands for support, sliding our feet along the smooth floor.

The water gets deeper until we're wading through it. Mitch retracts his spindly legs and brings out a set of paddles, swimming alongside us on his belly. Finally, we reach a point where the water is at our chests, and we're going to have to start swimming too.

"Shall we carry on?" I ask.

"We've come this far," Shen says.

My guide rope is nearly at the end of its tether, so I tie a second rope to it and unspool that instead.

After half an hour, the water is so high that my head nearly brushes against the vaulted ceiling as I swim. I start to feel nervous when I stop being able to make out the floor of the tunnel below us.

I'm about to suggest that we turn back and try the other tunnel when I catch sight of a weak light streaming through the murky water somewhere below us. "Do you see that?"

Shen dives to look while I tread water. He comes back up, wiping water from his eyes. "I think there's a side-tunnel on the right. It's quite deep, but it must lead upwards if there's light coming from it. I think we should give it a go."

"I'm up for the risk," I say, shrugging. "There's a light there. That's a better sign than anything else we've seen."

I'm out of guide rope, so while Shen sets up our scuba gear, I wrap the end of the rope around an old light fixture, leaving it for us to find on the way back. There haven't been enough twists and turns for us to get lost. Not yet, at least.

Shen holds my oxygen tank while I hook it over my shoulders. I do the same for him, and we pull on our mouthpieces. Then I kick off the curved ceiling, diving down towards the light. Mitch keeps close to us, his lifeguard protocol clearly making him wary of any underwater activities.

The mysterious light filters through the green. Beams of light drifting through the water were the first thing our ancestors saw, back when we were worms on the ocean floor at the beginning of Earth's history. If this sight was the first thing our ancient predecessors saw, then what will be the last? It should be something as important and unique as that first worm looking at the sun with brand-new eyes.

What if the last eyes are mine, or Shen's? What will be the last thing that we – that any human *ever* – sees? If it were up to me, I think I'd want to spend my last moments looking at Shen.

I turn to Shen, making an *OK* sign. He makes one back.

Mitch extends some sort of clamp from his hand, opening and closing it in his own version of *OK*.

The water gets lighter as we approach the light source up ahead. I'm focused on swimming towards it when I notice a stream of bubbles coming from my regulator. I slow down, reaching up to feel at my mouthpiece. There must be a leak. I turn to Shen, waving to catch his attention, then point at the regulator.

His eyes widen when he sees the bubbles. He points back behind us, wanting me to return to the surface, but I can already tell it's too late. We've come too far. My oxygen is already too low, and I won't make it back before it runs out. The stream of bubbles is getting faster and faster, hissing loudly like a boiling kettle. When I try to pull in a breath, it takes a huge amount of effort to get any air.

I've got no choice but to keep going and hope we reach shallower water quickly. I kick as fast as I can, holding my breath and aiming towards the light.

Shen takes my arm, kicking hard to propel me forwards faster. My lungs are burning, and I fight to draw in any air from the mouthpiece at all.

We're not going to make it. I need to breathe.

The surface isn't getting any nearer and I can't stop gasping fruitlessly for breath, even though I know it's not coming. I feel my vision go black, and then there's a surge of force behind me and we're being pushed down the tunnel at speed. Mitch has his arms around us, and he's driving us up and up and up until finally, finally, I break the surface.

Treading water, I tear off my mouthpiece and gasp and gasp, drawing in oxygen until the dizziness disappears and my vision comes back.

"I forgot the safety checks," Shen says, voice high and panicked.

I shake my head, still fighting to draw in breath after breath, unable to speak. The air is rotten and damp in the enclosed chamber, and I choke on the smell, dry-heaving.

"Lowrie, you nearly – you nearly drowned! Just because I forgot the safety checks!" He's panicking, just like I did outside the entrance, eyes wild and terrified.

I press my hand to his chest. "Then we're even," I say, the words hoarse and tiny. "I nearly killed you too."

"You were right, this was a mistake. We're going to get ourselves killed! What else have I forgotten? What else are we going to – *we can't do this.*"

I told myself the same thing outside the entrance, but now we're here, I'm absolutely certain that leaving would be the wrong thing to do. "No. We can do this," I tell him, "and we will. So what if we've forgotten things? So what if we make mistakes? This is all for our *parents*, Shen. We need to do this for them. We have all the skills we need to do this. We just have to believe in ourselves. And besides" – I try to smile – "we're here now. Going back would be just as dangerous as carrying on."

Shen breathes in deeply, and nods. "OK."

We swim a bit further until the tunnel levels out and we are able to walk through the shallow water, carrying our scuba gear on our shoulders. Once on dry land, Mitch shakes like a cat and draws his flippers back inside his body.

The light we saw through the water is coming from a bulb above a thick steel doorway fitted into the rock face. I call Mitch back from where he's exploring the tunnel ahead. Another DNA scanner is set at eye level. I press my finger to it, and the lock on the door clicks open easily.

CHAPTER 29

TIME	DATE	LOCATION	OBJECT	NOTES
16.10	03/02/2108	50.365506, -4.292160	Medieval reliquary gilt box containing a human toe bone. Eleventh century.	Found by SZ. Fell out of a box of clothing at a jumble sale. Origin unknown.

The door opens to reveal a small foyer enclosed by clear glass walls. I press my face against the glass, shining my torch through it. There's a giant warehouse on the other side. I can make out shelves full of boxes and crates, stretching out into the darkness. It's so modern and new and crisp that it takes my breath away.

I can't believe that this tidy storage unit can exist just metres away from a flooded stone cave. The part that I can see must be three football pitches long, and this is just one vault. Who knows how many huge caverns have been carved out of the rock to build the warehouses? What kinds of engineers designed this place? These caves must have undermined the whole structural integrity of the mountain. If I'd designed it, I would have kept the rooms long and narrow instead.

"There's no door," Shen says, pacing up and down the small foyer. "How do we get at the stuff?"

An ancient bot is activated by our presence and rolls towards us, chittering in welcome. I reach out and rub its head. It blinks, pink lights flashing across its screen as if it's blushing.

Mitch walks up to it, flashing something back at it with the lights on his head.

The bot, clearly delighted, lights up in a firework display of colours in reply.

"Shen! They're talking to each other!"

"They must have the same software," Shen says, grinning. "Neither of them can speak in beeps, so they're using the lights instead."

"Mitch must have been so lonely," I say, suddenly sad. "Not having anyone who spoke his language for all these years."

None of our bots speak using lights like this. No wonder Fitz and Mitch never got on. Mitch kept trying to copy the beeps he made and then ended up having to hang around with the dogs instead.

We watch the bots circling each other in joy, both using a complicated pattern of flashes and colours.

"Do you think that's why Mitch has been hanging around with us?" Shen asks. "Because he was looking for someone who understood him?"

"Maybe." My heart pangs.

The bot flashes at us, and I suddenly notice that there's a screen on its back. It looks like it's designed for humans to use.

I crouch down, looking at it carefully. When I tap the screen, it displays rows and rows of symbols. I squint at them, trying to work out what they mean. There's one I recognize – a picture of an apple – so I tap on it.

From somewhere in the darkness inside the warehouse there's a low grinding noise. Shen and I stare at each other, alarmed but intrigued.

We press up against the glass. I shield my eyes from the glare of the light, trying to see what's happening. A case has separated from the other shelves and is rolling towards us on a set of tracks. When it reaches the glass, it turns and rolls to the side, slotting against the wall. A hatch clicks open. Shen reaches inside and pulls out a handful of paper packets. I take one. It's ice cold, like it's just come out of a freezer. There's another symbol of an apple on the front. When I tear the packet open, small brown seeds spill out into my hand.

"We use the bot to ask for what we need," Shen says, delighted. "Just like the door – they didn't know what language the people who found this place would speak, so they made a system that uses pictures instead."

"Hieroglyphics!" I roll the dry seeds between my fingers. "When I tapped the picture of food, it brought us seeds."

"We just have to work out what the symbol for the Babygrow parts would be, and it'll fetch them for us."

"It can't be that hard," I say but doubtfully. "This place was built by humans just like us. They'll have used the same kind of symbols we would. Right?"

I kneel back down beside the bot and scroll through the other pictures on the screen, trying to work out what they represent.

Most of them are meaningless lines and shapes that I can't make sense of, until I see one that looks familiar. "That's a plough!" I say. "We found one at the river once, remember?"

And it's like that's the key which unlocks the code images for me, because I start to recognize dozens of items – all things we've found while mudlarking. There's a triangular shape that looks like an arrowhead. There's a woman in a dress and a little boy in shorts, holding hands. I think that must represent clothes. A thin screwdriver that looks like a dentistry tool. A button and zipper. A lock and key. A paint pot and brush. A spade and pitchfork. A clock. A book. A pen and pencil. A plate and bowl, knife and fork. All of them are essential items that have been used by humans for millennia.

"Whoever built this must have really been hoping the sterility would be cured, so this stuff might be used." This is a starter kit for life as a human being.

"It still might be," Shen says.

I shiver. "I don't think so. Do you?"

"No." Shen is quiet, arms wrapped around his chest.

"I think this whole place was a waste of time and money. Humanity is done for. Why is this even here?"

"They couldn't just give up. They kept fighting, right up until the last moment, just like us. I don't blame them."

"Let's get out of here as soon as we can," I say. "I can't stand it. It makes me too sad. Look for a picture that might represent electronics. A phone or battery, or something that might symbolize the Babygrow parts."

Shen taps on an image of a lightning bolt. The case full of apple seeds retreats back into the darkness, and after a moment of grinding, another box rolls up to take its place. The new crate is full of cables and wiring but no circuit boards.

"I think we need to be more specific. We need Babygrow parts rather than just generic electrical items," I say.

We try a few other symbols that seem related to computers, but none of them give us what we need. After the third attempt, I sigh. The image must be here somewhere. I need to think like Maya. What would she list the Babygrows as, if she was going to choose a symbol?

I notice the symbol of the lady and her son again, as Shen scrolls past it. Now I'm looking more closely, I can see that there's a little lightning bolt on the boy's T-shirt, just like the symbol for circuits. That could mean a robot child, surely. That would make more sense than clothing, anyway.

"That one," I say, tapping at it. "What if that's, like … family?"

The symbol expands, revealing a whole interface of other parts. They confuse me for a minute, until I recognize the plastic chest unit I opened in Alexei, and realise they're parts. Each symbol represents a different Babygrow part, from the full body kits to replacement components.

"The Babygrow parts are listed under family?" Shen repeats, stunned. "They did love the Babygrows, if they saw them as family… But then why didn't they let them inside the vaults?"

I frown. "It doesn't make any sense, does it? Plus, I've been thinking: Maya's posts make it sound like almost everyone had a Babygrow. So where did they all go? Why are there only three hundred of them left?"

"Something must have happened to them. Maybe there was another malware a while back that wiped them all out? We aren't going to find answers here. We need to fix our parents so they can explain everything."

"Right," I say, shaking my head. I scroll through the pictures of parts, skimming past the limbs and heads and cooling fans until I reach the smallest symbols, including some for tiny parts that are no bigger than a pea. I search for the one that looks similar to the burnt processor – round, with slightly angled edges. I tap on it.

The crates roll away again, and this time when they return, I know that we've chosen the right thing. The new box is full of processors, enough to build hundreds of new people. They are each so small and intricate that I'm relieved I don't have to try and make one from scratch – even with a magnifying glass, I think it would ruin my eyesight to try to solder one of these things.

"Got it!" I say, delighted.

When Shen and I high-five, the bot flashes pink and swivels in circles.

"Do you want to come with us?" I ask the bot, crouching down. Mitch is going to be so sad if we leave without it. "We can take you home with us. No one comes here any more."

The bot turns to Mitch, and they exchange a series of silver and gold lights that look to me how I imagine falling in love must feel.

"Soulmates," I whisper, but Mitch hears me and flashes orange, offended.

Shen sighs. "That was the most romantic thing I've ever seen."

Ignoring us, Mitch crouches down and scoops up the bot, before tucking it inside the storage drawer in his chest.

While we're packing the processors into our bags, Mitch keeps pulling the bot out again and flashing something at it in a series of lights, then waiting for a reply before putting it back. It's the sweetest thing I've ever seen.

"How are we going to get the parts out of here?" I ask. "There's no way we can swim with them. They'll break if they get even a bit wet."

"We'll find a different way out. I don't want you to risk using your scuba gear again anyway. There must be another way out without going back the way we came."

We finish filling our bags and haul them over our shoulders. I let out a wheeze at the weight. We've taken more than we need, just in case.

"We did it!" Shen says, sounding a bit amazed. He tugs me into a one-armed hug, reaching out to fist bump Mitch's shoulder at the same time.

We leave the warehouse, turning left instead of going back to the flooded tunnel on the right. We walk uphill, following the tunnel as it twists back and forth, until we turn the corner and come to a stop. The ceiling has collapsed, filling our path with stone and rubble.

CHAPTER 30

TIME	DATE	LOCATION	OBJECT	NOTES
22.41	07/04/2109	53.083409, -4.109218	Supplies of spare parts for the "Babygrow" body kits.	Found by SZ, LMBW and Mitch.

"*Tamade*," Shen swears hoarsely. "Shall we go back?"

I shake my head. "Do you feel that?" I ask, holding out my hand. There's a cool breeze blowing from somewhere up ahead. "If air is blowing, we must be close to an exit. The air has found a way through."

I walk along the wall of rock, keeping my hand out, trying to find the source of the wind. It's coming from high up on the wall, where there's a small gap between the ceiling and the pile of rubble. I climb up the rocks to peer through. It looks like it's just wide enough for me to squeeze into the narrow tunnel beyond. I can't tell how long it goes on for – far enough that my headlight can't reach the end, anyway.

"Maybe it leads into a chamber above this one," I say, climbing back down to Shen. "Like a natural cave or something. The builders who excavated the tunnels must not have known about it. They probably made the ceiling too thin and the roof collapsed inwards from the pressure."

"Do you think it's a way out?" Shen asks.

I shrug. "It could be. We should give it a go, anyway. You said yourself that you're worried about my scuba gear. This might be our only option."

"Maybe we should see if there's another route."

"I don't think we have time, Shen," I say. "Let's at least try this. It might save us a few hours, and we want to get back as soon as we can." It's eleven p.m. Finding the processors didn't take as long as I thought, but we have a lot of people to fix, and I have no idea how long it will take to replace each part. For every hour we spend here, that's another person in the community whose memories might be lost.

He agrees, but I can tell he's reluctant. I scale the rocks again and look into the tunnel. The crawl space looks even narrower now, but I'm sure there's just enough room to work my torso inside. "I'll go first," I say.

"Careful," Shen says. He climbs up the rubble to give me a leg up, and I pull myself into the opening.

As I wriggle in on my belly, the loose rocks shift under me. It's even tighter than I thought it would be. My chest and back scrape against the rock whenever I breathe out.

"OK?" Shen asks, his voice muffled. His headlight beam passes in front of me, casting my shadow into the tunnel ahead.

"Tight," I call back, "but OK."

He squeezes my ankle, and releases me. I rise up on to my elbows again and slide further into the space. My neck hurts from holding my head low enough to avoid hitting the roof. Slowly

I drag myself on, centimetre by centimetre, fingers creeping forward against the surface.

A metre or so in, a rock juts down from the ceiling. To get past it, I have to bring my arms back to my sides and twist my head and shoulders, pressing my cheek against the stone and easing through. There's no way to push myself forward except with the tips of my toes. I slither on, staring at the stone wall just in front of my face. I close my eyes, making my way through by touch. The rush of air into my lungs is roaringly loud in the silent space.

I'm nearly past the obstruction when my shoulder brushes against the rock, dislodging it slightly. I rear up in fright, convinced that the whole mountain is about to come down on top of me. My helmet smashes into the roof, filling my ears with a loud bang. It feels like the walls are squeezing in on me, making the small space smaller and smaller until suddenly I can't breathe.

"I can't – Shen, get me out! *Get me out, now!*" I scream, trying to turn around, but there isn't enough space. My breath is coming out in juddering gasps.

Two hands close around my ankles, sending warmth spiralling through my frozen body. A voice says calmly and quietly, "You can do this, Lowrie. I believe in you."

I sob. I'm breathing so fast that my back is scraping against the ceiling constantly, rubbing my skin raw through my clothes. I can hear a low grinding noise, and I can't tell if it's my bones working in my jaw as I tighten it in fear – or if the whole mountain is shifting above me, threatening to collapse and press me into nothing but rock.

"I can't! *Get me out get me out get me out!* I'm trapped!"

"You're not trapped," he says. His voice is steady, like this is totally normal. Why is he not terrified too? "I'm right here – ready to pull you out at any moment."

"The rock, it's – it's shifting! I'm going to—" I'm desperate to turn around, to look behind me and see what's happening. I imagine rock falling, cutting me off from Shen, leaving me alone in the darkness, without light, unable to move a muscle. "Shen, *please!*"

"It's in your head," he soothes, rubbing at my ankles. "The rock is stable. It's OK, it's OK. You've got this, Lowrie. You're OK."

I breathe through my nose, trying to calm down. He's right. I can do this. I'm so close. Now that I've relaxed a bit, I can even make out the chamber ahead with the light of my headlamp.

I'm so close to getting out of here. All I have to do is carry on a little further, and we'll be free and safe.

I have to do this. For Mum. For Dad. For Jia and Feng, and everyone else we know.

"Do you want me to pull you out?" Shen asks, as my breath slows down, grows calmer.

"No. I can do this."

I close my eyes and push myself forward, navigating by touch alone. Shen's fingers slip away from my ankles, and I hear him cheer me on. His voice buzzes in my ears, loud and encouraging.

The crawling goes on for ever in a slow, careful easing forward. Stopping for breath. Moving a bit more, stopping for breath. I start to panic again when I realise I've moved far enough inside the tunnel that Shen can't reach me any more to rub my feet. But I take deep breaths and keep going.

The surface is covered in a thick mulch of bird feathers. Pigeons must roost here. It's another sign that we're close to the surface. When my fingers reach the rock edge of the crawl space I'm unable to bear it for even a second more. I yank myself forward, scraping my torso along the rocks as I tumble out into the chamber.

I slump to my knees, gasping. I feel absolutely battered. I seem to be bleeding from every centimetre of skin. Pain shoots down my neck from when I hit my head, and my knees are numb.

"Lowrie?" Shen shouts, sounding high-pitched and worried.

"I'm OK!" I call back, looking around the chamber. It's even larger than the man-made tunnels. The walls are rough compared to the smooth machine-carved vaults. It's definitely natural. "Throw me the end of the rope?" I shout. "Tie the rucksacks to your end. I'll drag them through."

Once I've done this, I shout to Shen again. "Can you get through?" I ask.

"I think so. Are there any big obstructions?"

"Not any more. I knocked most of them aside." Next time, I think I'll push something in front of me to clear away the rocks. Then nothing can fall on me. Even better, I could send Mitch in first. He would have been able to scout ahead. I wish I'd thought of that before.

Shen moves more quickly through the crawl space than I did. He's not as scared, and he can pull himself forward using the rope tied tightly to this side. When he clears the crawl space, he's pale and dusty, with thin scratches covering the skin of his jaw and neck.

I immediately collapse against him, burying my head in his shoulder and letting out a muffled scream. His hands come up and wrap around my back. "I've got you," he says. He presses a breathless kiss to the side of my brow.

I lift my head to look at him.

"Breathe in," he says, pursing his lips as he takes in a long, slow breath. I follow it, latching on to his rhythm like a lifeline. "Breathe out." Shen holds me in place until I finally feel fit to move. "We're nearly free," he says then, pressing his thumb to the corner of my eye and rubbing away the damp tears clinging to my eyelashes. "It's over, Shadow."

I carefully brush a line of dirt from his cheek, bracketing his face between my palms. "I thought I'd never get to touch you again. I was so scared."

He smiles. "I'm not going anywhere."

Suddenly I know it's true. I don't need to worry about what might happen when Shen and I are left alone. It's already happened, and we're fine. We're still together, and I know now that there's nothing I could do that would make him leave me. Even if we got together and broke up, we'd still be in this together for the long haul.

So instead of letting go, I keep hold of his hand, interlinking our fingers and squeezing tightly.

There's a noise behind us, and I look through the tunnel to

see Mitch fold himself up into a smaller sphere and then roll through the tunnel.

"You are so creepy," I say, as he unfolds into his normal form. "Who *designed* you?"

Shen grins at us, looping the rope around the length of his forearm to pack it away.

Mitch reaches out to stroke the side of my face with a cold thin metal finger, slowly and intentionally weirdly.

I shiver, pushing him away with a laugh. "I'm pretty sure you have a sense of humour. A bad one but still."

Shen isn't listening. *"Lowrie,"* he says, sounding amazed. "Come and look at this!" He's moved further down the chamber and is staring at the rough stone wall. There's something drawn on the rock: slashes of red against brown.

I gasp. "Is that…?"

"Yes." His voice is trembling.

The walls are covered in red ochre line drawings of dancing figures and four-legged animals, painted in rough strokes and curved smears, surrounded by ancient handprints.

I realise I'm crying. This cave hasn't been disturbed in thousands of years. These drawings have been waiting in the dark, long forgotten, for thousands of years. I try to imagine the cavemen who drew them. I wonder if they had a language yet. I wonder if one of these mammoths was their god.

"Oh," I sigh. "Oh, *Shen.*"

He turns and wraps a palm around the back of my head, pulling me into a kiss. It feels natural, unquestionable. It's not dramatic or romantic. When or how we started this has never mattered, not when it's so inevitable. This is where we've been leading, all this time.

His mouth tastes dusty, with the distinct tang of minerals.

The kiss doesn't last long, and when he pulls away, we're silent, looking at the art and taking it in for long seconds that we can't really waste. But it seems wrong to leave straightaway, after we've found something so rare.

"Do you remember – before any of this, when we were talking about what humanity's last message to the future might one day be?" I ask.

He laughs. "Yes! And I thought that it would be cave paintings, because they'll survive longer than any of our buildings."

"Here it is. Humanity's last message."

Shen shakes his head, shadow trembling in the light from our head-torches across the years-old art. "This is getting a bit deep for me. We've not even got out of here yet."

"Well, at the very least I'm going to have to change my homework," I say, looking around at how dry the cave is. "I'm going to hide my time capsule in a cave, instead of burying it."

Shen kisses my neck. "It could still get flooded, though. Look at the vaults."

"OK, well – not a cave on Earth, then. One on the moon! That wouldn't get the slightest bit damp."

Shen looks up. "Wait, that's it! Space! What if we put a time capsule on a satellite? It could be designed to orbit the earth for years and then crash-land back on the planet at a certain point.

That would draw people's attention to it."

"*Ooh*. OK, you win. That's genius." I wonder absently where we might be able to get a satellite. I'm sure we could find one in an old warehouse somewhere. And if it really is just us left, for ever, then we have to leave a message somehow. One that will last into the future. For the octopuses.

Shen sighs. "I don't want to leave."

"We'll come back."

I'm crouching to pick up our rucksacks when I see something sticking out of the dusty silt on the cave floor. I tug it free, brushing away the dirt. It's a roughly carved stone figurine of a woman. She fits perfectly in the small of my palm. The face is coarse, but I can see the slash of two eyes and a mouth. I can even see the shape of her braids, running down her back. She's wearing her hair just like I wear mine.

"Shen, *look*." I hold out the small statue to him, and he cradles it between his hands. "It's…" I'm so overcome that my voice is shaking, emotion rising up through my chest and bubbling out with my words. "If it was made by the same people who painted these walls then this might be over *thirty thousand years old*."

I picture a girl sitting in this very cave, carving the statue one careful tap of stone at a time. It must have taken years; an entire life. It must have been her most treasured possession, and her children's, and her children's children's, passed down through the generations, used to tell fireside stories, maybe even worshipped.

Shen has gone pink. "This is older than civilization itself. Older than language. Older than agriculture. Older than domesticated animals. Older than writing. Older than *anything*."

I shiver, unable to stand the pure impossible time of it all.

I want to ask him to kiss me again, but that's not a step I'm confident enough taking yet, so it's easier to just lean in and press my lips to his, the ancient figurine pressed between us. The kiss is sloppy this time, more joy than focus. Shen lets out a little laugh into my mouth, fingers squeezing mine around the stone figure.

"I think we just found the ultimate treasure," I say. "That's it. There's no beating this. We can resign as treasure-hunters."

"Absolutely *not*." He nips at my lip, kissing me again and sighing. "I can't wait until this is over, so we can do that properly."

"We're so close!" I say. "Step one complete!"

Shen groans, tipping his head back and rolling it to the side to stare at me. "Don't put it like that. I'm exhausted – literally *drained of life*: pushed to the very limits of my endurance. And you make it sound like we've only just started."

"Well, we're *nearly* there."

"Soon we'll be able to tick *'save the world'* off our to-do list, then."

I grimace. "You know I don't keep a to-do list. Live fast, die young."

He winces. "Please don't. I need you to survive this, so I can teach you the joy of good list-keeping." He lets me go.

I want to push him against the rock and relearn the taste of his lips, but we have to keep moving. We don't have time to stay here all night, and I'm sure that's what would happen if I gave in to the urge to kiss him again. I keep catching him looking at my lips. I trail my hand down his forearm, interlinking our fingers. "Let's go home."

CHAPTER 31

TIME	DATE	LOCATION	OBJECT	NOTES
00.04	08/04/2109	53.083409, -4.109218	Limestone female figurine tinted with red ochre. Upper Palaeolithic, estimated to be from 30,000 BCE.	Found by LMBW.

The cave entrance is at least twenty metres above us, so we're going to have to climb up the rock face to get out. The rocks are loose and flake away under my feet as I grip on to the stone and pull myself up.

"Just pretend it's the wall of the east wing," Shen says, looking pale. "We climb stuff like this all the time."

"It's totally the same," I agree, not believing it at all.

"We've got this." Shen starts climbing.

I'm about to follow him when a slice of stone collapses below him. He quickly jumps away, swinging on to more solid rock.

"The east wing never did that!" I say.

He grimaces.

I blow out a long breath. "OK, then."

"We've got this," Shen repeats, but he sounds less certain this time.

We climb with Shen in front and Mitch bringing up the rear.

We're at about the height of the roof at home when there's a deafening creaking sound, and the rock around us starts shaking. Something above me snaps and a sharp stone breaks free from the cave ceiling. It falls past my hand, tearing open my glove and scraping the skin off my knuckles. Groaning, I tug off the scraps of ruined glove. My hand is slick with blood.

The whole cavern is shaking now, making it hard to hold on. I can hear the sound of rocks falling, hitting the cave floor far below. I try desperately to ignore it and keep going. We're so close to the exit, just one more foothold and we'll be free.

Another stone is dislodged from the roof of the cavern and nearly hits Shen. My muscles are screaming in pain, but I focus on pulling myself up as fast as possible. Mitch extends his legs and arms, bracing them on the rock above and blocking us from the torrent so we can climb. I can hear the crack and snap as the stones hit the robot's back. Whole slabs of rock are breaking off now, tumbling past us in shards the size of doors.

I grab on to the edge of the rock above me, feeling the brush of fresh air against my fingers. I tumble out and twist, grabbing Shen's forearm and pulling him through the hole after me.

We're just in time. There's another groaning creak and the roof of the cavern collapses completely in an avalanche. Mitch disappears beneath the rock. There's a screech of metal, a glint in the darkness, and then silence.

"*No!*" Shen shouts, horrified. "Mitch!" he sobs. "Is he…?"

I can't speak. There's no way Mitch could have survived that.

Mitch sacrificed his life to save ours. He died so we wouldn't.

I close my eyes, tears leaking out to run down my cheeks.

We're both shaking. We hold each other, waiting for the shudders to end, for our bodies to calm.

"We have to get back to the helicopter," Shen says finally. "Come on. Save this for later. We have to get home to our parents. Mitch wouldn't want this to all have been for nothing."

I turn and look at our surroundings through eyes filled with tears. We're on top of the mountain, breathing in clean air, wet with rain. The moon is bright tonight, and the stars shine in a sparkling expanse of glitter stretched out across the sky, framed by the range of hills. I can't help thinking of how pleased Mitch would have been to get out of the caves, how he would have gambolled around us, golden lights flashing on his head. He had only just found a friend, and now both of them are gone for ever.

We stumble on trembling legs back to the helicopter, leaving half our kit behind. I want to be somewhere with soft seats and warm air.

As soon as we climb into the cabin, I drink a bottle of water from the fridge in one long gulp. Then I take a deep breath. I can feel a great wave of grief and fear threatening to roll over me. I push back against it, refusing to let it overwhelm me, and turn to kiss Shen again.

I can't – *won't* – think about anything but him – about pressing him up against the dashboard and touching his cheek, his lip, the curve of his eyebrow.

He holds me tight by the hip and mouth, and keeps attempting to talk into the kiss, mumbling half-words about the helicopter and the flight, but I feel desperate and tender all over, and I don't pull away. Eventually his words dissolve into nothing but noise, his mouth sliding over mine, soft then hard and so much more instinctual than I'd imagined it would be.

Fireworks skitter through my stomach, and I let my fingers drift into his hair, smoothing through the short strands at the back of his head. He twists his fingers in the grey patch at my temple, bracing my face between his hands.

He bites my lip, and my hand jerks in surprise, accidentally tugging at his hair. He gives a full body shiver, right there in my arms. I can feel my mind going deliciously blank, every memory of where we are or what's just happened disappearing in the face of adrenalin and *Shen*.

I have an urgent need to rub the dirt away from his forearms until I can see the blue veins under his skin, the ones I've always wanted to run my tongue along. He shivers again when my fingers graze the knuckles of his hand, touching the raw pink scrape of skin he always chews on when he's nervous.

"Come here," he says in a low voice I've never heard before, and kisses me again. This time it's less desperate and more intent, with all of Shen's focus directed on just me.

I make a keening noise I didn't know I could make and tip against him until we slip down on to the seats. I lie half in his lap, half braced on the headrest.

He makes a gratifying noise and touches my stomach gently, murmuring, *"Wo xiang yong yuan zhe."*

A flush runs over me. I don't need to know what he's saying. I can tell from the way he says it.

After a while he speaks again, this time in English. "Helicopter," he says, sounding drunk. "Home."

"OK," I agree. However much we both want to carry on kissing, we have to go home. Now isn't the time for this, not when Mitch gave his life to make sure we got the processors out.

I carefully remove myself from his lap, not quite sure how I ended up there and press the controls to turn on the engines. Shen's hand remains on my collarbone, touching it lightly with the tips of his fingers. His eyes are fixed on it like he's trying to memorize the feel of the dip and swell.

I clear my throat, watching a pink blush spread down his neck and ears with interest. Somehow my hand has found its way to his chest and is rubbing across the lines of muscle over his ribs.

By the time the helicopter takes off, his fingers are tangled in my hair again, and we hold each other tight, curled together against the pain of losing Mitch, until we land in the hospital car park with a jolt.

MyWaves05

Today a new boy joined Darcy's class at school, and he's biological. We hadn't really explained to Darcy what that means, and what she is – so when this boy asked Darcy if she was "real" like him, it resulted in some very interesting questions after school.

Posted on 22 Mar 2039

Blueburnedskies on 22 Mar 2039
Replying to **@MyWaves05**
Oh jeez, I remember that. When we told
Hailey, she asked when she was going to turn
into a human like us. Nearly broke me.

> **MyWaves05** on 22 Mar 2039
> Replying to **@Blueburnedskies**
> Darcy was very quiet at first, but she's been
> asking questions about it all night, so we can tell
> she's processing it. I made sure I told her how
> much we love her, and that the whole reason
> she exists is that we wanted a baby so much we
> had to make her from scratch. Hopefully that
> will be enough to stop her getting too upset.

> > **Silentstar** on 22 Mar 2039
> > Replying to **@MyWaves05** and
> > **@Blueburnedskies**
> > Jason had nightmares for a while when he
> > found out. He kept waking, thinking that
> > wires were spilling out of his mouth while he
> > slept. I wish we'd never kept it a secret – that
> > we'd just talked about it openly ever since he
> > learned to speak. It's too much of a shock to
> > find out something like that, even if we think
> > it's more than a baby can understand.

MyWaves05

The biological boy in Darcy's class has been
getting bullied. They're best friends, and it's really
tough seeing how quiet he's become. He was such
a character when he was younger. But clearly
he's finding it hard to be among only Babygrow
classmates. Does anyone have any tips for how
to deal with the bullying? Darcy keeps asking me
what she should do to stop the others from going
after him, but I don't really have any suggestions.

Posted on 20 Jan 2040

MyWaves05

Today I was getting my car MOTed, and was chatting
to the mechanic about nothing much when I realised

he was a BG! I hadn't even noticed! I'd never been served by a BG before. I knew that some of them were eighteen now and starting to get jobs, but actually meeting that young kid working at my local garage brought it home. This is our world now. Babygrows are becoming adults. Wow.

Posted on 19 Sep 2045

MyWaves05

This is complete prejudice. It should not be acceptable for news sites to publish and promote this kind of vitriol in the year 2046.

Posted on 16 Aug 2046

THENEWWORLDPOST.COM

INTERSPECIES DATING: SHOULD BABYGROWS BE ALLOWED TO DATE BIOLOGICAL HUMANS?

Our opinions editor says NO.

Babygrows are robots. End of discussion. Would you date a bot? No. You'd be outcast from society as a pervert. The Babygrows might mimic humans, but that's all they are – a copy.

It's creepy for so-called "parents" to pretend that they're the real thing, and even more so for partners of the bots to do so. It's like having your own personal sex doll that someone raised as a child – gross! Count me out.

Humans should date other humans, and robots should not be programmed to experience romantic attraction at all. Nothing else is acceptable in a modern society. I'm sorry, but it's true.

TIME	DATE	LOCATION	OBJECT	NOTES
10.09	31/12/2108	51.501244, -0.141826	Mont Blanc "Meisterstück 149" black-lacquer fountain pen with gold nib, engraved with curlicues, circa 1924. Bic ballpoint pen, transparent white plastic with red cap, circa 2011.	Found by LMBW. Both pens were discovered down the back of a mustard-yellow leather armchair in the second reading room.

We're running inside the hospital before the helicopter's rotors have even stopped spinning, sprinting straight to the ward where our parents are, with the rucksacks full of computer chips. Everyone is still laid out where we left them. We don't have long before their memories are wiped for ever. We're going to have to move fast.

"Let's try it on Baba first," Shen says. "If it works, he can help us fix the others before we run out of time."

I nod, slightly breathless with nerves. What if I mess this up, like I did with opening the door to the vaults? What if I kill Feng? If this doesn't work, Shen and I are really going to be alone for the rest of our lives. Somehow, the thought doesn't feel as terrifying as it did at first. I think we could handle it. I think we could survive. It wouldn't be good, but I would learn to live with it.

I lay out the new processor and my toolkit. I run through the process in my mind twice before I touch anything, then double check a few things online. Finally, I explain to Shen exactly what I'm going to be doing, more to hear it out loud than so he knows what's happening. "I think I'm ready," I say finally. My palms are sweating, but I feel confident.

I was rushing when I tried to get into the vaults. I was fuelled by adrenalin, and not thinking straight. This time I'm more prepared, more cautious, more determined to do this right.

I remember every lesson Feng and Dad and Mum and Jia have ever taught me. I take a deep breath. And I pick up my screwdriver.

It takes five hours to fix Feng. When he opens his eyes and smiles at me, I have to turn away and bite back tears of relief. "Hi," I choke out. "How are you doing, Feng?"

"You did it," he gasps, as Shen hugs him, holding him tight. "How did you—?"

"We got some spare parts," Shen mumbles, pulling back. His face has gone pink. "Are you OK? Does it hurt?"

"I can't feel a thing." He cups Shen's cheek and leans over to squeeze my shoulder. "You did an excellent job."

"We learned from you," I say, trying not to cry. I still can't believe that I managed it, even though he's awake, talking to us, touching us. *We fixed him.*

"What time is it?" he asks.

I check the time. I'm completely disorientated myself. I feel like I've been awake for weeks. "It's seven a.m. You had a seizure at my house, at eleven yesterday morning. Do you remember?"

He frowns. "Not really. I remember helping Margaret at the hospital."

"We have to wake up Mama now," Shen says, before we can carry on talking.

Feng rubs his eyes, visibly gathering himself. He stands up. "All right. Let's get everyone else fixed up, shall we?"

Between the three of us, Jia is awake within three hours. It's quicker now I know what I'm doing, now that I trust myself to do this right. Finally, I wake Mum while Feng and Jia fix Dad.

And then it's done.

Mum pulls me into her arms as soon as she opens her eyes. "Darling," she says, smiling so widely her cheeks might crack. "You saved us?"

I burst into tears. "I'm so glad you're back."

Dad doesn't let me go for a long time, pulling Mum close too and holding us both tight. "What happened to you?" Dad asks after a while, brushing a thumb down my cheek as he hooks an arm over my shoulder. "Why are you covered in scratches?"

I choke on a laugh. "So much has happened – I'm not quite sure where to start! We got the processors to fix you from the Snowdon vaults. It took … a while."

Jia lets out a sigh. "I knew there would be some parts in there. We've never managed to get inside. I was going to try again, but I ran out of time. I never expected the virus to spread so quickly."

"The doors to the vaults needed human DNA to unlock," I explain.

She lets out a long exhale. "Of course. Why did we never think of that?"

"You mean, it wasn't that you didn't trust us to open the entrance for you?" Shen asks. "We thought maybe you didn't … you know … want to ask us to help you get inside."

"What? No!" Jia says at the same time as Dad asks, "Why would you think that?"

"You didn't tell us you were robots!" Shen says indignantly.

There's a long silence.

"Shall we go and get a cup of tea?" Feng asks eventually. "You look as if you need one immediately."

Shen and I meet each other's eyes. Shen's head is resting against Jia's chest as he's cuddled ferociously. "I think we've waited for the truth long enough," he says. "Here is fine."

Our parents exchange a glance, then Dad gives a curt nod. "Maybe we should have told you as soon as we started getting sick. But we … we…"

"We wanted to protect you for as long as possible," Mum says.

"Protect us!" I almost shout. "By *lying* to us?"

Jia flinches and Shen puts his hand over mine, in a calming gesture. I draw in a deep breath.

"We're the only ones left, aren't we?" Shen asks.

Jia nods. "The history you were taught is correct. Humans really did stop being able to conceive in 2024, and the only children born after that came from frozen eggs."

Mum picks up the story from Jia. "Before they all died, human scientists worked for decades to solve the infertility. But eventually they realised that they wouldn't be able to fix the problem in their lifetime. They knew that an artificial intelligence would need to fix the infertility instead."

"They turned to the Babygrows, didn't they?" I ask. "I read about them online. While the biologists were busy trying to bring back babies, everyone else in the world was programming robotic children of their own. They made a whole generation of babies completely from scratch, just so they had something to love."

Feng nods. "We are the Babygrow generation. Jia and I had already met and married when my human parents died. When Jia was asked to join the UK fertility research team, I emigrated here with her. We were assigned to the London branch, which is where we met your parents."

"We were later models," Mum says. "I was created about forty years after Feng and Jia. My parents were some of the last to die."

I eye her, surprised, trying to see if she's different from Feng and Jia in any way. Her body kit was exactly the same inside, when I was changing her processor. I suppose Feng and Jia must have had upgrades as the Babygrow system improved, like Darcy did.

"Doctor Ahmed and I worked alongside the last biological scientists until they died," Jia says. "There used to be more Babygrows, but a lot of them decided to turn themselves off after the last humans died. They didn't want to stay around in a world without people. We've been using the parts from their dismantled body kits to get by, but the parts are nearly all gone by now."

"You decided not to shut yourselves down?" I ask, amazed at the idea of Mum and Dad trying to contemplate what seems to me to be suicide. They must not think about it that way, but to me, that's exactly what it sounds like.

Jia nods. "We decided to stay awake so we could try to fix the infertility. We couldn't stop, not until we'd found a way to give our parents the grandchildren they wanted."

"So where did we come from?" I ask.

"Eventually our research reached a point where we needed to test our theoretical progress on a living human, to see if we'd managed to fix the infertility. So we spent several decades developing the technology to grow a human clone in an artificial womb, using the DNA samples we had complete genetic profiles for. There weren't many that were complete, but we had enough samples to clone two humans."

"That's – that's us?" Shen asked.

Feng goes silent, and Dad replies, "No, son. That was in 2204. Three hundred years ago."

We both gasp, horrified.

"But then—"

"How can—"

Dad holds up his hands. "I know this is a shock. You're actually the fifth generation of test subjects. We've been working to bring back humans for the last three hundred years, ever since the last human died. It's actually 2509, not 2109."

I blink, trying to take this in. Humanity has been extinct for three hundred years, and we had no idea? I can't even process it. No wonder all the buildings and tower blocks are collapsing around us. They're even older than we thought they were. It's amazing that London is still running at all. "Why have you kept this a secret? Why not just *tell us*?"

"There were lots of psychological issues with the first generation, who were aware of the circumstances of their birth," Jia says. "They couldn't handle the knowledge that they were the only members of their species. Since then, we've been very careful to raise the children in an environment as human as it is possible to create. That's why we lied about the real date – so you wouldn't work out you were the only biological humans."

Shen bites at his cracked knuckle and starts pacing up and down.

I sit on one of the hospital beds, staring at a painted mural of a meadow full of bunny rabbits. Everything they're saying makes sense somehow. What's more upsetting is that they still think they're going to be able to save humans. Even after hundreds of years of research, they can't see how pointless it is.

Humanity's gone. We lost. The end. Even cloning more humans doesn't seem to be an option, if they barely had enough complete DNA profiles to make me and Shen. If the technology for cloning had been perfected while humans were still alive, then maybe the population could have been kept steady that way, but it's too late now.

"I don't understand why you're still trying, to be honest," I say, scrubbing my hands down my face and across my eyelids.

Suddenly I'm completely, utterly, overwhelmingly exhausted. I want to fall asleep, right here in the ward. "From what you're saying – it sounds like you've spent three hundred years wasting your time."

Mum raises her eyebrows, looking over at Jia.

I ignore them, and carry on. "There's no way you're going to resurrect humanity now. You might as well give up and enjoy your lives. You can't spend all of eternity raising and testing endless sets of humans. I mean, we appreciate the effort and everything. But it seems kind of … hopeless."

Dad is hiding a smile behind his hand, but the others look horrified.

Shen squeezes his mama's hand. "You shouldn't think of it as a failure. You aren't our servants who only exist to try and bring humanity back. Your parents raised you as their children. They'd want you to be happy."

I breathe out through my nose. "Let us go. We're not that great anyway. Let us be the last."

MyWaves05

Darcy starts university next month! She's studying art and design at Nottingham. We're so proud of her – she's following in her father's footsteps! Any tips on the best bedding/cutlery etc. for hall rooms? It's been a long time since I went myself!

Posted on 16 Aug 2051

> **RomanceLass** on 16 Aug 2051
> Replying to **@MyWaves05**
> Hi – university professor here! I've been getting questions like this a lot now that more and more

BGs are heading off into the world. Make sure she signs up for the government student loans – they'll help support her body kit maintenance, which can get a bit of wear and tear in Freshers' year while she spreads her wings! I'd also recommend she gets a really good diary and to-do list app, to make sure she doesn't get overwhelmed when she's trying to juggle social, academic and family life.

Also, I love that she's studying a creative field. Not many BGs do, because scientific topics come a lot more easily to them. She must have creative parents who put a lot of time into developing her artistic skills – good job!

> **MyWaves05** on 16 Aug 2051
> Replying to **@RomanceLass**
> Thank you SO much for your help – you're a life-saver!

MyWaves05

60% of the staff at my hospital are BGs now. It's really great, seeing this new blood come in. I've heard a few rumours about BG bullying in the workplace from older generations who've not had much interactions with BGs before. It's sad – I'm 50, but I still feel like one of the young ones!

Posted on 16 Jul 2055

> **Silentstar** on 16 Jul 2055
> Replying to **@MyWaves05**
> Bigots. My Jason has had some of that. He works in programming, and apparently the rest of the (fully biological) team think it's strange for a BG to work on software advances for Babygrows – like he wouldn't want to help to fix the flaws in his own system? It's ridiculous.

MyWaves05

Ah, this list brings back memories. I'm feeling so nostalgic now that Darcy has moved out. I'm definitely getting some empty-nest syndrome!

Posted on 24 May 2057

12 MOST ICONIC BABYGROW SOFTWARE UPDATES

To celebrate the 30-year anniversary of the Babygrow, we're sharing our favourite mods for everyone's favourite software.

12 – The Mod that Wasn't

Lasting a grand total of six hours, this BG update back in 2041 sent all children into unstoppable hysterics before being recalled. The constant laughter occurred after an inaccurate calculation massively overexaggerated the parameters of the humour sensitivity.

Read more

MyWaves05

My daughter surprised us all by announcing at dinner that she's applied to become a police officer. It was unexpected, but it makes a lot of sense in hindsight. She's always wanted to help people. I was a bit worried that 28 is quite old to start a new career, but she said that everyone else in training is a similar age.

Posted on 4 Oct 2061

MyWaves05

What a milestone. It's so cool to think that a lot of us were the early BG adopters. Look how far we've come since then!

Posted on 16 Apr 2070

BABYGROW GENERATION OFFICIALLY OUTNUMBERS BIOLOGICAL POPULATION

Today the UK census results were announced and officially confirmed what has been suspected for a while now: there are more adults aged 18–45 who were created using Babygrow software than those who were born naturally.

There haven't been any UK biological births for the last two decades. The last biological child was born in Canada three years ago. It doesn't seem likely that the fertility issues will be fixed in time for the statistics to be reversed any time soon. Meanwhile, the babygrows are filling a vital void in the healthcare industry, which desperately needed professionals to care for the ageing biological population.

On a personal note, this site is soon to be run by an entirely Babygrow-populated newsgroup, as our last "bio", our opinions writer, is due to retire this week as she turns 75. You can leave her a goodbye message here.

CHAPTER 33

TIME	DATE	LOCATION	OBJECT	NOTES
11.22	10/01/2109	51.471419, -0.261938	The enamel face of a carriage clock, cracked diagonally, with one gilt brass hand still in place. Marked with Roman numerals and the name Putham + Sons. Nineteenth century.	Found by SZ blocking up a hole in a shed roof. Has been rescued and is now being used as a bookend.

We go home, leaving Feng and Dad to wake up everyone else. We managed to save them all. It's hard to believe we really did it. It doesn't feel real.

The first thing we do when we get home is take Victoria and Albert, who've been home alone all night, for a walk. Even when you find out that your species has long been extinct and everything you know is a lie, life goes on.

I expect things to look different now. But even though everything about our world has changed, my home is still the same as ever. I walk through the halls, staring around me with fresh eyes, like I'm in a dream. Three hundred years older than I thought. Three *hundred*?

When we get back from our walk, Shen and I do our traditional standing-at-the-fridge-door-eating-everything-we-can-grab.

It's nearly three p.m., and I haven't eaten anything other than a hasty ham sandwich since the day before. I was too distracted kissing Shen in the helicopter to even think about food. Shen and I haven't mentioned the kisses since then, and the thought of discussing it makes my stomach flip over with nerves.

When we're full, and the kitchen bots are beeping at us in fury, Jia ushers us upstairs. She makes Shen and I have baths before she inspects our injuries. The water is completely brown with dirt and dust and blood and sweat by the time I get out.

"I think you'll live," she declares after giving us both full medical check-ups.

"Jia, can I ask something?" I say carefully.

"Of course, poppet."

"You know the vaults? Why did the locks not let Babygrows inside? Surely the people who made them must have had Babygrow children."

Jia sighs. "I'm sure they did. But it never – how do I explain this? It never occurred to them, or us, or anyone, that the Babygrows would ever be the only ones left. We are designed to be used by humans. We exist to give them children. The idea of us being here after all the humans are gone – it was just unimaginable. There's no point to us without them."

"But that's – that's awful!" I say, aghast. "They loved you. Why wouldn't they want you to live on without them? How could they lock spare body parts away from you like that?"

"It's not a matter of love," Jia says. "It genuinely wouldn't have occurred to them. The vaults were designed to stay closed for thousands of years until they were needed by humans far in the future. The idea that Babygrows would still be around by then doesn't make sense. Either humans would be able to have biological children again, and so there would be no need for Babygrows, or humans wouldn't fix the infertility and we'd all go extinct. There's no third option – where only Babygrows would still be around thousands of years from now. There was never a future where we would still be here to even need to get inside the vaults."

"There should be a third option," Shen says fiercely. He's been listening quietly up until now. "That's wrong. You make it sound like you're some kind of servant or convenience. That's not what you are at all."

Jia cups his cheek. "Our parents needed us, and we were there for them until the day they died. That is what we were for. That's something to be happy about, not get upset over. Now, get some sleep, both of you! We can talk about this tomorrow. You've had a busy day." She kisses us both on the cheek and leaves.

Shen and I stare at each other. It's the first time we've been alone together since we kissed – since we did so much kissing, after I'd tried so hard for years to do none at all. I've already forgotten how to kiss him. It felt so easy in the heat of the moment, but now it feels impossible. What if it's not as good as last time? What if it was adrenalin and beginner's luck, and now it'll be just awkward and painful and wet (and the wrong kind of wet, not the nice shivery kind)?

Although last time I was covered in dirt and dust and blood

and he still wanted to kiss me. Maybe even if I have forgotten the general process of kissing, he'll still want to do it.

We stare at each other some more, until finally, Shen huffs a sigh and pats the space next to him – he's sitting on the end of my bed. I reluctantly sit down by his side, staring straight ahead.

He leans in and hesitates, biting his lip. Summoning my courage, I turn towards him and then reach out and hook a finger into the collar of his plaid pyjamas, pulling him in the last centimetre.

He exhales against my lips, bringing a hand to my face and hovering above the skin, like he's not sure if he's allowed to touch me. I tilt my head, pressing my cheek against his hand.

I'm close enough to see the hairs on his lower lip, the scarring of old spots on his nose. I breathe in the scent of mint from his mouth, waiting for the grossness to kick in. Now that we're back home, I expect the instinctive *this is Shen, what are you doing!* fear to take over. But there's nothing except warmth and surprising ease. I lean in, pressing our lips together. When my lower lip catches between his, I almost gasp. It's too much, too intimate.

Shen sighs into my mouth, and I feel the warm tip of his tongue skim across my lip. My whole body relaxes. I twist closer, reaching up to wrap my hand in the front of his shirt. His fingers slip into the soft, thin hair at the back of my head, and he tugs, just enough to encourage me in the right direction.

Shen sucks on my lip, then does that thing with his tongue again: small touches and long, wide swipes. When his teeth nip at the skin around my mouth, a moan bubbles out of me. It rises up my throat and crosses from my mouth to his. His tongue dips into the gap between my front teeth.

I pull away and wipe at the tender dampness of my mouth. "Good. Good, that was – that was good." I wince. Why did I say that? What am I going to do next, mark him out of ten?

"Yeah," he says, voice grinding like pebbles on a beach. I catch sight of the vivid red blush of his lips, roughened by our kiss. "Good work, team." He sounds slightly stunned, like he also hadn't thought it would work the second (third? fourth?) time around.

It definitely worked. My stomach is still twisting over itself.

"Do you want to – shall we get into bed?" I can't look away from his lips. Why can't I look away from his lips?

He turns to me with wide eyes.

"To sleep," I add quickly.

"Oh God please yes," he says in a rush, like I said the sexiest thing in the world. "I'm exhausted. I'm – I think I'm about to pass out right here, actually."

I wriggle my way into the smooth silk sheets with a newfound appreciation for the luxury of non-cave, non-helicopter surfaces. Earlier I placed the ice-age figurine on my dressing table, next to the locket that Mitch found.

There's an empty space in front of the fireplace where Mitch should be, and it hurts my heart. I only knew him for a few days, but it felt like he was part of the family. I roll over, turning to face Shen, so I can't see the lonely hearth. It's strange to have him in my bed for real, instead of as a video call. I can feel the weight of him tugging on the bedding. It's nice.

"What do you think the original Lowrie and Shen were like?" I ask.

"What?" He lifts his head. "Sorry, can we swap sides? I won't be able to hear you if we lie like this." I snort and roll over him so he can take my side. This time, he lies down with his hearing ear facing upwards. I repeat my question in a whisper.

"I don't know. Nice, I think." Shen's hand slides across the sheets and wraps around mine, lacing our fingers together. "Your donor must have been very beautiful."

I'd wondered for a while if Maya might be my DNA donor, but I don't think she was. The odds alone make it implausible. I like the idea, though. I smile at the ceiling. A golden cherub smiles back.

Out of all the buildings in London and the world, I wonder why Mum and Dad still live here. What kind of person would I be now, if they'd chosen to raise me in a normal terraced house instead of Mum's ancient ancestral manor? Would I have appreciated what I had, instead of taking everything for granted?

Maybe if I hadn't been given my every desire at the very moment that I wanted it for my whole life, I would have thought to question my world a little more. Shen too. We might have noticed all the secrets and fake histories a lot sooner, but keeping us happy kept us oblivious, living from day-to-day in an entertainment bubble.

I'm sure Mum and Dad didn't do it maliciously. They loved me and wanted me to be happy – so they gave me the world. But I never needed the whole world. I just needed them. That was always enough.

I suppose the opulence does suit Mum's personality exactly, though. I can't imagine her anywhere else other than here.

"I hope our DNA donors knew each other. I can't imagine having to live without you."

He breathes in. "Lowrie..."

"We haven't had any time to talk about what this is, between us," I say, soft and quiet in the warm comfort. I'm not sure if I'm allowed to call this a relationship yet, but I think that if Shen is anything, he's the opposite of the kind of person who runs at a sign of commitment. It isn't possible for me to say anything here that might make him think I'm moving too fast. There's no such thing.

"I love you," he replies immediately. "I've always loved you, my whole life, ever since we were children. I didn't think this was what you wanted, so I never said anything. But I've always wanted this."

"You have?" I whisper, unable to believe it. "But – you can't have done. When did you realise? Have you always known?"

He closes his eyes. "Not consciously but deep down, yes. I saw you sitting on the patio one morning last summer in those flannel pyjamas, hair unbrushed and Victoria in your lap. You were wrinkling your nose as you forced down a cup of coffee. The kind you don't actually like but make yourself drink because that's what grown-ups do. And that's when I knew I wanted to wake up every day seeing you like that."

I close my eyes, drawing in a long, shuddering breath while I try to memorize every word of his reply. When he reaches out to cup my cheek, I look at him again. "I feel the same, obviously.

I didn't want to do anything about it for a long time, though. I was scared that if we did this and it failed, I'd lose everything. It felt safer to not try. But of course I love you too. And I'm ready now. I don't want to waste any more time."

Shen's eyes fill with tears. He leans forward and touches our foreheads together, aligning our noses and finally our lips. We kiss until my mouth feels sore, until my breath hitches.

"How did I nearly miss out on this?" I whisper.

"I would have waited. I would wait for ever for you. You feel like home to me, Lowrie." Shen curls around me, pulling the duvet over us. He speaks into the darkness, slowly weighing each word before setting them free. He tells me all the things he must have kept hidden for years and years, waiting until the day I was finally ready to hear them.

"You're rooted so deeply into me, into the person I am – my opinions and sense of humour and feelings – that I think if you were torn away from me now, there would be nothing left of me at all," he says, voice sleep-soft and heavy, utterly relaxed. Not even one part of him is scared of revealing his heart to me. He trusts me completely, like he knows on some deep subconscious level that I would never hurt him, not even by accident.

At long last, I realise how wrong I was to be scared of this. I could never lose Shen, no matter how hard I tried. He's mine, and I'm his, and that's never going to change. Not if we're the last humans on the planet or just two of billions. I am him, and he is me. Regardless of heartache and romance and friendship, that's how it's always going to be.

OBITUARY OF RIZ STEVENS

It is with great sadness that the family of Riz Stevens announces his passing after a brief illness, on Saturday 7th May, 2090, at the age of 85 years. Riz will be lovingly remembered by his wife of 60 years, Maya, and his daughter, Darcy.

Riz was a passionate advocate for social change and spent years campaigning for Babygrow equality. In his spare time, he enjoyed drawing, baking and keeping chickens.

Those who so desire may make memorial donations in memory of Riz to the Gender Identity Research and Education Society.

pcdarcymw

I'm very sorry to announce that my mother Maya
Waverley passed away in her sleep last night at
the age of 93. She was a beloved mother, wife and
social activist, who made multiple changes to the
political landscape of this country. Her funeral is
being held tomorrow at 12 p.m. Please contact me
for details if you would like to attend. – Darcy

Posted on 30 Dec 2098

TIME	DATE	LOCATION	OBJECT	NOTES
23.19	08/04/2109	51.501244, -0.141826	*The next generation.*	*Found by LMBW.*

I jerk awake from a deep sleep with an idea. I stare at the ceiling, turning it over and over, evaluating it to make sure it holds up.

The answer for how to preserve a message for the future wasn't in buildings or underground. It was in technology – in a satellite. It was something different and unexpected, something that would never even occur to you unless you let yourself think outside the box. That's how we're going to find a way to end the infertility. Not by plodding along doing the same research and experiments that have failed thousands of times already. But by trying something new. Something technological.

I'm not clever. I'm not ambitious. But I am patient. I can spend hours staring at sand, searching for the spark of gold. I can polish my tools until they shine. I have determination. And there's the pearl of an idea in my head that I know will come clean with just a little bit of polish.

I let the idea sit in my brain and pull up Maya's posts, reading the last of her entries. When Riz's obituary, and then hers, are shared by Darcy, I can't stop tears slipping from my eyes. She felt like a real friend. I'm going to miss her.

I have so many questions I wish I could have asked her: what was it like being in a relationship with a trans guy? Did people assume she was straight, like they will with me because I'm with Shen? How was she brave enough to fall in love when she thought the world was ending? But she's long gone. She's been dead for hundreds of years. I'll never get that chance.

Her last post is a message to her daughter. I can barely control my tears enough to read it.

MyWaves05

I don't really post here any more, but I thought
I'd make an exception as it's my daughter's fiftieth
birthday today! Darcy, I have never been so happy
as I was the day you were born. I never thought
I'd be able to have a daughter – but I knew from
the first moment I held you in my arms that I
would die for you. I still would.

One day, if the scientists find a way, I hope that
you will be able to have children of your own. You
might then be able to understand the depth of the
love I have for you. Happy birthday, darling.

Posted on 19 Sep 2083

The idea I've been polishing in my mind grows clearer, glistening like a jewel. Babygrows are children. They aren't some temporary solution, designed to keep people happy while fertility is fixed.

They are the answer.

I asked Mum the other day what the point to any of this was. Why we lived here, kept London going, if it was all going to go to rubble in a few years anyway. I couldn't see the point of us being alive if it was all going to end whatever we did – whether we lived good lives or bad lives or wasted our lives doing nothing.

I know the answer. If you think that the world is going to end after you've gone, then you're not trying hard enough to find a way to live.

I realise now that every person can make a difference. However small a change, it counts. Maya never stopped trying to make the world a better place for her daughter. She tried every single day, until the moment she died.

If I thought that life wasn't worth living, it was because I hadn't found the way I could change things yet.

But I know now what I have to do. I can't sit here, quiet at the end of the world. I have to fill the world with noise. I have to shout and fight and give everything I have to make sure this isn't the end.

I might fail, but that's OK. Because what's the point of living, if you don't try? That's what makes the Babygrows human, more than anything else. They've been trying for three hundred years, even where there's no hope. They haven't ever given up, even long past the point they should have done. What's more human than that?

Shen stirs next to me. "Were you whispering?" he asks.

I flop over to face him. "Shen! Yes! Listen! I've been thinking about extinction!"

"Oh, joy," Shen replies mildly.

I take his hand. I'm almost trembling with excitement. I can't sit still. I jump out of bed and start to pace up and down. "I think I know what we have to do."

318

"What are you talking about?" Shen rubs his eyes. "What time is it?"

"I don't know, it's, like, eleven or something. It doesn't matter! Listen – they've been trying to solve the fertility problem for hundreds of years, and they've never come close to finding a solution. Clearly, they aren't going to solve it any time soon. But it doesn't matter – they don't need to. They've been doing completely the wrong thing!"

Shen sits up. He's fully awake and paying attention to me now. "What are you saying?"

I jump on to the bed and kneel in front of him, face to face. "The Babygrows, Shen. They're the answer. The future of humanity isn't biological. It's robotic."

Before the last human died, all of the brainpower on the planet was dedicated to creating human personality software – through the Babygrows. Each one of them has the personality of their parents. The last generation of humans made children who enjoyed the same things as them, who laughed at the same jokes, who had the same hair colour and shade of skin. Feng and Jia's parents were Chinese, so they are Chinese, and they have raised Shen to be Chinese too. Everything important – everything real – was passed on, even if it wasn't done genetically.

That's what no one else has realised. Humans did find a way to carry on their species, but it wasn't through the biology and cells that the Babygrow scientists have been messing with in the lab for all these centuries. People around the world worked as one, without even meaning to, to preserve all of their quirks and

individuality and humanity in code. They made artificial offspring, each one as varied as humans were.

"What if the Babygrows are the next stage of evolution?" I say,
voice trembling. "They aren't just here to try to bring the real
humans back. It's them. They're the answer." It's the two of us
that are the anomalies, perched on the handover point in Earth's
history.

Shen tilts his head. "Apes, humans, robots. Each step more
advanced than the last. It makes a strange kind of sense."

"The paintings in that cave aren't going to be the human creation that survives the longest. The Babygrows are! We never
considered a sentient kind of legacy. One that can evolve. Robots
are our message for the future." I lean forward and kiss him,
unable to resist. "The Babygrows are the next generation of
humans. They just don't know it yet!"

I am not human because I have a brain made of cells and
water and iron. I am human because I think in the same way
that my ancestors thought. I feel like they felt. I live like they
lived. However much my world has changed, however different my day-to-day life might be, that much is true. I think in
the same specific, unusual way as my great-great-great-to-the-
infinite-power-grandmother on the plains of Africa, with the
same cunning and intelligence and speed that gave her the abil-
ity to survive long enough to have children and pass on her genes.

That's what evolution is, when you get down to it. One person
who finds a way to do that one thing: reproduce. It's why the
world is full of crazy, unimaginable creatures, like eight-legged,

320

colour-changing membranes that breathe water. The octopus found a way to live long enough to pass on their mutations, and they did that over and over again, generation after generation, and they're still alive today.

The last generation of humans had to try harder to survive than any person before them. Their usual way of reproducing failed, but they did what every living thing does, and they found a way to carry on their line. They made the Babygrows so they could pass on their niche, their way of thinking: the essence of their species.

They evolved.

The Babygrows became the next phase of a species that's existed for millions of years and that I have no doubt will exist for millions more. That is what being alive means. That is why the Babygrows are alive. Because whatever humans are, at our essence, they are it.

Shen's creatures from the Cambrian age – the eight-metre-long millipedes with pincers – failed to survive. They're a joke now, a crazy fossil that we find in the rock and can't believe ever existed. Humans aren't like that. We aren't a dead end in the evolutionary chain, a future fossil that will serve as an example of what not to do if you want to survive. We are adaptable. We are intelligent. We are worthy of being alive. We are humans.

CHAPTER 35

TIME	DATE	LOCATION	OBJECT	NOTES
11.17	09/04/2109	51.507611, -0.121833	Crowd-sourced open code for Babygrow software, created by the last generation.	Found by LMBW.

The next morning, there's a community meeting. The room is full of familiar faces. Everyone woke up when their processors were replaced. Dr Ahmed was even able to replace Alexei's wiped memories with a backup. He's lost a year of memories, but he survived with nothing worse than a firm lecture from Dr Ahmed about backing up his hard drives more often. Hard-drive backups are apparently compulsory due to something called the Waverley law, which was introduced in the twenty-thirties after a Babygrow child nearly lost their memories. Maya made a difference, after all.

I can't help looking around the room at all the people with their familiar strange quirks that I've known all my life and wondering which traits they inherited from their human parents and which they developed for themselves over hundreds of years.

I'm helping to pour tea when I accidentally knock over a jug of milk. A cleaning bot rushes over to mop it up as I grab a washcloth. "Sorry! I'll do it," I say. "Don't worry." I'm on my knees, wiping up the liquid, when I realise that this is something I would never have done a few days earlier. It's only now that I know the truth about Mum and Dad and the other robots that I've stopped assuming that the bots will tidy up after me.

I squeeze the milk into the empty jug, frowning. Why did I ever think that was the case? Why did I feel entitled to the bots' service? It feels so tasteless now. I have no more right to their service than they would have to mine. Mitch was my friend, not my servant.

"How are you doing?" Mrs Maxwell asks me, while I pour her a cup of tea from the refreshments table.

"I'm – good," I say, surprised to realise that it's true. "How are you?"

"I'm excellent. And how's your dad? Is he OK?"

I grin. I'm pretty sure half the women in London have a crush on my dad. I once overheard the knitting circle describe him as "rugged". "He's, er, very well."

Mrs Maxwell and I turn to inspect him in a moment of mutual observation. Dad catches us looking and raises his eyebrows in awkward acknowledgement, then goes back to hiding in the corner.

"How are your hens?" I ask Mrs Maxwell, as she takes a biscuit.

"Very well, thank you, love. Maya has been laying the most enormous eggs recently, I don't know how she manages it."

I jolt, eyes widening. "Maya?" I ask.

"Yes? She's named after my mother."

I clear my throat. "Is – is your first name Darcy?" I ask, hardly able to believe it's possible.

"Yes, dear, it is! Why?"

"I – I've been reading about your mum." I can't believe it's her. I gape at her, amazed. This is Darcy. Maya and Riz's Darcy.

Darcy fumbles the biscuit, dropping it on to her saucer. "You have?"

"Shen and I found her purse in the Underground, and I started researching her. She actually helped me save you all."

"She – how—"

"We wouldn't have known to replace the processor if you hadn't had those seizures when you were little. Do you remember?"

Darcy blinks. "Goodness. That was a long time ago."

"Maya seems like she was an extraordinary woman. Your dad too. You're really lucky."

Darcy smiles. "I miss them very much." After she hugs me, I push another biscuit into her hand.

"Are we ready to begin?" Jia asks, standing at the front of the room. Everyone grabs their mugs of tea and settles in to listen to her talk through her findings.

I try to focus as she goes over the minutes of the last meeting, but Shen takes my hand and starts tracing the lines of my palm with his thumb, absently running his fingertips over mine and dipping down between my fingers.

A shudder runs down the back of my neck. I stare at his lips, open-mouthed, wishing very much that I could kiss him.

We have always touched a lot – hugged as easily as breathing, napped side by side, leaned our heads on each other's shoulders when lessons got boring – but now that we're together, the touches have suddenly multiplied. Today, he always seems to have a hand on me, trailing across my shoulder as he walks past where I'm sitting; brushing the hair back from my face absently; resting a hand on the small of my back as we walk. It's a different kind of touch, somehow more meaningful than our puppyish childhood cuddling.

I tune back into the meeting when Jia says, "We've managed to isolate and destroy the malware so that it won't break down our new processors. I've also updated our antivirus protection to guard against similar mutated malware attacks. We should all be safe in the future."

It seems impossible that such a small thing could have done so much damage. Evolution is always a matter of chance: a minuscule game of odds that somehow, improbably, pays off. So many species don't make it. They survive for a while until some act of chance ends them for ever, like the meteorite which wiped out the dinosaurs.

I have a feeling we'll survive whatever fate throws at us next too. Humans are lucky. Luckier than we deserve to be, probably. Luckier than any species has any right to be. But for now, at least, we can make our own luck. And I'm going to make sure that we choose to live.

"Thank you, Jia," Feng says. "And thank you, of course, to Lowrie and Shen. They saved us all."

325

A sea of heads turn to look at us, where we're sitting in the third row back. I wave at them, and call out, "We're just glad you're all OK!"

"Now, we have some maintenance jobs that need volunteers," Feng goes on, "then I'll let you all get home. It's been a long week. Firstly, there are two bots we want to retrieve from the Snowdon vaults. They were destroyed while helping to save us all, so we want to extract their hard drives and house them in new body kits. Is anyone willing to help assemble them?"

Shen and I instantly shoot our hands in the air, thrilled. Mitch and his friend are relics of an old world, just like me and Shen. We need to bring them back to us.

"Very good, very good. Next on the list… Mr Fields is looking to adopt a tabby cat. If anyone is expecting kittens soon, please let him know. I think that's all we need to discuss today. Thank you for coming, everyone," Feng says, nodding to dismiss the gathering.

I meet Shen's eye. We need to speak now, but I'm scared. I don't want to mess this up.

I always thought I was the confident one out of the two of us, but the truth is that I've been a coward my whole life. I've been too scared to trust myself to do anything. I was too scared to be with Shen, in case it failed. I was too scared to live my life the way I wanted, in case I let someone down. I was too scared to let myself learn the things my parents needed to teach me, in case I wasn't clever enough. I couldn't even open the vaults without having a scared breakdown.

All I thought I was good for was studying the past and finding and preserving lost things from the river. But now I know that I can do so much more than that, and that even if I mess things up along the way, it doesn't matter. Because doing anything is better than doing nothing. Trying is progess, and that's all you need to keep going.

The Babygrows have been trying for three hundred years to fix human infertility and they've never given up. How can I even think of not trying, in the face of that determination?

So even though I'm still scared, I stand up, and say, "Actually, before you leave, Shen and I have something we want to say to you all."

Shen adjusts his cuffs nervously.

I take his hand, pulling him to his feet and looking at the familiar faces of everyone I know. These people have taken us ice skating and swimming; they've invited us round for banana bread and sleepovers. Shen and I can do so many things, because they've taken the time to teach us their hobbies since we were old enough to walk. I'd be a different person completely without them. I doubt we'd have managed to rescue them at all without the skills they taught us. And it's time for me to give something back to them.

"We've been talking," I start and then stop. Shen squeezes my hand, reassuringly. I decide to just come out and say it. "We think that you're the next stage in evolution. Humans have gone extinct, and they need to stay that way."

A wave of muttering and shifting passes through the room.

Before anyone can interrupt, I quickly say, "You have just as much right to be alive as humans did. You're not just here to bring humans back from the dead, or fill in the gap where biological children should have been. You're real people."

I have to shout to be heard above their voices. "You've all been the best babysitters possible for Shen and me. But you don't have to just be babysitters. You can be parents too. When we were at the vaults, we saw boxes and boxes of parts. There are enough body kits there for everyone here to have a baby – more than enough. Enough for generations of Babygrows. And when they've run out, we can make more! You shouldn't be living without children because you're waiting for the sterility to be fixed. You shouldn't be dying when your body kits break. The population should be growing and growing!

"If you all have children, and they all have children, then in a few decades the whole world will be full of people again. That's the real way to bring humans back. Not by messing around with cells in a lab. But by raising children, the way your parents would have wanted you all to do." By the end, I'm yelling above everyone's objections.

Mum stands up, and says loudly, "Let her finish!"

There's something about her tone that makes them all fall silent.

I turn to her, pleading. "Mum, you said once that the point of being alive was to be happy with the people you love. And that the thing that made you happiest was having me. Well, do you not want everyone else to have that too? Don't they deserve that? Mum, Dad, Feng, Jia – you are the lucky ones. You got to have children. But everyone else here deserves that too, including Shen and me.

"We were alone while you were all unconscious. It was awful. It didn't feel like there was any point to living at all if we were the only ones. If you don't let us do this, if you take this away from us – when you said yourself that the only point of being alive was to love – then you're not the people I thought you were. And if you don't give yourselves this – if you don't admit that you deserve to be happy and share that happiness with children of your own – then maybe I don't know any of you at all."

Whether I want to admit it or not, I have a legacy. A heritage. As a human, and a daughter, and a descendent of some very intimidating ancestors, I can't ignore my birthright.

I was always scared of my responsibility. I didn't want to think about the people that depended on me, because I didn't know how to help them. But I know now how to fix this, and I want to do it. For Maya and Riz, and for my grandmother, who raised Mum from a doll in our attic and called her "daughter". For the parents of every single one of the people here.

I owe them this. They deserve it. Their legacy needs to continue, not just for a few more decades until the last of us dies or breaks down but for ever.

My ancestors didn't work so hard to build this amazing, crazy civilization just for it to end. Cavemen didn't draw on walls or walk on beaches so that they would one day be forgotten. People didn't spend generations creating techniques to extract ore from the ground and then turn it into breathtakingly beautiful necklaces just so we could return to the ground again.

Our culture is unique. It's incredible. If there really are aliens or octopuses out there that might find our cities one day, I want us to be here to show them everything in person. To explain it, not just leave pens and bracelets and bottles behind in the ground for them to find and wonder at.

If we need to change to metal skeletons and electronic brains to last that long, then that's what we're going to do. The human race has to exist. We've fought tooth and nail to survive against predators, famine, war and natural disasters for eons. This is what we do. This is what we were made for.

No species has ever survived by trying to cling to what's gone. You can't exist if you're trying to get back to an environment or culture or climate that's changed. You have to adapt if you want to keep going.

"Our old ways are gone," I say, when they've quietened down again. "That isn't what the world needs any more. That is not what we are. Whatever it was about our biological bodies that didn't work and stopped us reproducing the way we used to, it doesn't matter. That's over and done with.

"You can't be fussy about survival. You take what you are given. And what we have been given is a way to carry on. A new type of body that does work. It has its flaws like the old one, sure, and it might break again one day, so that we have to move on to the next thing. But it works, and we are going to use it. Because we have no other choice."

The world is changing too. Nature is breaking down the old ways and reassembling them: forests grow where cities once stood; rivers flow where concrete used to be. Nothing stops the endless march of progress. We have to do what London has done. We have to change. It'll be strange and uncomfortable and new, but it has to be done.

I raise my voice. "We are the human race. All of us, everyone in this room. And we are going to continue. We are going to thrive. Because there is no point to anything if we don't have a future. We are creating something for the next generation. And we aren't going to let them down!"

There's a stunned silence.

Eventually, Feng stands up. "Thank you, Lowrie and Shen, for raising this motion." He sounds quietly shocked. "We will discuss it in the same way we do every topic – in a calm, civilized fashion. Now, who would like to speak first?"

Darcy stands immediately. She opens her mouth to speak and then bursts into tears. "My mum would have wanted me to have children," she says, mopping her face with a flowery handkerchief. "I don't know why we didn't do this years ago!"

"It's wrong," Olivia Fletcher interjects. "It would be selfish! We weren't designed for that!"

I lean over and whisper in Shen's ear, "Do you think we should leave? I don't think this is our debate to have."

"Can we go mudlarking?" he asks.

I stare at his lips. "I suppose, if that's what you want to do. I had something else in mind, though."

He raises an eyebrow and tugs me out of the hall. Everyone is arguing so much that they don't even notice us leave.

I'm sure they'll let us know their decision later – although I think I already know what it's going to be. We're humans. If there's one thing we can do well, it's find a way to survive. A little thing like extinction isn't going to stop us. Not when there's still so much of the world left to explore.

EPILOGUE

London, England
16 August 2528

Hello!

This message – if anyone ever reads it – was written by the last two members of a biological species called *homo sapiens*. It is part of a time capsule which we launched into space on board a satellite. It is designed to orbit the third planet from the sun, which we call the Earth. It will remain in orbit for five hundred thousand of our Earth years. It will then decay so that the capsule falls back to the ground.

Hopefully the silicon wafer this message is engraved on will last long enough to be found by any future intelligent lifeforms living on Earth. There is also a data-storage device, which contains pictures, sounds and objects from our culture, as well as documents taken from our lives, so that you can understand more about us.

(See: bagpipes.mp3, fire-footage.mp4, kissing.mp4, heartbeat.mp3,hammering-nail.mp4,Bach-toccata-d.mp3, chuck-berry.mp3, male-female-child-anatomy.jpg, DNA-simulation.gif, pyramids.jpg, athletes-racing.gif, eating.gif, children-playing.mp4, ink-calligraphy.gif, horse-riding.gif, gymnastics.gif, last-messages-from-around-world.txt.)

We don't know if humans will still exist by the time you read this. The inorganic form our species currently takes is quite hardy, but it isn't indestructible. Maybe you're a human yourself but a gaseous version, or made of code in a virtual reality. Whoever you are, we hope that you are safe and happy.

We've done our best to pass on Earth in the healthiest state we can. Our species has done so much harm to this planet over the centuries. We have burned and ravaged and overturned Earth, from the deepest oceans to the final layer of the atmosphere. Hopefully we've fixed that by the time you inherit the planet. We're working as hard as we can to reverse our ancestors' mistakes for you.

If you're reading this, whoever you are, we hope that you love one another and create breathtaking art and care for this planet as well as it deserves. Please remember the human race, even if you don't know us yourselves.

We have to sign off here. Our son, Adam, is just waking up, so we need to intervene before he starts pestering Mitch again.

Yours, on behalf of humanity in its many wondrous and terrible forms,

Lowrie and Shen Zhang

P.S. If you're an alien, know that I love and respect you and everything you do, but please be nice to anything living on this planet. We really like it. — Shen

ENJOYED THIS BOOK?
WE'D LOVE TO HEAR
YOUR THOUGHTS!

🐦 #TheQuietBook   @Lauren_E_James
@WalkerBooksUK · @WalkerBooksYA

📷 @WalkerBooksYA

AUTHOR'S NOTE

This book was inspired particularly by *Seven Brief Lessons on Physics* by Carlo Rovelli and the essay "Aliens and Us: Could Post-humans Spread through the Galaxy?" by Alexei Rees in *Aliens: Science Asks: Is There Anyone Out There?*, edited by Jim Al-Khalili.

I also drew inspiration from *Ice Age Art: Arrival of the Modern Mind* by Jill Cook; the article "Hominin Footprints from Early Pleistocene Deposits at Happisburgh, UK" by Nick Ashton; *The Sixth Extinction: An Unnatural History* by Elizabeth Kolbert; *Other Minds: The Octopus, the Sea, and the Deep Origins of Consciousness* by Peter Godfrey-Smith; *Sapiens: A Brief History of Humankind* and *Homo Deus: A Brief History of Tomorrow* by Yuval Noah Harari; *A Brief History of Everyone Who Ever Lived: The Stories in Our Genes* by Adam Rutherford; and *The World Without Us* by Alan Weisman.

ACKNOWLEDGEMENTS

Thanks to everyone at Walker Books, especially Annalie Grainger, Emily McDonnell, Krystle Appiah, Emily Sharratt, Margaret Hope, Anna Robinette, Kirsten Cozens, Rosi Crawley and John Moore. I also want to thank Lisa Horton and Margaret Hope for the gorgeous cover.

This was a really tough book to get right. I wrote version after version, searching for the best way to tell Lowrie and Shen's story. Annalie went above and beyond as an editor to help me find the answer, and I couldn't be more grateful.

I couldn't have written this book without the unwavering support of my agent, Claire Wilson, who was there when I thought I'd never find the right idea. Thanks to the rest of the team at Rogers, Coleridge and White, including Rosie Price and Miriam Tobin.

Thank you to Sarah Barnard, Clare Samson, Alice Oseman, Emma Mills, Steph Whybrow, Lucy Powrie, Alice Hildreth, Catherine Doyle, Sara Barnard, Non Pratt, Charlie Smissen, Charlotte, Troy and Travis Smitten, Xiaoyue Wu, Shirley Barnes and Madison Woodward for the support. Biggest thanks go to Mum, Dad (who is deaf in one ear – sorry for never ever remembering which side to talk to you on) and my brother, Chris.

Portrait by Pete Bedwell Photography

LAUREN JAMES was born in 1992, and graduated in 2014 from the University of Nottingham, UK, where she studied chemistry and physics. She started writing her first novel during secondary school English classes, because she couldn't stop thinking about a couple who kept falling in love throughout history. She sold the rights to the novel, *The Next Together*, when she was 21, while she was still at university.

Her other novels include *The Last Beginning*, and *The Loneliest Girl in the Universe*, which was inspired by a physics calculation she was assigned at university. Lauren is a passionate advocate of STEM further education, and all of her books feature female scientists in prominent roles.

She lives in the West Midlands and works with Writing West Midlands, providing creative writing courses to children. She is an Arts Council grant recipient. She has written articles for numerous publications, including *The Guardian*, *Buzzfeed* and the *Children's Writers' and Artists' Yearbook 2019*.

You can find her on Twitter at @Lauren_E_James, Tumblr at @laurenjames, or her website: laurenejames.co.uk, where you can subscribe to her newsletter to be kept up to date with her new releases and receive bonus content.

ALSO BY LAUREN JAMES

"A FUNNY, GRIPPING, AND INCREDIBLY IMAGINATIVE STORY OF TRUE LOVE AND REINCARNATION."

LOUISE O'NEILL AUTHOR OF *ONLY EVER YOURS*

Katherine and Matthew are destined
to be born again and again.

Each time they fall hopelessly in love,
only to be tragically separated.

Maybe the next together will be different...

A LOVE THAT
TRANSCENDS TIME

A SECRET THAT
COULD DESTROY THE FUTURE

THE
LAST
BEGINNING

LAUREN JAMES

The thrilling follow-up to *The Next Together*

Sixteen years ago, a scandal rocked the world and
teenagers Katherine and Matthew vanished without a trace.

Now Clove Sutcliffe is determined to find them.

But in uncovering their secret, she could destroy
the world and lose Ella, her love of a lifetime...

Want to read more about
Katherine, Matthew, Clove and Ella?

Don't miss these two companion novellas
set in the world of *The Next Together* series:

ANOTHER TOGETHER

ANOTHER BEGINNING

Available as eBooks from all good retailers

THE
LONELIEST
GIRL
IN THE
UNIVERSE

·LAUREN JAMES·

"A WHITE-KNUCKLE RIDE..."

SARA BARNARD AUTHOR OF *BEAUTIFUL BROKEN THINGS*

Romy Silvers is the only surviving crew member on a spaceship bound for a new planet. She is the loneliest girl in the universe, until she begins to communicate with another spaceship. Then Romy discovers that sometimes there's something worse than being alone...